The Thornhill Secret

Caroline Curran

The Thornhill Secret

Caroline Curran

authorHOUSE®

AuthorHouse™
1663 Liberty Drive
Bloomington, IN 47403
www.authorhouse.com
Phone: 1-800-839-8640

First published by AuthorHouse   11/08/2011

ISBN: 978-1-4567-9385-2 (sc)
ISBN: 978-1-4567-9386-9 (ebk)

Printed in the United States of America

Any people depicted in stock imagery provided by Thinkstock are models, and such images are being used for illustrative purposes only.
Certain stock imagery © Thinkstock.

This book is printed on acid-free paper.

For my parents

With all my love

PROLOGUE

Beads of sweat sprang out on her forehead as she pushed tiny wisps of hair away from her eyes. As she opened the library door, the moonlight guided her to the hiding place. The secret closet would now become her refuge.

Feeling her way along the bookcase, she found the lever. As she turned it to the left, the heavy door creaked open. The air was thick and heavy with the smell of old books and wood. Something touched her hair. She flinched and moved her hand to wipe away the remnants of a spider's web. As she closed the door, she heard footsteps on the parquet floor, getting louder and louder. Closer and closer to her hiding place. Her heart pounded. She felt as if it would leap out of her chest. She wanted to scream, but she had to stay calm. The heat inside the room was stifling. The thick dust clung to her nostrils. It was difficult to breathe. A shaft of light under the door penetrated the inky blackness. The wooden floor creaked. Suddenly the door swung open.

"Ah, there you are. Why are you hiding here? Did you think I wouldn't find you?"

CHAPTER ONE

New Hampshire, Summer 1925

The shrill ring of the telephone penetrated the silence in Todd Thornhill's study as he sat behind a magnificent walnut desk, looking out over the gardens. At sixty-years old, with thinning snow white hair, he ran his department store empire from his estate in the Ossipee Mountains in New Hampshire, with occasional visits to his office in Concord. He could never escape from the telephone. *A great invention, but it never seemed to stop ringing. There is always something happening at one of the stores*, he thought, puffing on his cigar.

"Hello. Thornhill," he barked.

"Mr. Thornhill, Sir, just to let you know that Sam King wants to see you." It was his assistant calling from Thornhill Enterprises Executive Office in Concord. Sam King, his Chief Accountant, was a financial genius. He kept a tight hold on the purse strings, but when it came to the annual audit, he was a thorn in the proverbial Thornhill backside.

"Can't a man spend his own money?" Thornhill had bellowed at him the previous year.

"Why, of course, Sir. However, there also has to be a certain amount of accountability." The man wasn't easily shaken and still went about his nit-picking. Thornhill had gotten one of the best accountants in the business, so he had to like it or leave it.

"Sir. Are you still there?"

"Yes. Thanks for telling me. I'll drop by tomorrow afternoon, around three o'clock." After he'd hung up, Thornhill sat looking out of the window of his study. He lit a cigar and took a long drag. Eleanor was always saying he smoked too much, but at his age, why bother to give up?

The department store business wasn't an easy one. There was a lot of competition from Macy's. Thornhill had started out in 1910 with a small place in Concord and within four years he'd opened stores in Boston, New York and Concord. Thornhill's Department Stores had become a household name and the money started to roll in almost instantly.

With the fruits of his labour, he'd managed to build and furnish Thornhill Manor. This imposing house sat nestled in the mountains. It had two turrets on either side of the building, rather like a house Todd had seen when he visited Lake Geneva in Switzerland in 1912. The bay windows let in the stunning views over Lake Winnipesaukee and the surrounding mountains. It was spectacular in the fall. The russet, golden brown landscape covered the mountains like honey poured over morning waffles.

The house sat amongst four thousand acres of land, some of it farmed, but most of it forest. He sold agricultural products to local communities. He'd even set up a fund from the profits from the stores and the estate to help his workforce in times of hardship. A little bonus in their pay packet at Christmas always brought a smile to their faces.

"Eleanor, the workforce is the backbone of any company. Look after your employees and you'll get the best out of them," he'd said to his wife of thirty years.

He glanced at the photograph of Emily, his niece. He thought of that fateful decision that he'd made in April 1912 when he'd decided not to travel back to New York with his younger brother Gilbert. After visiting the famous Harrods Department Store in London to gain some ideas for his stores in the States, Todd had taken an earlier passage from Southampton. Gilbert had managed to get a ticket on the White Star Line's new flagship *Titanic*. When the ship struck the iceberg and sank on that bitterly cold April evening, only 706 people would survive out of a total of 2223 passengers and crew. Gilbert did not make it to a lifeboat and would never see the United States and his family again. He had left a wife, Miriam, and three young daughters, Emily, Elizabeth and Mary, of whom Mary was just two months old.

Todd's grief at the time of this family tragedy made him feel like his heart had been ripped from his body. He was proud of Gilbert and Miriam's girls, especially Emily, the eldest, who was now twenty-five years old. He encouraged her interest in horticulture. The rose garden outside of her bedroom was coming along just fine and he'd arranged for the latest garden furniture to be sent up from New York. His face suddenly clouded over when he thought of that young fool James Flynn who had been spending a lot of time with his niece. *I can't stop her from seeing him*, he thought; *she knows her own mind. Young Flynn well, I've heard all about his womanising. News travels fast here.* Todd stubbed out his cigar. He couldn't help thinking that he had to do all he could to protect his niece. *I won't let that good-for-nothing hurt her*, he fumed.

———•———

The black Model-T swept up the driveway as a brisk wind threaded through the trees. The train ride and then the drive up from New York in one of Uncle Todd's new chauffeur-driven motorcars seemed to take forever. Uncle Todd was proud of the fleet of cars that his close friend Henry Ford had sold to him recently.

Emily Thornhill was in a state of excitement. She was home for the holidays. She'd just spent some time in France, perfecting her already fluent French and writing some short stories that she hoped one day to publish. She couldn't wait to see her family. Her sisters, fifteen-year old Elizabeth and ten-year-old Mary, were already here. They'd travelled over from Cape Cod. It was wonderful that they'd all be together for a couple of weeks.

When they heard the car horn, Mary and Lizzie came bounding out of the house, under the watchful eye of the housekeeper, Mrs. Banbury. Lizzie's billowing copper-coloured hair was in sharp contrast to her younger sister's honey-blond locks, which were short and curly. Emily's was brown, medium-length and straight and it was now tucked neatly under a black cloche hat. She had added a small ostrich feather at the side.

Emily smiled as she hugged her sisters. Lizzie was the wild one, usually getting up to all kinds of mischief. In fact the last time they were here at Easter, she took a nasty tumble from one of the trees. "I'm fine. No broken bones," she'd proudly announced, smiling impishly as the others all heaved a sigh of relief. Emily was very protective of Mary, who was much quieter.

"Mary, each time I see you I swear you've grown another two inches," Emily said. "You'll be almost as tall as I am before long."

"Oh, I'd love to be tall and beautiful like you Emily," Mary said, jumping up and down as her sister laughed.

"Mary, I'm sure you'll grow up to the one of the prettiest girls in New Hampshire."

"Lizzie, how did you get that bruise on your arm? You haven't been climbing trees again have you? Aren't you getting a little bit old for that?" Emily said to her sister who was trying to hide behind the fountain.

"No I haven't been climbing trees. I knocked it on the library door if you must know."

"Ouch I bet it hurt," Mary said wincing.

"Well, you won't die then Lizzie. You're made of strong stuff. You're a Thornhill remember," Emily said laughing as they chased each other around the fountain.

"Now then let's get you all in the house," the housekeeper said, interrupting the high jinks. "Miss Emily, your aunt and uncle are waiting for you in the library."

"Thank you Mrs. Banbury," Emily said, catching her breath.

Todd was flicking the end of his cigar into the fireplace as Emily crossed the room towards her aunt. Eleanor was looking down at her embroidery; her glasses perched on the end of her nose. She looked up and smiled at her favourite niece.

"Emily my dear, how wonderful to see you." She put the embroidery aside and they embraced.

"It's so good to see you too aunt and you dearest uncle." Emily said turning to Todd who was now standing behind his wife. They kissed on both cheeks.

"How was your journey, my dear?" Todd sat next to Eleanor and lit his cigar. Emily suppressed a smile. She knew how much her aunt disliked this loathsome habit.

"Rather long, but we stopped for tea and cakes along the way . . . ." Emily stopped herself mid-sentence.

"I hope you haven't spoilt your appetite," her aunt reprimanded. "Cook has made a sumptuous dinner and we'll be having some of your favourites tonight."

"I'm looking forward to it, Aunt."

"Why don't you run along, Dear, and get settled in your room. We'll talk later at dinner," Eleanor said, kissing her niece's forehead.

"Oh, Emily I'll show you my new shotgun tomorrow. Just had it sent up from New York. It's a Browning A5 Herstal, manufactured in Belgium. What I would call a beautiful piece of craftsmanship," her uncle said, puffing on his cigar.

"Todd Dear, can't you put that out? The smell does tend to linger in this room," Eleanor chided.

"Of course Dear."

"Well, Uncle, I do look forward to seeing your new shotgun," Emily inserted.

"You will, my dear, you will. I won't be short of something to shoot around the estate. We have plenty of game." *I'd like to pump a couple of rounds of buckshot into that no-good boyfriend of hers*, he thought, as his niece left the room.

"Emily, where are you?" Elizabeth Thornhill shouted as she hurried down the garden path towards the rose garden.

Her sister was sitting on a wooden bench, staring into the fountain.

"There you are. I've been looking for you everywhere." Emily looked up as her sister approached and sat down beside her.

"Mary is having an afternoon nap so I thought we could go for a walk. It's such a beautiful day," Lizzie smiled as the sun bathed her copper-coloured hair.

"I think it's too hot to walk, Lizzie. I prefer to stay here for a while. I want to write in my journal." she said, and clutched the brown leather book to her chest, as if her younger sister was about to snatch it from her.

"We'll have some shade amongst those trees, Em," Elizabeth said, trying to reason with her.

7

"No, you run along and I'll see you later." Elizabeth knew that once her sister made up her mind about something it was difficult to change it.

"Well, I'm going to see the new foal that was born a few days ago. Aunt Eleanor told me it was the colour of honey. Can you imagine?" She hurried off with all the energy of a fifteen-year-old.

This was one of Emily's favourite places: in her beloved rose garden amidst the sweet scent. She had helped to select and plant some of these blooms only two years ago and they were coming along fine. She often collected the petals and kept them in her linen closet.

Emily had graduated from Miss Porter's School for Young Ladies in Farmington, Connecticut. It was one of those places where young ladies were taught how to be creative. Needless to say, she had excelled at the arts particularly reading and writing short stories and poetry. She also loved history and spoke French and Spanish fluently. She was a little bit older than the other girls, and she'd even helped one of the teachers with the French class.

She had also developed her passion for gardening, which was unusual at a place like Miss Porter's.

"Oh, back home on Long Island, Robinson, our gardener, does all that. Why ever would you want to do such a thing, Emily?" one of her fellow pupils had scoffed.

Miss Porter was an advocate of outdoor pursuits and Emily loved swimming and horseback riding. Now, at Uncle Todd's estate, she could ride her horse, Minstrel, along the long country roads without a care in the world. When she wasn't writing or reading, then riding was her passion.

Emily opened her journal. As she started to write the date in the top right-hand corner, she heard a noise behind her. She looked up towards the trees, expecting to see her boisterous sister coming towards her, full of tales of the honey-coloured foal that she'd seen in the stables. Instead, a tall sandy-haired man with cornflower blue eyes, with a shotgun slung over his shoulder, was walking towards her.

"Emily, Darling. How wonderful to see you." He reached over, took both of her hands and kissed her on the cheek.

"James, I was wondering when I'd see you," she smiled coyly.

"When did you get back from Europe?" James Flynn was the only son of Charles Flynn, the Estate Manager.

"Last week. I spent a few days at the Cape, which was glorious, but I've missed my mountains."

"How was Europe?"

"Simply wonderful. Did you receive my postcard?"

"I sure did. Was Paris as wonderful as they say it is?"

"Absolutely. I just love sitting at one of those quaint little sidewalk cafés eating croissants and drinking café au lait. There's so much to see. The Eiffel Tower was simply a dream to visit," she said, her eyes lighting up.

"Sounds wonderful."

"It is and you must visit one day."

"My dear, we shall go there together. I hear it's one of the most romantic cities in the world."

"It is and spring is a good time. All the daffodils are in bloom."

"I knew you'd have to mention flowers," he teased.

She laughed. "I can't help it, James."

"How was the journey? Did you meet anyone interesting on the boat?"

"It seemed to take an absolute age. I met up with a very nice family from Baltimore. They had been visiting their daughter who was at school in Switzerland."

"Well, I'm glad you came back to us," James said, looking into her chocolate-coloured eyes.

"Now tell me, how is Yale?" she asked.

"Well, I'm glad that my course is finished for this year. I don't have to be back until October," he said, propping his gun against a nearby tree and sitting next to Emily on the wooden bench.

"What's it like, studying journalism?"

"I really enjoy it. I've just completed an internship at the New York Times."

"Good for you. The budding journalist." She laughed. You know I thought about it myself, but I'm not sure that Uncle Todd approves of a woman going to University," she said in a disappointed tone.

"Well, we have some of the finest professors at the School. I wasn't sure whether I would like it, but it's going well. I'd wanted to go to Harvard Law School, but I wasn't quite rich enough to get in," he said sarcastically.

Emily looked away, embarrassed. She closed her journal and smoothed down her hair.

"So what are you going to do now that you've returned from your trip?"

"I'm not sure. I would like to go to college," she said hopefully.

"Then why don't you. At Yale, they only admit women students at graduate level, but you could always try Bryn Mawr College. One of my friends at Yale has a sister who is studying there," he said optimistically.

"Well, I'm not sure I want to go all the way to Pennsylvania and to be perfectly honest I don't think Uncle Todd will let me."

"Oh for goodness sake Emily, you are a grown woman. I honestly don't think he could stop you," James said, trying to hide his annoyance. To James's view of the situation, Thornhill was a master manipulator. He felt sorry for Emily.

"Well, we'll see what happens. I'm really fond of European history and I had so much fun travelling around France. *C'est vraiement un pays magnifique.*" She liked to practice her knowledge of the language regardless of whether or not anyone could understand what she was saying.

"I'm impressed. Your French is getting better and better," he teased.

"How would you know?" she said, playfully striking his shoulder.

"These are wonderful roses. My father told me you helped plant them," he said, changing the subject.

"Yes, that's right." Emily was quite proud of her horticultural talents. During one of her visits a few years back, Uncle Todd had asked one of the gardeners to help her design a rose garden.

"I like what you've done."

"Tell me, how's your writing coming along?"

"Quite well. I wrote some short stories when I was in Paris. I quite like writing poetry, but I never had much chance to write any whilst I was away. I've been reading a lot of it though."

He held her gaze. "Who's your favourite poet, Emily?"

"Well, I rather like Robert Frost. You know he lives here in New Hampshire. He came to stay with us last year. After dinner, we all gathered around as he read one of his poems. It was wonderful. Aunt Eleanor has invited him to stay with us in a few weeks, but unfortunately he's out of town. What a pity. Anyway, Uncle Todd has asked Leo Burns to join us for the weekend."

"Leo Burns, I've never heard of him."

"Oh haven't you? Well, he's an up and coming young writer. Uncle met him a few months ago in Providence, Rhode Island and thought he would make an interesting houseguest." *Did he now*, James thought.

"You know James, I'd be happy if you would join us for dinner."

James smiled as he stood and picked up his gun. He knew the chances were slim of being able to join the family. Old man Thornhill hated his guts. The feeling was mutual. He thought the department store tycoon was the most arrogant man he'd ever met. Regardless, he was willing to go along with the little charade. He did love Emily and she did have a habit of wrapping her uncle around her little finger. *I guess I'll have to put up with them and that ridiculous sister Elizabeth, who looks like an overgrown red setter, bounding everywhere*, he thought. Whenever she saw him, she always had an expression on her face as if she'd swallowed a mouthful of sour plums.

"Sounds like a good idea. Well, I must get back to my hunting. I'm just helping father with a few things before I head off to New York for a few days. Enjoy your roses." He turned and walked back towards the woods.

He reached his father's cottage and opened the door. He put away his shotgun, not in the least bit concerned that he hadn't shot a thing all morning. His thoughts wandered to Emily as he poured himself a drink. He really loved her, but her uncle watched her like a hawk. He wondered if they had a future together. *If I do marry her, I get the in-laws*, he thought, taking a gulp of his scotch.

He sat there for a while and then remembered the appointment. It would take him a few minutes to walk over to their agreed meeting place, he realised, as he finished his drink.

James left the cottage and arrived at the stable block to wait. He waited for a few minutes and then decided that she wasn't coming.

Women, you can never rely on them, he thought, as he crushed his cigarette under foot and returned to the cottage.

———•———

Eleanor Thornhill had one of her migraine headaches. As she lay on her bed in her second floor bedroom, Emily quietly knocked at the door.

"Come in," she murmured, exhausted by the mere effort of saying those few words.

Emily closed the door, trying not to disturb her aunt. She remembered how Eleanor had told her that when she moved into the house with Uncle Todd in 1915, she'd insisted on having a bedroom that was facing the west so she could see the sun setting. This was probably the last thing on her mind now. She looked pale as Emily sat in one of the chairs. The curtains were closed and her young maid Mary Riley had prepared a cold compress with some eucalyptus oil, which she pressed to her brow at regular intervals.

"Emily, dear child. Come closer. I need to speak with you."

"Don't tire yourself, Aunt. You must rest. We can talk later." *Surely whatever she has to say to me can wait,* Emily thought.

"No, I need to speak to you. This needs to be said." There was a hint of annoyance creeping into her voice. Emily pulled the chair closer to the bed and leaned forward so her aunt wouldn't be too uncomfortable and have to raise her voice to be heard. She had no idea what her aunt wanted to talk to her about.

"James Flynn." Her aunt's voice brought her out of her reverie. "I saw you talking to him this morning near the Rose Garden."

"Yes, Aunt. Such a charming . . . ."

"He has little or no interest in the working of the estate, not like his father. He's got the temperament of that feisty mother of his who selfishly committed suicide when the boy was only fifteen, leaving his father to raise him. I'm not surprised he's turned out the way he has." She sighed and pressed the eucalyptus-soaked cloth to her brow.

Emily, taken aback at this outburst from her aunt, sat in silence. It didn't make sense. James seemed like a nice enough sort of young man. *A bit cocky, worldly-wise, but isn't everyone who's lived in New York?* she wondered.

"Emily dear, I don't want you to be as unhappy as I've been." Emily looked at her aunt with a puzzled expression. She'd always assumed that her aunt and uncle were happy. Not always overly affectionate, but never unpleasant to one another. In fact, Emily always thought that Todd pandered to Eleanor's every whim.

Eleanor had married Todd when she was twenty-five. At the time, she thought she was the happiest woman alive.

"Your Uncle was very eligible and so handsome," Eleanor told her niece. "People always thought he was a confirmed bachelor. Well, he surprised everyone, including himself when he married me." She managed a smile. "We'd met at my friend's beach house in Maine. He'd asked me if I liked the sea, as we walked towards the terrace. In the distance the waves crashed against the shoreline. I remember it as if it were yesterday. He told me his family used to spend the summers at Orchard Beach. I remember just standing there looking out over the Atlantic Ocean. Although it was a cool summer evening, menacing grey-black clouds were building up in the distance. I knew there would be a storm and there was that night. Some properties were damaged along the coast." She pressed the cool cloth to her brow. "It only seems like yesterday, but it's over thirty years ago."

Emily moved closer to the bed, as Eleanor tried to raise her head off the pillow.

"Don't you worry yourself, my dear. It will pass." Eleanor managed a smile. "Just be careful, Dear. You know Uncle and I do worry about you. Now will you read one of your poems to me, Emily?"

"Of course I will." Emily kissed her aunt on the forehead and then sat on the window seat. She opened her book and started to read, but within a few minutes her aunt had drifted off to sleep. Emily closed her book and crept towards the door. As she closed the bedroom door behind her, she saw Mary, the young housemaid. Emily liked the young Irishwoman and she'd become somewhat of a confidant; despite the fact that they were classes apart, they were almost the same age.

"Hello Miss Emily. How is Madam? Does she still have her headache?"

"I'm afraid so Mary. Thank you for preparing her compress. I really think it helps. She's resting now. Perhaps you could check on her in an hour or so, see if she wants some of her herbal tea."

"Yes Miss, I'll do that."

"Thank you Mary. Now I must go to my rose garden. There's always some pruning to do and then I'm going to a party."

Todd Thornhill's car pulled up outside the entrance of Thornhill Enterprises in downtown Concord.

"Thanks, Charlie," Thornhill said to his driver. "I'll be through in about an hour."

"Sure, Sir. I'll be waitin."

Thornhill took the elevator to the third floor executive boardroom where he knew Sam King would be waiting for him. His secretary had arranged the meeting for three o'clock. It was just two minutes after when the heavy wooden door swung open.

"Sam, er, please don't get up. Can I get you a drink?"

"No, erm, I'm good," the accountant said, nervously straightening his tie. Todd Thornhill sat at the head of the table.

"My assistant said you wanted to see me about something in the books," Todd said and leaned back in his chair.

"Yes. It appears that several sums of $1,000 have been leaving the account, but I can't seem to find a paper trail."

"Well, I think it's probably some transfer to the Trust Fund. You know the one we have for the employees. Helps them out now and then and . . . ."

"I already checked that. It doesn't appear that they turned up in the Trust Fund," King interrupted.

"I'm sure there's an explanation. I must admit I'm not always party to every single cent going in and out of the accounts. I leave that to the experts." He lit a cigar and blew the smoke across the table.

"Mr. Thornhill, there is no easy way to say this. We think someone is withdrawing these amounts."

"What? You mean . . . ."

" . . . . stealing from the company," King said, finishing his sentence.

"You can't be serious? You mean fraud?"

"I mean fraud," Sam King said, as he pushed his glasses back on his face.

"What can we do to find out who is doing this, Sam?"

"We set a trap and then, *bam,* catch them red-handed," he said, slamming his fist on the table.

"Well, you will have our full cooperation. Thanks for your time. Sure you won't have that drink?"

"Yes, Mr. Thornhill, quite sure."

"Well let me know if there's anything else and, er, Sam . . . ."

"Yes Sir."

"Don't mention this to anyone else. I don't want to alarm anyone. We'll get to the bottom of this and clear things up."

"Sure, Sir. No problem."

"You know, you and your family must come up to the house for a weekend. We'll do some hunting."

"Sure, thanks. I'll keep that in mind," he said and closed the door behind him.

Todd Thornhill walked to the drinks cabinet and poured himself a large scotch. If Eleanor were here she'd be upbraiding him for his drinking. He swallowed the amber-coloured liquid in one gulp, oblivious to the burning sensation as it slid down his throat.

What can I do about this little problem? he thought, lighting a cigar.

"So how many people are coming tonight, Emily?" Elizabeth asked her sister, as they sat in the car for their short drive over to Oakwood House. Their neighbours, the Willoughby's were throwing a twenty-first birthday party for their youngest daughter Cora.

"Well, I'm not sure, but knowing the Willoughby's, a couple of hundred. They like to impress. Oakwood House makes Thornhill Manor look like a garden shed. It's huge, Elizabeth, almost to the point of being grotesque."

"Well, I'm sure there'll be lots to eat and interesting people to meet, don't you think, Em?"

"Yes, but I think Jamie will be there and I'll only have eyes for him," she sighed.

Elizabeth rolled her eyes. "Oh, how could I forget," she said, as a white silk glove came flying through the air. Elizabeth caught it and tossed it back to her sister.

"You know there'll be lots of nice young men there, Lizzie. Aren't you even interested in any of them? What about Jason Bridge, the man who works for the *Laconia Herald*? He seems nice enough."

"Jason Bridge I might add is a few years older than me."

"Well, he always likes to talk to you. You both seem to get along well."

"He's just a friend. I've met him a couple of times and we've had a good laugh and that's all, my dear match-making sister."

They arrived at the entrance to Oakwood House to the sounds of Paul Whiteman, *The King of Jazz* and his Orchestra on the phonograph. By the time the car door had opened, Cora Willoughby was running down the steps to greet them.

"Emily, Elizabeth, how good of you to come. I wanted to have a little intimate dinner for my birthday, but Daddy bless his heart insisted that his little baby had to have a big party."

"How sweet of him, Cora. We're absolutely delighted to be here, aren't we Lizzie?" Emily said, nudging a rather bored-looking Lizzie in the ribs.

"Why yes, we sure are," Lizzie said, imitating Cora's melodious-sounding voice.

"Yes, well, let's step inside, shall we," Emily said, dragging her sister away before Cora noticed.

"Lizzie, I wish you wouldn't do that. You have this awful habit of mimicking. Why do you do that?"

"Oh don't be so serious. Cora never even noticed. That silly voice of hers just makes me sick. "Oh, Daddy's little baby," she said, putting her two hands up to her chin in a coy-like expression and fluttering her eyelashes. Emily tried not to laugh at her sister's antics.

"Ladies, a photograph please." A young man stepped out of the shadows and placed his camera and tripod in front of them before they had a chance to object.

"There. Thank you Ladies and enjoy your evening." He said packing up his tripod and moving onto his next victim.

"Well, I need a glass of champagne after all that excitement," Emily said blinking. "And you my dear sister can have a soda. We don't want anything to stunt your growth." They both laughed, as they made their way over to one of the white-covered tables in the garden, which was laden with a champagne fountain and hors d'oeuvres.

"What are you two laughing at?" A wisp of smoke from a newly lit cigarette drifted towards them, as the Thornhill girls turned around to see James Flynn standing at the end of one of the tables.

"Wouldn't you like to know?" Emily said flirtatiously, as she moved towards him. This was Lizzie's chance to escape and find something more interesting to do than listen to all that boring chit-chat.

"See you later, Emily." She waved and headed towards the pool area before her sister had a chance to react. A marquee had been set up nearby with tables and chairs and a small band was playing music. There were lots of people milling around. The sky was as black as ink and, as she looked up, she could see lots of little stars, twinkling. *If only I could see just one then I could wish upon it,* she mused.

"Oops, sorry I . . . ." Lizzie said colliding with a fellow guest sending the drink he was carrying crashing to the ground. She felt the icy cold liquid strike her skin.

"Oh, how clumsy of me," Lizzie said, reaching for her handkerchief.

"Lizzie, it's you. Well, I might have known," Jason Bridge said with amusement.

"Hey, what's that supposed to mean?" she teased him.

"You are a true free spirit, Lizzie, that's what I like about you. Now let's get you something to drink, shall we?" They found a couple of garden chairs away from the crowd.

"When are you going back to Cape Cod?" Jason asked, interrupting Elizabeth's thoughts. Elizabeth was very young when her mother committed suicide, and had fond memories of the Cape where they had lived as a family. For the past two years, Aunt Eleanor, Elizabeth and Mary had spent some time at the sea. Uncle Todd wasn't so keen on the experience. It reminded him too much of Gilbert and Miriam and the cosy family environment they'd tried to make for their girls, only for it to be cut short by not just one tragedy, but two.

"I'm not sure, Jason. It will all depend on if we can find another house to rent. Uncle Todd sold Daddy's house a few years ago, so we don't have a place to go." She looked sad as Jason reached over to squeeze her hand.

"Never mind, we'll have lots of fun here in New Hampshire." Bridge was well aware of the Thornhill sisters' background and the tragic death of their father at sea and the subsequent suicide of their mother. One of the perks of being a journalist was access to information and lots of it.

His thoughts were interrupted by a drum roll. Their host for the evening, Evan Willoughby, was standing on an elevated platform with his wife Katherine on one side of him and his daughter Cora on the other.

"Ladies and gentlemen, gather around please. I am so glad you could all come here this evening to celebrate the twenty-first birthday of our dear sweet Cora. It only seems like yesterday when she came into this world. Now look at her, a young woman engaged to be married." A ripple of applause swept the crowd, as an enormous cake was wheeled in. It was made of vanilla and strawberry ice cream and layers of chocolate sponge. It was topped with twenty-one red roses. The inscription next to the cake was equally stunning: *To our darling Cora, may your life be filled with lots of joy and happiness.*

The photographer who had taken a snap of Emily and Elizabeth when they arrived now stepped forward and took one of Cora blowing out her candles, as a ripple of applause swept the crowd.

Suddenly, the sky lit up with fireworks. The crowd cheered and more champagne was poured.

By eleven o'clock dancing to the Fred Winner Orchestra was in full swing and the guests were served with a midnight buffet of smoked salmon and scrambled eggs.

Thora Banbury stood by the dressing table in one of the six guest rooms. She moved a glass dish to the other side of the table and could see a faint line of dust where it had stood. *That girl never cleans as well as she should,* she thought, running her duster across the table. The Thornhill family were expecting some houseguests for the weekend. President Coolidge's Secretary of Commerce and his wife would be here, as well as the young writer Leo Burns. *Miss Emily will be pleased,* Thora thought, *she likes to meet new people with similar interests does Miss Emily* and smiled as she closed the door.

Since she'd started work at the estate the previous year, she had grown fond of the family. The young girls brought some life into what could, at times, be quite a depressing place. It was her job to oversee the running of the house in consultation with Mrs. Thornhill and to ensure that the servants all did their chores correctly and efficiently. She knew she could rely on most of the staff to pull together, but in her opinion, some of them were lazy good-for-nothings, out to make a quick dollar and then leave a mess behind them.

She made her way down to the staff dining room.

Mary Riley slammed the copper pan down on the counter. She'd been up since the crack of dawn. She'd heard the fireworks from the Willoughby estate at around half past nine last night just before she'd climbed into bed exhausted. *All right for some, partying while the rest of us have to clean and do god knows what around this place,* she thought.

"Morning, Mrs. Banbury," she mumbled.

"Morning, Mary, you're up early. What happened, couldn't you sleep?" she said sarcastically. "Thought it was your day off today?" *That girl is up to no good,* she thought.

"It is. I've just lit the fire in the library and finished washing the dishes from last night. I'll be off shortly."

"I see, well, don't be late. We've got a busy week ahead of us. Mr. Thornhill has some important guests coming up for the weekend and we have to prepare all the guest rooms. It does them good to give them a good airing." All the six guest bedrooms and four bathrooms would be used during the visit.

"Alright, I'll be back around seven," Mary said, trying to disguise the annoyance in her voice. She was entitled to some time off and didn't come on duty until seven o'clock the next morning, so even if she stayed out until midnight it was none of Mrs. Banbury's bloody business. She took a deep breath, not wanting to put herself in a bad mood. She didn't want him to see her like that. She just couldn't wait to see him again.

"Oh, before you go, have you put fresh flowers in Mrs. Thornhill's room?" Mrs. Banbury enquired.

"Yes, Ma'am, exactly like you asked." Her mouth twitched as she tried to hide her annoyance.

"Fine then, well, I'll see you later," Mrs. Banbury said and swept out of the room.

Mary had said that although she was born in Ireland, she didn't feel Irish, but American. Her green eyes and fiery red hair, which matched her temperament, gave away her ancestry. Her family had lived in New York since they had travelled from Wexford in the south of Ireland in 1901, when Mary was just a baby.

Mary generally enjoyed her life on the estate, especially having her own room and its en-suite bathroom. Todd Thornhill was good like that. He took care of his staff. If Mary had still been living in New York or even Wexford, she would have to share a room with her three sisters and forget about having a nice bathroom. *A tin bath in the middle of the room and an outside toilet that was always clogging up, that's what I could expect*, she thought.

Mary was wiping her hands on her apron, as one of the bells on the wall tinkled. She looked up to see that it was Miss Emily calling from her room. Mary made her way along the corridor to Emily Thornhill's ground floor room. She knocked on the door and walked in. Emily was sitting by the window looking out onto the rose garden.

"Morning Miss. Can I get you anything?"

"Yes Mary. Can you bring me some tea with honey. I have a sore throat and I do think the tea will help it."

"Of course Miss," Mary said, and turned to go out of the door.

"Mary, have you ever been in love?" Mary Riley was stunned that Emily had been so forthright. She hesitated a moment.

"Why yes, Miss." Mary was herself in love, but she had to keep it a secret. People would be shocked. The scandal would ruin both of them. He'd promised her that they'd be together one day.

"Oh, I can't bear the waiting. I'm in love, but I can't say anything. Uncle Todd doesn't approve," Emily laughed, her eyes lit up with happiness.

"Well, I'm sure it will all work out for the best, Miss. I'll go and fix your tea." Mary returned to the kitchen. She knew who had caught Emily's eye. Hers wasn't the only eye that he'd caught. They not only shared confidences, but they also shared the same beau. James Flynn was crossing the boundaries of class. Sweet Emily and the feisty redhead from Ireland. Mary laughed as she waited for the water to boil.

She had met James a few years ago, not long after she'd started working at Thornhill Manor. It was a chance meeting in a New York department store where her older sister worked. Mary had travelled down to New York for a few days to spend time with her family. At the time she had no idea who James was or his connection with New Hampshire. They met a few times in New York and then continued seeing each other whenever he visited the estate. They had to keep things quiet though. Old man Thornhill would have a fit if he thought Flynn was cheating on his niece. *He should talk*, Mary laughed.

CHAPTER TWO

Balmoral, Scotland, Summer 1950

The taxi pulled up outside the black and gold gates. She paid her fare and picked up her battered suitcase. She could see the Castle at the end of the gravel driveway. The agency in Aberdeen had contacted her. They were looking for a replacement housemaid for a couple of months up at Balmoral while the Royal family enjoyed their summer break. She couldn't believe she was here at the holiday home of their Majesties King George VI and his consort Queen Elizabeth.

Balmoral Castle in Perthshire had been purchased in 1848 by Prince Albert of Saxe-Coburg Gotha, the husband and consort of Queen Victoria. At the time it wasn't big enough for Victoria and her growing family, so the Prince had a new castle built in 1852 on the same site. With its white turrets and small windows it sat nestling in the Scottish countryside on the banks of the River Dee and now provided an escape for the monarch and his family away from the hustle and bustle of the London court. Back in Victoria's day, the Royal Family had divided their time between Buckingham Palace in London and Osborne House on the Isle of Wight in southern England. Things hadn't changed much, just the people and some of the residences. The Court now moved between Buckingham Palace, Windsor Castle on the outskirts of London and the Palace of Holyroodhouse in Edinburgh.

"Good day Miss. Let me take that case for you. It must be heavy," the porter said, opening the gates. "They are expecting you. Don't worry about this, I'll bring it up to the house just as soon as I've closed up these gates." He gestured towards the house. "Now, you just follow the path around to the left and, after the small garden, you'll find the servants' entrance."

"Thank you," May said, smiling nervously. She made her way along the pathway, catching the faint scent of lily of the valley, hyacinth and roses. Daffodils swayed in the wind, bobbing up and down in greeting for the new arrival. The sun had been shining during her short taxi ride from Braemar, but slate-grey clouds were gathering and sweeping across the landscape, as she heard the first rumble of thunder over the hills.

May stood hesitantly at the servants' entrance looking at the brown door with its ornate knocker complete with ferocious lion's head. *That knocker could summon the dead*, she thought, as the first drops of rain started to fall around her.

She was reaching for the knocker when the door suddenly opened. A tall man with grey hair and a long pointed nose stood looking down at her. He was immaculately dressed in a black suit and white shirt with a high-necked collar. His shoes shone and you could see your face in them.

"Yes. Can I help ye?" he said in his thick Scottish accent. May stood, holding her handbag, and raised her eyes from under her brown felt hat.

"Good morning. I'm May Hamilton. I have a letter." she said, fumbling in her handbag.

"Aye yes, the new housemaid," he interrupted. "Yer'd better come in." His bushy eyebrows twitched as he directed her through the door.

"Sit there, Lassie," he said, and pointed to a chair next to the fireplace. "Findlay's the name. I'm the Head Butler. I'll introduce you to the housekeeper, Mrs. Tremayne. She's busy now with all the preparations. There's so much to do before their Majesties arrive in the next few days. Yer've come at the right time, lass. Aye, we need an extra pair a hands."

May was shown to her room, given her uniform and assigned to work with one of the other housemaids.

"Bessie will show you what's what," Findlay had explained. "Then you'll spend a half a day with Mrs. Tremayne. She's a stickler for detail and tidiness. A wee bit of advice. You'll do well to pay attention to everything she has to say," he said, raising his eyebrows and staring straight at her.

May took heed and joined the small army of staff running around the big house dusting, sweeping, polishing and making all the preparations for the royal visitors.

After three weeks, May had been assigned to *afternoon tea duties* as one of the regular maids had left unexpectedly the previous day. The rumour mill was rife. Everything from thieving from the kitchen stores to an unexpected pregnancy following an affair with one of the footman. May didn't know who to believe, but was glad of the opportunity to meet royalty. Her granny had shaken the hand of old Queen Mary fifteen years previously when she had visited Camden Hospital in London.

May brought a tray to Queen Elizabeth promptly at four o'clock. The Queen liked Earl Grey Tea with lemon, finely cut cucumber sandwiches and two delicious-looking slices of homemade Battenburg cake. May bobbed a curtsey and set the tray on the small table near the fireplace.

"Thank you, May." Queen Elizabeth, the former Lady Elizabeth Bowes Lyon, smiled at her and then helped herself to some tea. They used to call her the smiling Duchess and she and King George, or Bertie, as he was known within the family, had practically saved the monarchy after her wayward brother-in-law Edward abandoned everything and ran off with the American Divorcee Wallis Simpson in 1936. The country had been plunged into a terrible crisis and Elizabeth had helped her shy, stammering husband in the early days of his reign. She even arranged a speech therapist for him, to help him cope with the many speeches a King was expected to make.

"Well, how is life here at Balmoral? Are you settling in?"

"Very well, Your Majesty. It's such a beautiful place." May's eyes quickly scanned the room and rested on the dressing table where a ruby and diamond tiara sat waiting for its appearance at the dinner party their Majesties were giving that night for the Duke and Duchess of Braemar.

"Yes, it is rather a delight. The King and I adore this place. When the children were young, they used to ride their ponies over the hills and play tennis here. Now they still ride, but now it is horses. Princess Elizabeth often comes up here for the weekend with her new husband and my grandson. It's so different to London. There's so much smog now in the city. At times, one can hardly breathe," she sniffed. The Queen delicately touched her pearl necklace.

May stood to attention hoping that the Queen would not see her legs shaking.

"Will that be all, Ma'am?"

"Well, I wanted to ask you, May. Would you be a dear and help me this evening? You see, my Ladies Maid is unwell and we do have this dinner. It would be frightfully kind of you if you could help me dress. I've already mentioned it to Mrs. Tremayne." She started to pour her tea, something the Queen liked to do herself.

"Of course, Ma'am." How could she refuse and why would she want to? This was a wonderful honour. May bobbed a curtsey and closed the door behind her, thinking of that wonderful tiara. What would her old granny say when she told her she'd helped to get the Queen ready for one of those posh do's? Her thoughts turned to the delicious-looking Battenburg cake that she'd brought up on the tray. She was lucky, as Cook always made several of them. One cake was made for their Majesties, one for the senior household and one for the rest of the staff. Needless to say, they were devoured within hours of appearing on any of the tables, regardless of which part of the house they went to.

I hope that someday I can cook like that, May thought to herself. *I'll have me own little place I will. No fetching and carrying for the likes of this lot, no sir,* she thought, as she made her way back to the kitchen.

The Queen's bedroom looked out over the flower beds and rolling Scottish hills and this evening it was softly lit by candles and two bedside lamps. May laid a pair of white and gold-trimmed evening gloves on the edge of the bed.

The Queen picked them up. "Yes, they will go perfectly with the gold edge of my evening dress." Queen Elizabeth was wearing a diamond drop tiara that had once belonged to her mother-in-law, Queen Mary.

"Now, where are my pearl-drop earrings?" she said, staring at May.

"Here, Ma'am."

The Queen took the earrings and sat at her dressing table. "They match my tiara and I also have this pearl ring, which the King gave me shortly before our wedding in 1923. It belonged to his grand mama, Queen Alexandra," she said, twirling the ring around on her right finger.

"It is beautiful, Ma'am." She couldn't take her eyes off the Queen. *This jewellery must be worth a fortune*, May thought, licking her lips.

"Thank you for helping me tonight," the Queen said, snapping the earrings into place. "These dinners can be rather tiresome. Same old faces, but we have to smile and do our duty," she said, laughing.

"It's been my pleasure, Ma'am." May was overwhelmed. She had never seen such beautiful jewellery and clothes.

"Do you have any family, May?" the Queen asked, putting on her long white gloves.

"Yes Ma'am, a sister in New York. I haven't seen her for a little while. One day, I'd like to visit her. She writes that America is the land of golden opportunities," she replied, and looked out of the window dreamily.

"So I hear," the Queen said pensively. "The King and I visited the United States in 1939. Everything was arranged and some months before we were to leave, my dear Mama, the Countess of Strathmore died. Well, we absolutely could not cancel."

"Yes Ma'am." May didn't know whether she should answer or just stand there and nod. She thought back to the time when she was younger. Speak when you are spoken to, was what was drummed into her as a child in Edinburgh.

"President Roosevelt and his wife were so sweet. We would also stay with the President and Mrs. Roosevelt at their private residence in Hyde Park, New York," she said, thinking back to the early part of her shy husband's reign.

"Well, I didn't want to wear sombre black, because of Mama's death. What a dilemma." May stood next to the Queen listening attentively.

"Well, my designer Cecil Beaton told me that white can also be used for mourning, so he made all my lovely dresses in the most adorable fabrics. All in white. I was so relieved," she smiled.

"I still have fond memories of the President and his wife. You know, they served us hamburgers or was it hot dogs, I can't remember. Anyway, Bertie and I thought it was funny. I heard from one of our equerries that the President's mother was absolutely horrified that they had served us such food. I didn't mind and neither did the King." She smiled at the memory. "Princess Elizabeth and her sister Margaret Rose were quite jealous when we told them what we had eaten," she laughed.

"We got such a send-off when we left. The Americans were so kind at a time when we were on the verge of war and we didn't know what was in store for us," she said pensively.

"Well, thank you again, May, you'll like America." The Royals had a knack for dismissing you in the most polite way. Sometimes it was a look or a word.

"I'm sure I will, Your Majesty. Enjoy your evening." She gently closed the door to the Queen's bedroom.

———•———

A few days later, May was sitting at the kitchen table polishing some spoons.

"Mrs. Tremayne wants to see ye," Mr. Findlay said, as he shuffled into the room. May didn't question why the Head Housekeeper wanted to see her. It was a regular occurrence. Do this and do that. It was never ending, but it would all be over soon. Then she could go back to London and then think about a trip to America to start up her little venture. She wanted to open up a tea shop with her sister. Nothing fancy, just selling a decent brew with a few homemade cakes and an assortment of sandwiches. *Well, one had to have some dreams*, she thought, as she made her way to the Housekeeper's office. She knocked lightly at Vera Tremayne's small office near the servants' kitchen.

"Come in." The door creaked as May opened it.

The imperious Vera Tremayne sat ramrod straight in her chair. Her mouth moved in a nervous twitch. She had worked at Balmoral for more than twenty years. Her first job was as a personal maid to Queen Mary, who now lived in London at Marlborough House, and was now much too frail to make the long journey to Scotland to stay with her son and his family.

"Sit down, May," she said. She took off her glasses and sighed as the young maid approached her desk.

"There's something I have to talk to you about," she said. May looked anxious as she sat there, her hands across her lap.

"We've had a report that a pair of pearl-drop earrings belonging to Her Majesty have gone missing." Mrs. Tremayne looked at May for her reaction.

"What's that got to do with me?" May was struck with fear. She couldn't believe that she could be accused of such a thing.

"You have access to her Majesty's jewellery collection. Who else could have taken them?" Tremayne looked at her accusingly.

"Well, it wasn't me. The last time I saw those earrings was last week before the dinner for the Duke and Duchess. Perhaps they're just mislaid. These things hap . . . ."

"They're not mislaid," Tremayne snapped. Her eyes bore into her. "We've searched everywhere. Where are they, May? Come girl, own up." May felt as if she had been accused, tried and now was waiting for her sentence, all in the space of five minutes.

"I haven't got the earrings," May said as a sob caught in her throat. She couldn't think why they were accusing her.

"Go back to your room and stay there. We're going to conduct a search of all the staff rooms. We'll get to the bottom of this. Mark my words." May was petrified as she made her way back to her room. She bumped into Sally, the parlour maid in the corridor.

"What's wrong with you? You look as if you've seen a ghost."

"They're saying I took some jewellery belonging to her Majesty. I don't know what they're talking about," she said through fresh tears.

"Get a move on you two. There's no time for tittle-tattle. Their Majesties don't pay you to conduct idle gossip in the corridors." They jumped as they heard the booming voice of Findlay echoing down the corridor.

May got back to her room and threw herself on the bed. She cried all day and well into the evening. She heard a tap on her door. It was Sally with a tray for her.

"Here you are Love. Look what cook sent up for yer. Some of her nice shepherd's pie. I know it's yer favourite. I've also made you a nice pot of tea. Get that down you. A cuppa always tastes better when it's made by someone else." Sally put the tray on May's bedside table.

"I didn't do anything, Sally. Why are they blaming me?"

"Well, you know what these toffs are like. They always blame the likes of us. When they pass yer in the corridor, they look as if they've got a bad smell under their noses."

"The Queen's not like that though. I spoke to her, she asked about me family and . . . ."

"May, they don't give a fig about us. Don't let those sweet smiles fool yer."

May couldn't stop the tears falling down her cheeks. *Poor lass. Just when things were going so well for her*, Sally sighed as she closed the door.

———

The next morning a fine mist hung over Balmoral Castle, as May knocked gently on Mrs. Tremayne's door.

"Come in." May opened the door to find the housekeeper standing by the fire.

"Sit down, May. Would you like a cup of tea, Child?"

"No thank you, Madam."

"You know why you are here. We've had this theft and we've now interviewed all the staff. It all points to you, May. You've been spending a lot of time around the Queen."

"Did the Queen actually accuse me, Madam?" May asked, gaining some confidence. If she was going to be dismissed anyway she had to defend herself. Her old granny would've been proud of her. She couldn't let this old cow walk all over her.

"No she didn't. All the evidence . . . ."

"All the evidence. Who are you anyway, a bloody policeman?" May suddenly realised she'd said too much. That's it now. They won't give me another chance.

"That's enough backchat from you, young Miss. How dare you raise your voice to me. Policeman, you'll get policemen all right.

They'll be searching all the rooms and, guess what, your room will be at the top of their list. I'll personally see to it. Now go to your room until I call you again."

May ran back to her room. She went inside and closed the door, her heart beating ten to the dozen. She fastened the lock in case Sally came looking for her.

Now then, let me see, she thought. She slid her hand behind the radiator. Just inside the panel, there was a little leather pouch. Inside were two shillings and the most beautiful pair of pearl-drop earrings. She held them up to her ear.

So pretty. They'll be a nice down payment on my little coffee shop in America, she thought, putting them back into the pouch and placing it behind the radiator.

———•———

The police who searched the servants' quarters found a couple of candlesticks, a gold ring and a set of six silver teaspoons in a wardrobe belonging to a groom to his Majesty. The poor lad didn't have a clue how they'd got there.

"They all say that, Son. Do you think they flew there all by themselves?" the policeman barked at the petrified boy.

May had heard all about the find. It didn't matter that they had a culprit. She was for the chop. After her insolence to frosty-faced Tremayne there was no going back. She was dismissed and left Balmoral a few days later. *Glad to see the back of the place. Do someone a good turn and look how they treat you.* Never mind, she had her little *nest egg.* The police said the young groom had probably sold the earrings to some pawnbroker and then they were sold on, no questions asked.

After all the excitement at the Castle, May stayed at a small bed and breakfast in Aberdeen for a couple of days before catching a train back to London. She'd decided to go to the United States to stay with her older sister in New York. Always opportunities presenting themselves, her sister had written last year. *I think a fresh start in America will be just the job,* she thought, as she stepped off the train at Kings Cross Station. *I mustn't forget about my little tea room either.*

"Paper, get yer paper. King's housekeeper found dead, read all about it,' the young boy selling newspapers yelled.

May looked at the news board as the headline page flapped in the wind: *King's Housekeeper found dead at Balmoral.*

"Paper, Miss?" the young boy thrust the paper at her as she hurried through the station.

She gazed at the headline. *Well, well, who said those that doubt don't get their just deserts.* She walked into the Lyons Café on the corner and ordered herself a tea and two slices of toast.

Those dark Balmoral corridors were death traps during the night. You never knew what might happen.

CHAPTER THREE

New Hampshire, July 1999

It was a morning in early summer when I headed north. I was looking forward to a couple of weeks in the mountains. I'd spent many childhood summers at my great aunt Elizabeth's estate in New Hampshire, but I hadn't been up there for a few years. We usually met up when she came to New York on one of her culture trips. She was a trustee to the Metropolitan Museum of Art and she also sat on the committee for the preservation of Grand Central Station. Alongside Jacqueline Kennedy Onassis, she had campaigned fearlessly for this gem of a piece of architecture to be restored to its former glory and Elizabeth Thornhill's name regularly appeared in articles printed in the Bulletin of the Association for Preservation Technology. The last time I'd seen her was at a reception at the Museum earlier in the year. A friend of mine was exhibiting there and I'd gone to lend some valuable support. Over a glass of champagne my great aunt and I had managed to catch up on some news. It was a double celebration. I'd just turned thirty and she'd just celebrated her eighty-ninth birthday. Despite the vast difference in age, we liked to keep in touch. She was as sharp as a pin and I admired her strength of spirit and her love of the arts. I had long wanted to explore my ancestry and we certainly had an interesting family history. I loved chatting to her over coffee or a glass of wine, as she told me about her younger days at Thornhill Manor. We shared a common interest in keeping the family spirit alive.

My visit to New Hampshire wouldn't be all play and no work. As a writer, I never travel anywhere without my laptop. On this occasion It was tucked safely in the boot of my car. I'd been working for the past few months on my latest book, a biography of Queen Katherine of Aragon, the Spanish Princess who became the first wife of Henry

VIII of England in June 1509. Some of my friends had asked me why write a book about Katherine. Well, it was a question I had no difficulty in answering. I love history. No, let's make that I adore history. My work took me to all those wonderful country houses and castles that are such a rich part of English history. I believed the story of this strong and determined woman needed to be told. Her battle with her husband over their divorce was inspiring. I believe Henry VIII seriously misjudged how strong and powerful she was. Her nephew Charles was the Holy Roman Emperor and his forces had sacked Rome. Pope Clement VII, the only person who could grant Henry a divorce, was now under the thumb of Emperor Charles and there was no way that he would upset the Emperor or his aunt Katherine. It's nice to think that families could stick together even back then.

There was another reason for my interest in English history. My father was English and part of my childhood had been spent in Cheshire in the northwest of the country. He had been a Professor of English history at Chester University and I had frequent trips to London with him as a child to places like Hampton Court and the Tower of London. Tears welled up in my eyes as I thought of my parents, who had died a few years back. They would have been proud to know that I'd graduated in journalism from Yale two years ago.

After graduation, I'd rented an apartment on the ground floor of a converted New York brownstone on East fifty-four Street, not far from Lexington. It's a spacious place with the original wooden floors, a cosy fireplace, a small walled garden and a couple of French windows thrown in for good measure. My walled garden is packed to the brim with my tomato plants. It's strange; no matter when I put in the seedlings they all seem to come up together. I then find I have more tomatoes than I know what to do with.

I've just finished decorating my apartment and putting up some of my favourite pictures. I loved the apartment when I first saw it, but the only drawback is that the owner of the building lives next door. *Don't do it, it's a recipe for disaster,* a colleague had told me, but I'd lived in places before where the owner was on the premises and it had worked out. Anyway, the outgoing tenants told me how nice she was. What a joke. They saw me coming alright. They'd have sold their own grandmother just to get out of the lease. Amazing how people can really fool you with their cheesy smiles. If ever there was a reincarnation of Medusa, well she lives next to me. She hasn't got anything better to do than snoop and tell me not to hang flowers next to the shutters. Little does she know, but they're plastic flowers. I might be okay growing tomato plants, but I draw the line at flowers. I've never been good with them. I sometimes think that I need something that responds to neglect.

The other day, when the old crone told me not to leave my bicycle outside the front entrance, she gave me such a look; I seriously thought the flesh was going to melt off her face. That reminds me; on the next Halloween holiday, I must ask her how much she would charge to frighten people. She'd make a fortune.

The cars were bumper to bumper through New York State. Menacing grey clouds scurried across the horizon. The rain pelted the windscreen making it difficult to see the road. The road up to Aunt Elizabeth's was full of twists and turns and it had been a while since I'd driven up there. The bad weather was left behind on the Interstate, however, and it didn't seem to delay my journey. By the time I drove through the gates of the estate just after midday, the sun was shining again, as I wound my way amongst the trees.

I hadn't spent much time up here during the winter. The roads could get blocked and as much as I liked it here, the thought of getting snowed in didn't really appeal. I'm one of those people who easily succumb to cabin fever.

One of my favourite rooms at the Manor is the library. The shelves were packed with first editions and I'd spent many blissful hours looking through the books, carefully turning their pages. I'd even come across a book that a former housekeeper had written during her time here in the twenties and thirties, *Recollections of an Estate*, by Thora Banbury, which had been published in the 1950s. It gave a detailed account of what the Manor was like and included some fascinating photos and little anecdotes of when famous people came to stay. I'd sat for hours looking through it trying to picture what life was like in the earlier part of the twentieth century.

Back in the 1920s the Manor had had a staff of more than twenty, including a housekeeper, an estate manager, parlour maids, two gamekeepers, three gardeners and a couple of stable hands. They all contributed to making this one of the most successful estates in

New Hampshire. I knew that Todd Thornhill was well connected and that ex-Presidents had visited, and there was a rumour that Todd had even invited the famous actress Louise Brooks here for the weekend, much to the annoyance of his wife Eleanor.

As well as providing for the needs of its occupants, the estate often supplied the local villages with flowers, vegetables, dairy products, game and poultry. There were also horses, as Todd liked to ride with his nieces Emily and Elizabeth. Aunt Eleanor didn't ride, but did like to walk around the estate.

The long winding roads that snaked around the estate had originally been built for carriages, and had also been used for the first motor cars, those sleek highly polished black machines with their running boards and large headlights. One can imagine them making their way along the roads, the swaying trees like a guard of honour to welcome them and their occupants as they reached the main house. The roads were also ideal for long hikes and bike rides and these same trees also provided some welcome coolness from the sun.

The ten-bedroom manor house suddenly loomed in front of me. It looked elegant set against the clear blue sky and swaying trees as I swung the car around the statue of Venus and parked in front of the main entrance. Every time I see this statue, it reminds me of my frequent visits to Florence, Italy where I saw Boticelli's *The Birth of Venus* painting.

As I climbed out of the car, I heard the front door opening. My aunt's housekeeper stood on the steps. She managed to run the place with minimal help from a domestic who came in twice a week.

"Hello, Victoria, welcome back." A warm smile spread across her face as she approached the car. *She has put on a few pounds since I last saw her*, I thought, as I approached the front door. The result of tasting too much of her own delicious food. Well, who could blame her? I'd give my right arm to be able to cook like that. Her shoulder-length grey hair was held back with a metal hair slide and she wore tortoiseshell glasses, which belonged in another era.

"Hello, Mrs. Winton, how are you?" I grabbed my bags from the backseat and walked with her towards the house.

"I'm not too bad, but my arthritis has been playing up again," she said and clutched her shoulder, as if she was expecting another twinge of pain to hit her. "Your aunt's waiting for you in the library."

Dropping my bags in the hallway, I passed the long sweeping staircase as I made my way towards the library. The smell of beeswax from the parquet floor mixed with the pungent smell of old books drifted in the air as I entered.

"Ah, Victoria, how lovely to see you, my dear." My great aunt got up from her chair, stretching out her arms.

"It's nice to see you too, Aunt Elizabeth," I said, kissing her. She was the only relative that I had left on the Thornhill side. My own parents had died in a boating accident when I was fifteen and I'd spent most of my time in boarding schools, with the odd visits to my father's relatives in England and with intermittent visits to the Manor.

"I'll ask Mrs. Winton to bring us some tea," she said, pulling a cord by the side of the fireplace.

"Tea would be lovely, thanks." After my long drive, I was grateful to have something hot to drink. It had been a few hours since my coffee at breakfast and I'd only managed to drink some mineral water on the drive up.

Elizabeth Thornhill had never married. She had inherited the Manor in 1955 from her Uncle Todd, who had died of a heart attack. Her white hair, which had once been the colour of copper, was now short with a permanent wave. As a young woman, she had been something of a tomboy. She would ride her bicycle around the estate and wasn't frightened to wear pants and sweaters when most women her age were happy to be decked out in the latest Paris couture.

Our tea arrived and as my aunt poured the hot steaming liquid into the china cups, I looked around the room. I'd forgotten how impressive it was. The large fireplace reminded me of one I'd seen at Hampton Court Palace, near London, during my book research. I'm pretty tall and I'd managed to stand up in it, looking up into darkness, but seeing nothing. I expected something to come hurtling from above and hit me on the head any minute. To think that in the days of King Henry, they use to cook whole animals on a spit in those fireplaces.

The floor-to-ceiling bookshelves were packed with editions of Dickens, Scott Fitzgerald, Wharton and even one or two of the Bronte sisters. Several tired-looking leather chairs were scattered around the room. The library's bay window overlooked the garden with a backdrop over the lake and mountains.

Hanging on the wall above the fireplace there was a portrait of Todd and Eleanor Thornhill.

"We had it cleaned and restored a few months ago. It had been in the attic and we discovered it last year when we had one of our spring cleans," Elizabeth said, sipping her tea.

Todd Thornhill, a self-made millionaire who had owned several department stores in New Hampshire and Massachusetts now stood behind his wife, his hand on her shoulder. He had sandy-coloured hair and brown eyes. He had thin features, but I understand that later in life he'd put on a few pounds which had played havoc with his bad back.

Eleanor's beauty and elegance seemed to radiate from the portrait. Her porcelain skin and piercing blue eyes lit up her face. Her dark brown hair was swept up in a chignon with little tendrils falling at the side. She was wearing a high-necked cream lace dress and an emerald choker with matching earrings. Her hands were crossed in front of her and I could see the sapphire and diamond ring on her right hand. That ring now belonged to Elizabeth Thornhill.

After we finished our tea, I left my aunt in the library and followed Mrs. Winton to the ground floor guestroom, which had once been my great aunt Emily's.

The sunshine poured in through the French doors, making the room quite warm. I opened them and was met with a welcoming cool breeze which carried the scent of roses wafting in from the garden. An inquisitive wasp buzzed around the door, and then quickly changed direction as I shooed it out with part of the curtain.

A four-poster bed with what looked like a handmade quilt dotted with pink roses took up most of the space in the room. The fireplace made the room cosy, as evenings in the New Hampshire Mountains could be cool even in the summer. In the bathroom, the washbasin, bath and shower stall were as old as the hills and whilst they looked very interesting, I silently prayed that they would work. I could just imagine a modern-day plumber standing here scratching his head in confusion if he had to tackle this lot.

I longed for a refreshing shower after my journey. I stepped into the shower stall and turned on the taps. I heard a cranking sound and the water speeding through the pipes. It suddenly burst out of the shower spout with such a force that it almost knocked me off my feet. Well nothing like an invigorating shower to wake me up, I thought, as I covered myself in a lovely soapy mass. I changed into white linen pants and a pale blue t-shirt and made my way to the library, where Aunt Elizabeth was still reading the newspaper.

"Is your room comfortable enough, Victoria?" she said, taking off her reading glasses.

"It's wonderful. The bathroom is interesting. Some of my New York friends are renovating their bathrooms with older washbasins and here I am with the real thing."

Elizabeth laughed. "Well, some things never go out of fashion. The bedroom is one of the nicer rooms. It was always used by my older sister Emily."

"Oh yes, I remember you telling me. It has a wonderful view of the garden."

"It does and you know, when we were growing up, she was so proud of the garden. She planted some of the roses outside her room."

I smiled, thinking of the gorgeous blooms that I'd noticed. "I'm really looking forward to staying here for a couple of weeks," I said.

"I'm pleased to hear it. I think it will do you good to have a change of scene. New York is a nice city, but it's always good to have some fresh air." I totally agreed with her.

After I'd split up with my fiancé a few months ago, I found it hard to spend weekends in the city. I remembered our walks in Central Park, the visits to the Opera and the theatre and all the different restaurants that we could choose from. I was always so busy with my writing during the week. Many deadlines to meet, rushing around visiting the publisher, and not to mention all the research that goes with it. I hardly noticed he wasn't there, but weekends were another thing. We had managed to enjoy one of my favourite cities, the Big Apple.

I discovered he was having an affair with his secretary. Everybody else seemed to know what was going on except me. Despite my busy schedule, I'd invested a lot in that relationship and thought he was the one, but he had to go and ruin everything. We'd had such great times together. We were like kindred spirits. I'm not sure I believe in that hogwash now, but at the time, well, I was just about floating on air. I felt that we had a lot in common, as his parents had also died in an accident.

"I thought we'd have dinner on the terrace. Mrs. Winton is making something special for us." My aunt said interrupting my thoughts.

Our dinner was simple, but delicious. Tomato and basil soup served with sesame bread rolls, and a spinach and iceberg lettuce salad. This was followed by a cold meat platter of ham and turkey. Mrs. Winton was famous for her cheesecake and this time she didn't disappoint. I polished off two slices before I realised how hungry I was. I hadn't noticed until I sat down to devour the feast set before me.

I left my aunt on the terrace sipping her coffee and returned to my room.

Sitting on the bed, a cool breeze drifted over from the French doors. Just as I was about to close them I heard a noise. I stepped outside, and looked across to the woodland. One of the branches was moving as if someone had recently swept past it.

———•———

The milk in the jug had turned sour. He threw the contents down the drain and placed the jug on the draining board. The faint smell of sour milk hung in the air and he had to fight back a wave of nausea. His head throbbed as he went to the fridge to get a fresh carton. When he opened the door and checked the shelf, there were no cartons.

He cursed himself for drinking the whole bottle of wine last night. He'd been thinking again of Sarah. It had been five years since her death. He remembered the call from the police. She'd been forced off the road by a drunk driver. Her car rolled and burst into flames. It's hard coming to terms with the loss of your wife, but even more difficult when they don't find out who was responsible.

He'd hired a private investigator, but that had drawn a blank. *I hope whoever did it can't close their eyes at night*, he thought. He swallowed two aspirins and took a large mouthful of coffee. I'll take it black today he smiled to himself, suddenly wincing as his throbbing head reminded him of his over-indulgence. He headed for the bathroom and showered, letting the cool water wash over his face. As he changed into blue jeans and a white t-shirt, he thought about his nine o'clock meeting with the lady of the house. She was worried about poachers. One or two of the fences had been torn down on the estate and there were unexplainable tyre tracks off road near one of the fences.

Well, I best be on my way. I don't want to keep her waiting, but I'll just stop by the kitchen up at the Manor, see if I can beg a cup of coffee with milk.

Simon knocked at the kitchen door and walked in. Mrs. Winton, who had been like a mother to him, smiled as he came through the door.

"Morning, Simon, and how are you today?"

"So, so. I could really use a cup of that coffee, Mrs. W."

"Sure and how about a blueberry muffin? I've just taken some out of the oven."

"Sounds great." He pulled up a chair. "I'm meeting the boss at nine, so I don't want to be late."

Elizabeth Thornhill's housekeeper of almost thirty years knew only too well that her mistress was a stickler for time. If she wanted to see you at the certain time then god help you if you were late. She looked over at Simon. He was so like his father. They'd been good friends and he'd helped her when she had first arrived on the estate, a few years after Elizabeth had inherited it. The place had been closed up after Todd Thornhill died, and the previous housekeeper who'd been around since the 1920s had just died. She'd already retired, but they'd given her a grace and favour apartment at the top of the house. A sort of thank you for all she'd done over the years.

"Victoria arrived last night. She's grown into such a lovely girl, Simon," she said, placing some potatoes into a pan of water.

"Has she now," he said, finishing his coffee and the last few crumbs of the blueberry muffin.

"You can't mistake that family resemblance. She's got that lovely coppery-coloured hair, just like Miss Elizabeth had when she was younger," Mrs. Winton said, but Simon wasn't really paying attention. However, his head didn't feel like the size of a football now as the aspirin set to work.

"Well, I must be off," he said, kissing Mrs. Winton on the cheek.

Mrs. Winton knew that it would only be a matter of time until Elizabeth Thornhill suggested, albeit politely, that she retire. She had hinted at it a few times.

"Your grandchildren, don't you want to spend more time with them?" she had urged. It would be hard to leave, unless she was offered a nice little grace and favour apartment at the top of the house. Sadly, that part of the house was closed up now. *We simply don't have the funds or staff to look after it,* Elizabeth had said. The box that she was living in now, well you couldn't swing a cat in it.

After her husband Eddie died in 1975, she lost the will to carry on. They'd met when she went to live in New York where her sister lived. *It was so difficult and only for Elizabeth Thornhill, I'd have jumped over the cliff,* she thought, as she finished another potato. Her two children had married and she sometimes visited them and her grandchildren in Boston. She loved their get-togethers over clam chowder.

The only black sheep in Eddie's family was his younger brother Arthur. In and out of trouble since he was a young boy, he'd served fifteen years in *Alcatraz* for armed robbery and blackmail. He was finally released in 1963 just as the prison was closing and had settled in Massachusetts with his wife and son.

She finished peeling the rest of the potatoes and put them into the pan of water with the rest of them. She chopped up some tomatoes for the salad and put them into a bowl.

There, always good to be prepared. You never know what might happen, she thought, as she piled some of the blueberry muffins onto a plate and took them to the breakfast room.

My bedside clock told me that it was twenty to eight. I wrapped the duvet around me. My friends laugh at me because they call it a comforter. *Oh, Victoria, you're too European*, they exclaim. Well, it doesn't matter what you call it—that nice big lumpy mass of goodness that you throw over yourself and snuggle into.

I dragged myself out of bed and then had a long soak in the claw-footed bath. I was looking forward to catching up on my book. It always took longer than I thought, but I enjoyed the research. I dressed in blue jeans and a lemon t-shirt and made my way to the breakfast room.

"Oh, sorry Mrs. Winton. I didn't see you." I said narrowly avoiding a collision with my aunt's housekeeper.

"Has my aunt had her breakfast already?" I said helping myself to some orange juice.

"Yes. She's gone to see Simon Flynn." I knew from my conversations with Aunt Elizabeth that he was the current Estate Manager, one of a succession of Flynn men who had held this post on and off over the years since the estate had been built in 1915.

As I helped myself to some fresh fruit and Earl Grey tea, I thought about my book and some research I needed to do. I was just organising my thoughts when I overheard voices coming from the garden.

"That's good, Simon. You know how I worry about the roads around the estate. Uncle Todd was very proud of them. We have to keep them in good order."

"Just leave things to me, Ma'am, I'll make sure everything's okay. We often have trouble after spring rains with loose soil and leaves and a couple of rock falls. I'll see that those fences are repaired too."

I grabbed a blueberry muffin as I came out of the house. Simon Flynn had dark brown hair with tiny flecks of grey. He towered over me and must have been well over six foot tall. He stood with his hands in his pockets, deep in conversation with my aunt.

"Morning, Aunt Elizabeth," I said.

"Morning, Victoria," she said smiling.

"Hello, Mr. Flynn," I said, as I held out my hand. I hadn't seen him for a few years. *He must be in his late thirties*, I thought looking into his sparkling blue eyes.

"Victoria, you look so grown up." We shook hands. He had a firm grip and I could feel his eyes wash over me. The tell-tale flush reached my cheeks before I could turn away. My face lit up like a beacon.

"My niece has blossomed into a striking-looking woman, hasn't she, Simon?" My face was burning up so much I was convinced the glow could probably be seen from the international space station. All my New York boldness appeared to have deserted me. Perhaps I'd lost it somewhere along Interstate 91.

"Are you going into town today, Victoria?" Aunt Elizabeth enquired.

"No, I need to work on my book. I have a deadline looming."

"Well, don't work too hard, Dear. Do let Mrs. Winton know if you need any lunch."

"Okay, but I'll probably fix myself a sandwich. See you later." Flynn was still looking at me as I kissed Elizabeth. Although I hadn't seen him in years, he bore a resemblance to someone. Someone I'd seen, but I couldn't remember who, where or when?

"Bye, Mr. Flynn."

"Please call me Simon." A broad grin spread across his face.

As I walked back towards the rose garden, I could still feel his eyes follow my every move. Normally, I'd be rather flattered, but now I felt a little uneasy.

When I arrived back in my bedroom, a cool breeze was threading through the room. I closed the window and plugged in my laptop. I didn't have the luxury of a desk, so the machine was balanced precariously on my lap as I sat next to the window. My deadline was looming faster than I'd realised, but once I got going I became lost in text. After about an hour, I'd managed to write a rough draft of about 2,000 words, part of the chapter where Katherine of Aragon refuses to divorce Henry VIII as he wants to marry Anne Boleyn. Not finished, but getting there, I thought, as I sat back in the chair. The telephone interrupted the silence. It was Connie from my agent's office calling about progress on the book.

"Hi, yes, I am having a few days up in the mountains, but my laptop is chained to my waist," I said reassuringly. I'm quite serious about deadlines. When I say I'm going to do something by a certain time then I do it. It always amazed me when I was at Yale when we had papers to turn in when some of my fellow students breezily strode into class on Monday morning empty-handed. "I didn't have time over the weekend; I went to watch the game." Just one of the excuses, I'd heard over the years. Makes me wonder what he's doing now. He's probably some high-powered lawyer charging $300 an hour and still going to the game.

"That'll be fine, tell him I'll send the rest of the text in about two weeks." I switched off my cell phone and stared at the text floating across the screen. I think that's it for today. Tomorrow is another day. I was starting to sound like Scarlet O'Hara. I made sure the text was backed up on a floppy disk and switched off the laptop. I decided to take a shower and change. I stepped into the shower stall and let the warm water wash over me, creating a safe soapy haven. I towelled myself dry and then I dressed in a pale blue cotton shift dress and low-heeled white pumps. I sat down in the easy chair facing the window and closed my eyes for a few minutes. It was so relaxing here at the Manor.

I soon fell asleep. When I awoke, I saw that it was dusk. I reached for the lamp next to my chair. My eyes drifted to the bookcase on the side of the room. Emily Thornhill loved to read and write, according to Aunt Elizabeth. Nice to think those genes have been passed down to the following generations. Some of the books looked as if they hadn't been moved in years. As I took one of them off the shelf, little puffs of dust drifted into the air. It was a book of poems by Robert Frost entitled *New Hampshire.* Published in 1923, I knew it had won the prestigious Pulitzer Prize. I opened the page at one of my favourites *Fire and Ice.*

After reading it, I closed the book and put it back onto the shelf. It didn't quite line up with the others. I moved it from side to side and tried again. I realised something was blocking it. I looked at the space where the book had been. I put my hand at the back of the shelf and touched something. It felt like a box. I removed two of the other books and then pulled the box out of its hiding place. It was black with a Japanese scene on the front of it, depicting Mount

Fuji, that familiar landmark near Tokyo. The mountain majestically overlooked a Japanese village with a typical house near a bridge surrounded by trees. It had various other illustrations on the side of it. It reminded me of a music box I'd received as a gift from my mother when I was twelve. Apparently, Uncle Todd had given this box to my grandma Mary following one of his trips to Japan. I'd also seen a similar box on Aunt Elizabeth's dressing table.

I tried to open the box, but I couldn't. I slid my hand at the back of the shelf. Perhaps the key had fallen behind, but I found nothing. I looked at it for a moment. Was this also a music box? Then why was it locked? Perhaps it's something else. My curiosity got the better of me as the minutes passed. I had to find the key. This box must have belonged to Emily. All three Thornhill girls had been given similar boxes.

I decided to put the box back where I'd found it and try to look for the key. I made a couple of quick searches in the obvious places—the top drawer of the bedside table, on top of the wardrobe—but there was nothing. Disappointed at my attempts, I soon realised that it was time to go down to dinner.

Elizabeth was sitting at the long dining room table that could easily seat twenty people. She often invited friends from her Conservation Committee to dinner at the Manor and the dining room with its oak table was ideal. I had a small version of the table in my New York apartment, which I'd received from my great aunt as a graduation present.

"Good evening Victoria, did you manage to do some work?"

"Yes, I made some progress and I should meet the deadline." We joked about those dreaded deadlines that always seem to control our lives.

During a dinner of roast lamb, fresh mint sauce and Mrs. Winton's famous roast potatoes with vegetables from the garden, I heard all about my aunt's latest conservation projects. The Division of Forests and Lands had been planting more trees adjoining the estate and various study groups were expected to visit the Manor in the coming weeks. There were always requests for groups and individuals to visit. It offered such wonderful views and opportunities for wildlife projects. She told me that the KNC TV station had recently completed a documentary on the wildlife that inhabited the forest.

Although I'm very interested in the environment, I was anxious to steer the conversation again onto the subject of Emily Thornhill. At an appropriate moment, I jumped in.

"Did Emily spend a lot of time in her room?" I asked during an appropriate pause in the conversation.

"Why do you ask?" My aunt looked up from her apple pie and cream.

"I noticed she had a lot of books."

"Well, if the weather was bad and she couldn't sit in her rose garden, she loved reading and also liked writing poetry and short stories. My sister loved to sit in her room engrossed in the latest F. Scott Fitzgerald, or read from Tennyson's Charge of the Light Brigade: Half a League, Half a League etc., I know she enjoyed her stay at Miss Porter's because she was able to indulge in her passion for reading and writing. I have some of her poems. Let's go to the library."

We sat down in front of the fire. My aunt produced a box that had once contained shoes and now housed the poems and some personal effects of her sister Emily. I thought it was quite sad that these possessions were now kept in an old shoebox. Although I'm the last person to hold judgement. My apartment was full of bits and pieces from my book research stuffed into whatever kind of box or tin I could lay my hands on.

My aunt passed the box to me and I lifted the lid. Inside was a small blue book containing Emily's poetry, a couple of other pieces of paper and then, out of the corner of my eye, I caught sight of a small key. Could this be the key to the Japanese box that I'd found at the back of the bookcase? When my aunt reached over to stoke the fire, I slipped the key into my pocket. There were also some postcards in the shoe box, which I left on the sofa.

"Well, I'm quite tired," I said, stifling a yawn. "I look forward to reading the poetry." I hurried back to my room; I couldn't wait to try the key.

I placed the blue book on the bedside table. The poetry can wait, I thought, as I pulled two books off the shelf and slid my hand at the back, trying to find the Japanese box. It wasn't there. A rush of panic washed over me like a wave. I was sure that this was the place where I'd found it. I tried the next shelf, removing two books. It was there.

Panic over, I quickly removed it and then put the key into the lock. The key turned in the small rusty lock and I lifted the lid to reveal a jewellery box lined with salmon-coloured velvet with a mirror on the inside of the lid. As the lid was raised, I could also see a small compartment. A tune started to play as I pulled the two orange tassels aside to open up the compartment. *Greensleeves,* a tune that had been around some time. In fact I recognised it from my research into King Henry VIII. It was one of his favourites and legend has it that he composed it for his mistress at the time Anne Boleyn.

On the right-hand side of the box, tucked into the corner, was a small section for rings and small items. Of course, there was no jewellery in the box now, as Emily's possessions had been given back to Eleanor and everything had been passed on to Elizabeth.

No, wait, what are these? Tucked deep inside the ring pad was the most exquisite pair of pearl-drop earrings that I'd ever seen. I wondered why they were still here in this box. Had they been overlooked when the box was emptied of Emily's jewellery? If so, why put the empty box behind the books? I quickly realised that this box had obviously remained hidden after Emily's death.

I slid my hand to the back of the box to check if anything else had been hidden. At the back of the box I found a brown leather book. I opened it up. Inside the inscription read:

> *To my lovely Emily, with love from Uncle Todd,*
> *Christmas 1924*

My hands shook as I carefully turned the pages. On each page I saw the date followed by a beautiful handwritten script. I'd found Emily's journal for 1925.

CHAPTER FOUR

New Hampshire, 1925

Thursday January 1ˢᵗ

I can't believe another new year has passed us by. I've had the most wonderful Christmas. It was snowing on Christmas evening as we all sat down to a sumptuous dinner. Last night, I danced until two in the morning and Aunt Eleanor scolded me for drinking too much champagne.

This is my first day writing in my new journal. I've never kept a journal before, but now I think it would be nice because I can look back on it when I'm old. Well, that's a long time off, but now I will just sit here a while and enjoy one of my favourite places.

Monday February 16ᵗʰ

He told me about it today and how to get into it. Uncle Todd spends many hours in the secret closet. The room smelled of polish, old books and leather. It wasn't very big, but he said it gives him the peace and tranquillity he needs. There was a large armchair and a reading light that Uncle uses when he needs to. He said that his eyes were not as good as they used to be. We both laughed at that.

"Emily, look, just behind this book there's a lever. You pull it to the left and hey presto the door opens." He beamed. He was proud of his little secret. "Then when you're inside, press this button and the door will close over."

"You can come here if you want to; although I know you prefer to be outside in your rose garden," Todd had commented.

"Well, you never know when you might need to use this place to get away from something or someone. It will be our little secret," Todd had said, kissing Emily on the forehead.

Aunt Eleanor couldn't understand why my Uncle needed this place. I think I understood. When one is always at the beck and call of people as he is, you need a place of peace and tranquillity. He'd also told me that he wanted a place he could go to contemplate and read. Quite frankly, he wanted to get away from all the noise, including Eleanor's moaning about how many cigarettes he smoked and how much he drank.

I have my garden, Aunt Eleanor has her west-facing bedroom and her sunsets and Uncle has his reading closet.

Friday March 20th

I'm going to meet James tomorrow. I'll take the train from Concord to New York.

"Stop here. I'll walk the rest of the way." It had started to snow and within minutes her feet were cold and wet. She cursed herself for not wearing her boots.

"Are you sure, Miss? It's no trouble if I take you directly to the hotel. It's only two blocks and look at the weather."

Edward, one of her uncle's drivers in New York, had collected her from Grand Central. She had needed a break. She'd told them she was meeting a friend for lunch at The Pierre on Fifth Avenue and then would spend the afternoon at a new exhibition at the Metropolitan Museum of Art. It was a chance to get away from all that bickering up at the estate and the thousand and one questions about James. *I don't know if I can stand it much longer*, she thought, as she alighted from the car.

"Don't worry, Edward. I have an umbrella," she said turning up the collar of her fur coat as she stood on the side of the road.

"As you like, Miss," he said, doffing his cap.

"And Edward."

"Yes, Miss."

"Not a word to my uncle. You left me at The Pierre, is that clear?"

"Of course, Miss." Emily watched him drive off as the snowflakes settled on her brown felt hat and shoulders. She hailed a taxi. It stopped at the curb and she climbed in.

"The Windham Hotel, please." As the taxi pulled away, she breathed a sigh of relief. So far so good. The hotel loomed in front of her, tall and imposing as the taxi drew up outside. She paid the driver and climbed out. She hesitated at the revolving doors as the hotel doorman touched his cap in greeting.

They could meet here free from the servants' gossip and Uncle Todd's spies. It would not be the first time and probably not the last.

Saturday April 11th

> *I'm going to miss the estate when I leave for Europe tomorrow. I'm going to visit Paris and stay with Mademoiselle Dumont, who used to teach at Miss Porter's. Uncle Todd and Aunt Eleanor have been wonderful. We talked and talked yesterday about the garden. One of the gardeners is going to look after it whilst I'm away.*

Friday July 10th

> *I've come back to one of my favourite places. I have a lot of favourite places, James always teases me, but Cape Cod is truly a place where I can think and relax. The Bay is lovely at this time of year and I often walk along the endless stretch of golden beach looking at the white-painted houses with their wraparound porches.*

Today the sea looks angry. It's the same sea that took Papa away from me.

Ever since dear Mama's death a few years ago, although I had wanted to spend more time with my aunt and uncle, I didn't want to forget where I was born. I still miss Papa and I still can't forget the veil of grief that seemed to shroud our house after we found out that he wouldn't be coming back after his voyage to England. No more sitting on his knee on the front porch. No more nursery rhymes. Mama never stopped crying after Papa was gone. Her eyes always seemed to be puffy and red from the sobbing. It seemed that a smile never crossed her face again.

Uncle had persuaded Aunt Agnes, Mama's sister, that staying at the estate in New Hampshire and having my own private governess would be best for me. Miss Breen was nice enough, a bit strict sometimes, but I enjoyed her lessons, especially French and history.

Mama was so kind and thoughtful. I remember on my thirteenth birthday, she stood in the living room holding out a package. "Emily dear, a gift from Papa," her voice breaking as she handed me a white box wrapped in pale blue ribbon. He must have left it with her before he left for Europe. My fingers trembled as I removed the pale blue ribbon, so silky in my hands. I lifted the lid and saw a tiny photograph of my parents inside. It was from their wedding day. Why did you have to go? We all miss you so much.

Saturday July 18th

I saw James today for the first time since returning from Europe. I've really missed him. I know it's only been three months, but it was nice to sit with him in the rose garden. He can charm the birds out of the trees, I know, but he also makes me laugh. I feel so sorry for him sometimes.

51

I know how he feels. His mother also committed suicide. He doesn't talk about it much, but he told me that when he was young she used to encourage his love of swimming. "Come on, James, you can do it," she had shouted from the sidelines during a swimming competition. Whenever I speak to James about his father, he doesn't want to know about it. Mr. Flynn has been working for Uncle Todd as the estate manager for a few years now. I'd overheard Uncle talking one day on the phone when he said that Flynn Sr. had been away at the time of his wife's demise with one of his lady friends. Maybe that's why James blames him for his mother's death. The relationship is very strained and I think James is quite relieved that he's been in New York for a lot of the time. He wasn't sure if he wanted to return to the estate for the summer holidays. His father insisted, saying that James spent far too much time hanging around the fast set.

Wednesday August 19th

We've just got back from Oakwood. Elizabeth, Aunt Eleanor and I had been invited to a lunch party. The Willoughby's have the most wonderful swimming pool. It's the perfect place to sit around and have lunch or take a swim. We did both, of course, as the weather was glorious. We set up a little phonograph and a laid a carpet on the grass for our dance floor.

I saw Jason Bridge talk to Lizzie. He was teasing her about her swimming skills. She's one of the best swimmers I know, not as good as James, but pretty good.

I wore one of my favourite dresses today—pale yellow chiffon with a dropped waist and a bow at the side. I saw Jason looking at me. He smiled at me and I smiled back. He is rather good looking. I have him in mind for my sister, but she won't hear of it. He asked me to dance, but I refused. It was too hot.

I could see James looking at us from across the other side of the pool. He was sitting under a parasol, finishing off his second scotch. I sometimes think he drinks too much. He walked over to me and grabbed my hand. Before I had a chance to react he dragged me towards our makeshift dance floor. Jason Bridge was watching the two of us when I saw Lizzie bounding over to him.

"Come on Jason", she said. "Dance with me. Better luck next time," she teased him. Only Lizzie could break the ice with a witty remark like that. Did I see a look of disappointment on Jason's face as he looked at me? I'd managed to get James jealous. I could smell the alcohol on his breath as he pressed his face next to mine. He twirled me around the dance floor with such aggression that I thought I was going to fall over.

I was hot. I wanted to get something cold to drink and I was hungry. I finally managed to persuade him it was a good idea. I was a little disturbed by his behaviour. Even as I was helping myself to chicken and salad from the buffet, he seemed to be breathing down my neck. I caught the stale smell of whisky whenever he whispered to me. Ghastly stuff.

Tuesday September 15ᵗʰ

I had a lucky escape this morning. I was working in the rose garden, kneeling down turning over the soil when I heard a noise; like something whistling through the air. At first I thought it was a bird that had gotten too close to me. I turned around and looked up to see one of flower pots hurtling towards me. I just managed to step out of the way just in time before it hit me. The terracotta pot crashed into a hundred pieces at my side. They are pretty heavy things and when I told the head gardener what had happened, he thought it might have dislodged after the *storm we had a couple of weeks ago. New Hampshire is famous for its storms.*

Sunday November 8th

We'd had such a lovely evening. The meal was wonderful and I met Leo Burns who talked about his writing. I was glad that James had joined us. I could see that Uncle Todd wasn't very happy, but he can be rather grumpy now and again. I sometimes wonder how Aunt Eleanor puts up with him.

James was jealous that I was speaking to Leo. I think James might be having an affair. I always ignored what my aunt and uncle had said about him. "He's no good for you. He'll break your heart," they kept saying to me. At the time, I just thought they were exaggerating, but now I'm beginning to think they are right.

Sunday November 15th

James brought me home from the Willoughby's party last night. It was Cora's twenty-first birthday and we really enjoyed the fireworks. Once again, our wonderful neighbours had outdone themselves and the birthday cake, well, it was truly amazing; one of the biggest I've ever seen. There was even a photographer taking pictures. After some years, I am still trying to persuade aunt and uncle to hold a party at Thornhill Manor. Uncle said he couldn't bear the thought of people trampling over his precious lawns.

Sadly the evening did not end on a happy note.

"I just don't know, James. My aunt and uncle have been so kind to me since my parents died and . . ."

"Yes, I've heard it all before, Emily. What I'm asking now is that we go away together. We find a place of our own and, who knows, once I've found a job, we can get married." He drew on his cigarette.

"I'd prefer if we got married and then found a place of our own. Uncle Todd will never allow us to live together before we are man and wife and it would break Aunt Eleanor's heart."

"They run your life, Emily, and treat you like a child. You are twenty-five years old. You can make your own decisions."

"You've no idea how kind they've been to me over the years since my parents died. They practically raised me and my sisters."

"So what, that happens in most families when a parent dies, the other relatives look after the children. Why do you try and make them out to be saints? Todd Thornhill is the biggest crook that ever lived and . . ."

"You can call him what you like. He doesn't think too much of you either. He thinks I don't know, but he despises you. I'm loyal to you, James, but sometimes I have to wonder," she said, breaking free from him and running into the house.

"Emily, come back." He followed her and caught her arm. "Let's not part like this. You know I only want what is best for you."

"Leave me alone." Emily ran down the corridor towards the library. She could hear James in the distance. As she opened the library door, the moonlight guided her to the hiding place. She found the bookcase. Her hands reached behind and found the lever. She pulled it and the door opened. When she was inside, she closed it. The thick dusty air was filled with the smell of books. He would never find her in here.

CHAPTER FIVE

New Hampshire, 1999

The next morning I woke up feeling completely exhausted. I shouldn't have been surprised. It had been well after midnight when I had finally closed Emily's journal. I'd read quite a large chunk and certainly enough to intensify my interest in her. I'd been transported back to the 1920s by the writings of a young woman whom I'd never met, but with whom I now felt a connection. I couldn't believe some of the things I'd read. She'd mentioned the plant pot falling; was someone really trying to kill her or was it just an accident? I was also intrigued by this so called *secret closet*. Did it still exist? More questions. I was now more determined than ever to find out the answers.

I managed to crawl out of bed and plodded into the bathroom. I turned the shower onto the strongest setting possible with the ancient plumbing but it was still effective. It certainly woke me up and I was grateful that Mrs. Winton had left me a small tray with a much needed cup of tea—a nod to my English roots and frankly nothing like it first thing in the morning.

My head was clearing and as I gulped down a few mouthfuls of tea, I decided to go for a jog. I must admit that jogging around the Thornhill estate is a completely different experience from the hustle and bustle of New York's Central Park. It was a welcome change to hear birdsong instead of New York's national anthem, a.k.a. the sirens from emergency vehicles. The air was cool with no humidity—absolutely perfect.

As usual when jogging, I set off at a steady pace and tried to build up as I went along. The air was cleaner here, of course, but I still have a soft spot for Central Park. I'm one of the lucky ones I guess. I can have both.

As I rounded one of the corners, I spotted Simon on horseback in the distance.

"Morning, Simon," I said and slowed down to a trot, trying to keep pace with his horse.

"Hello, Victoria, you're out and about early," he smiled.

"Well, it's such a nice crisp morning and I couldn't pass up a chance."

"Do you like to ride?" he asked, and pulled at the reins.

"Yes, I do, as a matter of fact, but I haven't ridden for a couple of years."

"Would you like to join me for a ride one of these fine mornings?" he asked, and looked expectantly at me.

"Yes, why not, but I'm not very good."

"Don't worry; we have a nice mild-mannered horse back at the stables. I'm sure you'll be fine." He rode off. We would meet the day after tomorrow, nine o'clock sharp.

When I got back to my room, I found a note on my bed. It was Mrs. Winton to say that breakfast would be served on the terrace from eight o'clock. It was now half past, so I hurriedly removed my jogging clothes and stepped into the shower.

Later, as I entered the breakfast room, I found my aunt sitting at the table drinking some iced tea.

"I could really use some of that," I said. "I've already had my hot tea, but I've just been running and I haven't cooled down yet."

"I'm so glad that you are enjoying your time here, Victoria."

"Aunt Elizabeth, tell me a little bit more about Emily," I said, helping myself to a blueberry muffin. She leaned back in her chair, looking slightly uncomfortable.

"Well, she was ten years older than me. You know, all the young men were half in love with her. She seemed so much more alive than most of us." She closed her eyes. "Emily used to stay here with Uncle Todd and Aunt Eleanor during her school holidays. She loved riding, walking and spending hours in the rose garden. She was particularly close to Aunt Eleanor. They shared a wonderful interest in gardening. The budding horticulturist, that's what they used to say about Emily." Aunt Elizabeth beamed with pride.

"She was very young when she died wasn't she?" I probed.

"Yes, she was. We were all devastated." She lowered her eyes.

"How did she die?"

"She fell from her horse and died from the injuries a few days later. It was tragic." I knew Emily was, among other things, an accomplished horsewoman. Did something startle the horse? Did it slip? That's always a possibility, as I knew only too well. It had happened to me a couple of years ago when I found myself buried under a heap of brown muscle.

Well, I decided to give the explanation of Emily's death the benefit of the doubt, but I still had a feeling that something wasn't quite right.

"Victoria, you must understand that it was such a difficult time for all of us. My poor Mama had died a few years before. She had never recovered from the sudden death of my father on the *Titanic*." I had a sudden feeling of guilt as I listened to Aunt Elizabeth. I knew that my great grandmother Miriam had committed suicide by jumping from the widow's walk of her Cape Cod house into the sea below. The thoughts of such a horrible death made me shudder.

While Elizabeth and Mary went to live with Miriam's sister, Emily spent most of her time at Thornhill Manor. Todd and Eleanor simply adored her.

"It had been hoped that our family could stay together after the tragic deaths of my parents, but Todd and Eleanor had fought tooth and nail to raise Emily, as they had no children of their own. Emily had a private governess until she reached the age of fifteen and then she became a boarder at Miss Porter's school in Farmington, Connecticut. During the holidays, she travelled up to New Hampshire and stayed with Todd and Eleanor."

I'd heard some of the story before from Grandma Mary. If Aunt Elizabeth knew anything else she wasn't going to admit to it.

It was time for me to do some investigating into Emily's death. I just had this feeling that something wasn't quite right.

———•———

I arrived at Moultonborough Library just before ten. There were only three other cars in the car park, which I thought was strange for a weekday. I pushed open the swinging doors. I always expect other people to be as fond of libraries as I am. The Library, housed in a former bank building, had high ornate ceilings, parquet floors and large windows. A perfect setting to pore over the books, I thought. The smell of old books and polished floors hung in the air as I walked through the door. It reminded me of when I joined my first library as a child. It was a quaint old place on Christian Street in Chester. I was a big fan of the English writer Enid Blyton and would devour the stories about the Famous Five and the Secret Seven, not to mention Anna Sewell's adventures of Black Beauty.

I walked up to the enquiry desk. A middle-aged woman with short black hair sat staring at her computer screen.

"Good morning, I'm looking for some information." The woman looked up. Her glasses perched on the end of her rather long nose, at the top of which I could see the tell-tale red marks.

"Yes Ma'am, what type of information?"

"Well, I'm looking for some past news reports and information concerning a death in 1925."

"Ma'am all our records going back that far are kept in the archives section on the second floor. Just take the elevator on your right and contact the enquiry desk on that floor. My colleague will answer any queries you may have." She turned back towards her computer screen.

I made my way towards the elevator and pressed the button. The second floor was also an impressive room with high ceilings, parquet floors and long wooden tables. On the wooden tables, the only sign of modernity were the computer terminals.

I made my way over to the enquiry desk, where a young blond-haired woman sat looking at some index cards.

"Hi there, I'd like to search for some information for 1925 to 1926 please."

"Yes, Ma'am, come this way." We walked over to one of the computers.

"What exactly are you looking for, Ma'am?"

"I'm looking for details on the death of Emily Thornhill of Thornhill Manor; she died in 1925," I stated hopefully.

"Well, you can start your search by using a key word or a phrase. It's best to fill out all these boxes," she said, and pointed to the screen. "It gives you a better chance of finding something. We also have some things on microfilm."

"Thanks a lot." I completed the advanced search form and looked hopefully at the screen as the young woman walked back to her desk.

A few minutes later, the search revealed that ten records had been found. I felt a sudden rush of excitement as I started to scan through several articles that the system had called up. The first one that caught my eye had appeared in the *New Hampshire Chronicle.* It was a photo of Emily and her friend James, which had been taken in November 1925. They had attended a party at Oakwood House. Emily was wearing a knee length fitted dress, long gloves and her hair was up in a chignon. She was wearing a headband with a large ostrich feather at the side. James, dressed in a tuxedo, stood next to her. His hair was swept back off his face and he smiled confidently into the camera. He was holding a cigarette in his right hand. He had his right arm around Emily's waist. There was no mistaking the resemblance. James was the spitting image of his grandson Simon, but a little younger.

I skipped to the next record and started to read an article from the *Laconia Herald* on November 26th 1925.

The headline caught my eye:

Heiress dies suddenly after fall from horse
Thornhill multimillionaire devastated at the death of his niece

By Jason Bridge

Emily Thornhill, 25-year-old niece of Todd and Eleanor Thornhill, died last night at the family's estate near Moultonborough. Sources close to the family say she had been seriously ill since falling from her horse while riding on the estate.

I knew the offices of the *Laconia Herald* were about a fifteen-minute drive away and I thought I'd drop by their offices later to see if I could dig up some more information.

The other articles from the Internet and microfilm records reported the tragedy, but said nothing to suggest that it was anything other than an accident. I printed the articles and made my way out of the library. I felt sure I might be on to something.

"Hello again, Victoria. Catching up on some reading?" I turned around, startled. Simon Flynn stood looking at me. As I fumbled for my car keys I dropped my bag on the floor. The copies of the articles poked out of the side. Fortunately the text and photographs were on the inside. I quickly picked up the bag, stuffed the paper further inside and fastened the strap.

"Hi Simon, I was just following up on a few things for my book. These historical books take so much time and energy," I laughed. I was thankful that I'd managed to close the strap on my bag before he had time to glance at the articles. I really didn't want to alarm my aunt if he twigged on to the reason for my visit. I knew how close she was to Simon. He was the grandson she never had.

"Oh yes, your aunt told me about your latest book. Did you get all the information you wanted? It's only a small library. You may have better luck in Laconia," he said, as he opened my car door.

"I found what I was looking for, thanks." I smiled at him and then excused myself and set off for the offices of the *Laconia Herald*.

———•———

As I drove down Laconia's Main Street, I saw the usual collection of shops familiar in a small town; a pharmacy, a hairdresser, a book store, a shoe shop and a florist. I turned the car into Church Street and parked outside a diner. A sign with *Frankie's Diner* hung over the red and white door. I hadn't realised it had been a few hours since I'd eaten breakfast and my stomach was growling at me.

I sat down in one of the available booths. The place was tastefully decorated for a diner. Cream-coloured curtains hung from the windows. The mint green-coloured seats and cream tables gave the place a cool natural feel. I decided to have the basil omelette with a side order of green salad. That would take care of the hunger pangs that I'd tried to fight off for the past hour. I also ordered an apple juice.

The middle-aged waitress with dyed red hair and heavy make-up brought my order fifteen minutes later.

"There you go Ma'am. Can I bring you any salad dressing?" she said, placing her pencil behind her ear.

"Oh no thanks. Urm, by the way, I'm looking for the office of the *Laconia Herald*. Is it nearby?" You know what they say about a smiling friendly waitress; an open invitation to local information.

"Yes, it's just a few blocks from here. Turn left when you leave the diner. Go along Main Street until you reach Chainey's Garage. Then you turn right onto Piclow Road and the *Herald's* office is on the right-hand side of the street. You can't miss it."

"Thanks a lot." I ate my meal as if it was going to be my last. Hunger now satisfied, I paid the check and made my way out of the diner, deciding to walk to the newspaper office. I needed the exercise and it's not always easy to find parking spaces in small towns.

CHAPTER SIX

New Hampshire, 1925

"Jason, I think someone is trying to kill me."

"What? That's preposterous. Who would want to do such a thing?"

"Take a look at this." She handed him the anonymous note, which had been slipped under the bedroom door the night before. The letters had been meticulously cut and stuck onto some cheap quality white paper:

EMILY
LEAVE JAMIE ALONE or you will die.

"I can't imagine who sent this. Oh Jason, I'm so frightened. Do you think whoever sent this is serious?"

"Of course not. This is someone's idea of a stupid joke."

"Some joke," she said through her tears. "It's scaring the living daylights out of me."

"You haven't mentioned this to Flynn, have you?"

"No," Emily said softly.

"Well, don't."

"You don't think he's behind it, do you? Why send me a note? We love each other. We've talked about going away together . . . ," she sobbed.

They sat in silence, Emily dabbing her eyes. Jason was concerned for his friend, but he didn't know what to do.

"That's not all. A few days ago, while I was working in the rose garden, one of the plants pots from the top of the house came hurtling towards me. I just barely got out of the way."

"That could be a coincidence, Emily."

"That's what I thought, but then when I received the note . . . ," she said, and wrung her hands. "I know he's seeing someone else."

"Do you have proof? Have you seen him with someone else?"

"Jason, I just know it." Emily walked over to the window seat and sat down.

"How do you know this, Emily?"

"For goodness sake, call it a woman's intuition or whatever you like. I overheard one of the maids talking about another servant who visits her journalist lover in New York. Now if that's not a coincidence, I don't know what is. James has been interning at the New York Times."

"Have you confronted him over this?"

"No. I'm not sure it's a good idea. I just don't know what to do, Jason. Sometimes I get so angry I think he can just go off with his fancy woman and just leave me alone."

———•———

The dining room looked wonderful and the scent from the roses, lilies, sweet peas and tulips floated through the air. Eleanor always enjoyed arranging the flowers herself with the help of Mrs. Banbury. There was so much to choose from now in the gardens. Their special guests, President Coolidge's Secretary of Commerce, Mr. Hoover, and his wife Louise would join them for the weekend. She now had the perfect excuse to fill the room with her favourite blooms from the estate.

"I'm going to have an arrangement for each of the six tables," she'd informed her housekeeper. The gardener had delivered the blooms earlier that morning and Eleanor and Mrs. Banbury had put the flowers in small tubs.

"We can't have them too high otherwise our guests won't be able to see each other across the table." Eleanor was especially pleased that Leo Burns would be visiting. She knew how much her niece enjoyed literature. The one thing that she wasn't looking forward to was the presence of that loathsome boy, James Flynn. She didn't have the heart to tell Todd that Flynn would be a guest at the dinner. Emily had asked if she could invite him for dinner and Eleanor didn't have the heart to say no. Todd would not upset his favourite niece;

thankfully, there would be no scene. Emily would sit on the right of her uncle, but Flynn would be on a table as far away from them as possible.

"Everything is ready, Ma'am, for this evening," Thora Banbury said. "I hear Cook is preparing the most wonderful venison from the estate and she's using only the best vegetables that she could find. She's also making crème caramel as only she can make it," she offered. "Mr. Thornhill also asked that we serve French wines this evening, Ma'am," she said, and clasped her hands together.

"Thank you so much, Mrs. Banbury. I know I can always count on you to make sure that everything is perfect. Now I must go and get ready. Our special guests are due within the hour."

"So Leo. What are you working on at the moment?" Todd Thornhill asked, handing the writer a glass of red wine.

"Oh, a collection of short stories with the main theme of horses."

"How very interesting, Todd smiled. "Very important animals. I've got a few of them here on the estate. I don't know what I'd do without them. You know Burns, you must meet my niece. She adores the creatures."

"Ah Emily. Let me introduce you to Leo Burns."

"Mr. Burns, I am pleased to make your acquaintance. My uncle has told me all about you."

"Nice things I hope." the writer said smiling mischievously. "The pleasure is all mine, Miss Thornhill," he said, kissing her hand and making Emily blush. Their eyes held for a few seconds.

"I'd like to introduce a friend of mine, James Flynn."

"How do you do. Pleased to make your acquaintance," Flynn said, extending his hand.

"And yours, Mr. Flynn."

The colour drained from Todd's face. Eleanor, earlier that evening, had suddenly told him that Emily wanted to invite this degenerate to the dinner. It was too late to say no and Emily might cause a scene and not show up. How embarrassing would that be in front of the guests? Eleanor had been planning the weekend for some time. *Get lost,* he wanted to shout at Flynn, but he had to keep his temper in check.

"Mr. Burns, I wonder if you will be so kind as to read a poem to our guests tonight?" Emily enquired.

"I will be delighted, Miss Thornhill." He smiled and kissed her hand.

Todd watched the expression on Flynn's face. He was delighted to see that rogue squirm. Flynn's jealously of Leo was written all over his face.

"Dinner is served, Madam."

"Dear guests, let's go into the dining room, shall we?" Eleanor exclaimed.

"Excuse me Sir. There's a telephone call for you. It's your office in Concord."

"Well tell them I can't be disturbed. I'm having dinner with my guests. They can call me in the morning. Isn't it tiresome, Herbert, when someone is always trying to contact you?" he said to the Secretary of Commerce.

"Sir, they are quite insistent. They must speak with you straight away."

Todd Thornhill flung his napkin on the table and pushed out his chair. "Apologies; I will just see what this is all about. Pour Mr. Secretary some more wine, will you, man," he barked at the waiter standing near the door.

"Yes Sir," the ashen-faced waiter replied.

Todd grabbed the receiver off the hall table. "Why are you calling me at the house? This had better be good. I'm in the middle of an important dinner and . . . ."

"It's Sam King, Sir. He's been found dead."

"Dead, what do you mean, dead? I only saw him last week. What was it, a heart attack? I always thought he was doing too much he was always . . . ."

"No Sir. His body was found in Lake Laconia. It had washed up near the jetty. A young fisherman found it about seven this morning.

Police say he'd probably been in the water for eight to ten hours by the looks of the body."

"Do they think it was suicide? How did he end up in the lake? I can't imagine he was into midnight swims." The assistant cringed at Todd's insensitivity.

"The police found one of his business cards in his coat pocket and called the office. The night security gave them my number. Police think he was mugged and then dumped in the lake. His wallet was missing and his watch was stolen. They'd even removed his shoes and glasses."

Todd leaned back in his chair. "Well, we've lost a really good accountant."

"We have indeed, Sir. What's going to happen now?"

"Sam's deputy can cover for a while and then I'll think of something. I'll need to stop by the office in the next few days and see if there was anything outstanding."

"The police have been looking around Sam's office . . . ."

"Who gave them permission? Do they have a warrant? They can't just breeze into places without a warrant." He slammed his fist on the table. "Who do these cops think they are?"

"We were going to call you, Sir, but they said it wasn't necessary."

"Well, they would say that wouldn't they. Let me know if they come back and find out who's in charge of this investigation."

"Of course, Sir."

"What is it, Todd?"

"Oh Eleanor, I didn't hear you. Some bad news, I'm afraid. Sam King's been found dead. Floating in the Lake. The Police suspect foul play."

"Oh dear god. His poor wife and children." She steadied herself on the table.

"Now Eleanor, calm yourself Dear, we must get back to our guests."

"Yes, our guests. I'll make sure we send our condolences to his wife and family. "

"Ladies and Gentleman, may I propose a toast to our guests of honour here this evening," Todd said addressing the room. "To a very good friend of mine, Herbert Hoover, and his charming wife Louise." Glasses clinked and the Hoovers smiled.

Emily turned to Leo Burns who was seated on her right. "Mr. Burns, I'm intrigued by these stories you are writing about horses."

"Please call me Leo." He said taking a sip of his wine.

"Leo it is and you must call me Emily."

Well Emily, I grew up on a farm in Massachusetts and we had horses, so I thought it was a good idea. We also had lots of cows, but as a subject for a short story they obviously didn't appeal." he said laughing.

"I can understand that." Emily said smiling. "So you obviously ride, Leo?"

"I do indeed, but not as often as I would like to."

"Well, you must join the group tomorrow. We've planned an outing. I know that Mrs. Hoover rides, quite well I hear. Why don't you join us?"

"Oh I might take a walk around the gardens. Clear my head and get some thoughts down on paper. This is such a beautiful place to live. I understand you like gardening."

"That's right. Something I developed whilst at Miss Porter's in Connecticut."

"And do you have a favourite flower?"

"Yes, the rose," she said without hesitation. "but I also like hyacinth and lily of the valley. Such wonderful fragrances".

"Interesting selection." He said sipping his wine, his eyes never leaving Emily. Flynn was seated at another table and was surveying the scene like a general watches over his troops. He wasn't the only one watching Emily. Todd, in between gulps of wine and a slightly flirtatious conversation with Louise Hoover, glanced at Flynn. He could tell by the look on Flynn's face that he was jealous of Emily's conversation with Burns. *I'm thoroughly enjoying myself watching that little scum bag squirm,* he thought.

"Now Louise, you must join us tomorrow for our ride. We've plenty of good horses for you to choose from."

"I haven't ridden for a while, Todd. You know in my younger days, I'd ride out for hours and go hunting in California with my Papa."

"I'm sure you'll be fine. Won't she, Herbert?"

"She sure will. Let me tell you Todd when Lou sets her mind to something there's no stopping her," he said, and they laughed.

"Gentlemen, let's leave the women to their coffee and conversation, shall we. Please join me in the library; I've been saving a bottle of port for just such an occasion as this evening." Todd rose from his chair and the male guests, with the exception of Flynn, made their way to the library. Flynn had just about had as much of this charade as he could take. He needed some air. He needed to speak to Emily. He waited until she'd said goodnight to Burns.

"Emily," he said, grabbing her by the arm. "I'd like a word with you."

"James, did you enjoy the evening? See, I told you that I could get you an invitation. Uncle Todd always . . ."

"Come with me to the terrace, I need some fresh air."

"But James, I can't leave our guests, it's . . . ."

"Come now, or I'll make a scene. What's it to be?" Emily could see that he was serious. He had a strange look on his face. An almost blank expression as if there was nothing behind his eyes. No soul, no warmth or feeling.

They stood on the terrace breathing in the cool night air. James attempted to put his arm around Emily, but she shrugged him off.

"Don't touch me," she said. Flynn lit a cigarette and breathed deeply, exhaling from his nostrils. The smoke hung in the air.

"What's wrong with you, James?"

"What's wrong with me? I'll tell you what's wrong. What was that doe-eyed display at the dinner table?"

"I don't know what you're talking about."

"You know exactly what I'm talking about. All that whispering and giggling. You had that writer practically eating out of your hand. I thought the man was going to eat you, the way he was looking at you."

"Oh, don't be silly. The cat can look at the Queen. Don't tell me you're jealous. Ah, poor little James . . . ." She saw him raise his hand and before she had a chance to react, she felt the sharp sting on her cheek.

"How dare you. You monster!" Emily said, clutching her cheek. "I hate you, get away from me."

"Emily, forgive me. I don't know what came over me." He tried to grab her arm, but Emily swept past him and ran towards the rose garden. One of the thorns caught her dress and a tiny strand of pink silk was left hanging on the bush as she stumbled towards the house. Tiny pieces of hair had broken free from her chignon. She tried the side door near the servant's quarters, but it was locked. She banged on the door and it was opened by Mary Riley, whose bedroom was close by.

"Oh Miss, whatever happened to yer?"

"Mary. I just need to sit down and compose myself for a moment."

"And why do you need to do that, Emily?" Emily spun around and saw her Uncle Todd standing in the doorway. His tie was pulled loose and his jacket was slung over his shoulder. *Where had he come from?* Emily wondered.

"Tell me, where is he?"

"Uncle please, I went out onto the terrace to get some air and then came back to the house through the rose garden. Silly me, I stumbled and caught my dress. It was dark and the next thing I saw was a light shining from Mary's window."

"Don't lie to me. If Flynn has laid a hand on you, so help me, I'll show no mercy. I'll break every god damn bone in his body."

Emily and Mary stood in the small hallway leading to the servants quarters as Todd ranted and raved. Emily walked over to her uncle and held his hand.

"Uncle, you mustn't worry yourself. Thank you for your concern, but everything will be fine."

"Well, Emily, I think you should go to your room. All our guests have retired for the evening." He straightened his tie and put on his jacket.

"Mary, thank you for opening the door. Not a word of any of this to the other servants, is that clear?"

"Yes, Sir. It's clear, not a word." Emily and Todd Thornhill closed the door behind them.

"Oh, Mrs. Banbury, I didn't hear you," Mary said. Standing in the shadows, the wily housekeeper had heard everything. *Well, well, Mary and the old man,* she mused. *Who'd have thought? I wonder if he knows that Flynn is not just courting his niece, but this stupid girl. I'll never keep pace with all these comings and goings.*

"Just getting some hot milk. Couldn't sleep with all this commotion," Mrs. Banbury remarked. The girl wouldn't dare question her excuse. "Well, back to bed, girl. You've got to be up early in the morning to help with the breakfasts."

———•———

The sideboard groaned under the weight of a hot and cold buffet of eggs, bacon, hash browns, fresh fruit and freshly baked bread rolls. The Hoovers had taken their breakfast earlier and were now enjoying a stroll through the garden. Eleanor and Leo Burns were seated at the table when Todd walked in.

"Morning," he grumbled. He now regretted his little tryst with Mary the previous night. It had been a risk, but Emily was the last person who he'd imagined would catch him. She was naïve, but not that much.

After most of his guests had finished their drinks in the library, Todd had excused himself, saying he had to go to his study to make an urgent phone call. Saying he might not return, he bid his remaining guests a good day. Todd's study was close to the servant's quarters and he knew Mary would be waiting. *It's all Flynn's fault, I know he assaulted Emily, but she's protecting him. I'll sort him out. What happens when there's a thorn in my side? Well, I deal with it.*

"Todd Dear, you look a little tired. Didn't you sleep well?" Eleanor and Todd had separate bedrooms. He'd said it was better that way as he was an early riser and he didn't want to wake her.

"A little yes, but I'll still go riding later." He helped himself to some scrambled eggs and hash browns.

"Well, don't overdo it today dear. Remember your bad back," his wife said, sounding concerned.

"To hell with my bad back. I need to get out in the fresh air. Nothing like it." He said shovelling a fork full of eggs into his mouth. "So, Leo, what are your plans for the day?"

"I'll just enjoy the scenery. I have a magical view from my room. I rather think it will be conducive to writing."

"Todd, according to Mrs. Banbury, Emily is not coming down to breakfast. She's taking it in her room. After the dinner last night, she's feeling under the weather."

That's a joke, thought Todd. *Under the weather indeed. I'm going to get to the bottom of this business if it's the last thing I do.*

"Yes, Eleanor. I'm sure she's fine. It's a pity she'll miss the ride. Anyway, don't worry now. Eat your breakfast."

The houseguests left the estate the next day, after thanking their gracious hosts for their hospitality and extending the usual invitations to visit with them. Emily couldn't come down to say goodbye to them, particularly Leo. She had enjoyed his company, and had wanted to show him some of her short stories, but she couldn't face anyone, not after what had happened with James. She had no idea where he was. She assumed he was at Flynn cottage on the estate, but maybe he had gone back to New York. One of the servant's would be able to tell her. She heard a soft knocking at her door.

"Who is it?" she said her voice hoarse from crying.

"It's Mary. I brought you some tea with honey. I know it's your favourite."

"Come in, Mary." She would know where James was. Emily had seen them talking to one another a few months back during a summer barbeque.

"I'll just set the tray here, Miss. Let me pour you a nice cup of tea. That throat doesn't sound too good, Miss. I hope you're not getting a chest infection. Cook said one of the gardeners was struck down the other day. One minute he's mowing the lawn and the next he's taken to his bed."

"Mary, have you seen James Flynn these past two days?" Emily wasn't entirely sure she could trust the maid.

"No Miss, but Mrs. Banbury said he was at the cottage last night. He wouldn't answer the door to one of the stable hands when he dropped off some venison for him. We had loads from the hunt yesterday. Flynn told the boy to go away. Apparently he sounded as if he'd been drinking."

"Mary, I need to get a message to him. Would you be able to give it to him?"

"Well, I don't know, Miss I . . . ."

"It would mean a lot to me, Mary."

"I'll try, Miss. He might not even answer the door to me."

"Just knock at the door. Tell him you've got a note from me and then slip it under the door. Simple."

Before Mary could change her mind Emily tore a sheet of paper from a notepad she always kept at the side of her bed. She sat at her desk, quickly scribbled a few lines, folded the paper and then gave it to the maid.

Mary stuffed the note in her pocket and left the room. She smiled to herself. So she fell for the *he's in his cottage and won't answer the door routine. Gullible Emily, what James sees in her I'll never know*, she thought, ripping the note into tiny little pieces and flinging it in the bushes.

CHAPTER SEVEN

New Hampshire 1999

I arrived at the *Laconia Herald* just as a tall thin man in his mid-forties with bright red hair was rolling down the blind. I knocked and opened the door.

"Just closing for lunch, Ma'am." He looked as if he was on his own in the office. I immediately felt guilty. Perhaps he had to go home for lunch to a nagging wife or an elderly relative? As a townie, I always forgot that shops and businesses in the country closed for lunch. I remember a couple of years ago when I was visiting a store in Vermont. One minute there were ten people milling around the place and then just as the clock struck twelve, everyone disappeared and the lights went out. I was one of the stragglers and received a severe ticking off from the store assistant.

"I'm sorry, I just have a small question. It'll only take a few minutes," I asked with a warm pleading expression on my face.

"Okay. Step inside." He flipped over the door sign from open to closed. He certainly didn't want to risk another last-minute visitor.

"Take a seat. Are you visiting these parts? I haven't seen you before, Miss er," he stopped, with a quizzical look on his face.

"Yes, I'm visiting from New York. My name's Victoria Green."

"Jim Houghton, editor-in-chief. Nice to meet ya." Houghton shook my hand and made his way over to his desk.

"What can I do for you?" Houghton leaned back in his chair and pushed his glasses back onto his face.

"I read some information about the death of Emily Thornhill in November 1925. In particular an article written by a reporter from the *Herald*, a Mr. Jason Bridge."

"And why would you be wanting information on something that happened more than seventy years ago, Miss Green?" he asked, his eyebrows almost touching the ceiling.

"I'm researching my family tree and I . . ."

"Are you related to the deceased?"

"Yes, she was my great aunt. I'm staying up at the Manor."

"Ah, with Ms. Elizabeth Thornhill."

"That's right."

"How is she? We haven't seen her for a while."

"She's fine," I said impatiently.

"Well, about this story. Of course, I wasn't around at the time, but I recall seeing something in our files some time back." Houghton became circumspect, and looked surprised with my interest in an event that had taken place more than seventy years ago.

"From the article by Bridge in 1925, it sounded as if there was more to Emily Thornhill's death than just an unfortunate riding accident," I said. I reached inside my handbag for a copy of the article that I'd got from the library earlier and passed it to Houghton. He read it with the intensity and speed of a seasoned newspaper man.

"Bridge remarked on the rumours that were circulating at the time and I wanted to know if he may have found information on the death that perhaps he didn't or couldn't print?" Houghton put the article on his desk and took off his glasses. I could see the tell-tale red mark across the bridge of his nose.

"Jason Bridge was one of the best reporters that has ever worked at this newspaper. I met him on my first day on the job as a rookie reporter. It was about twenty-five years ago. Bridge was semi-retired then. He still popped into the office now and again. He liked to keep in contact. You know, to see what was happening around. He didn't speak very much about this particular story, though, but I know it was one of the first he did after he had graduated from Brown University and came to work here. Some of his old files and records should still be in the cellar. Would you like to come back another time to have a look?"

"Yes, sure. How about ten o'clock tomorrow?" I couldn't believe my luck. I would have a chance to go through the files.

"That'll be fine," Houghton said, and stood up. As far as he was concerned the meeting was over and he wanted to have his lunch.

"Thanks a lot. I'll see you tomorrow." We shook hands and I put the article back into my handbag. I left his office and hurried back to my car.

As I was driving back to the Manor, I thought about the articles I'd found at the library, my conversation with Jim Houghton and what I might find the following day amongst Bridge's archives. A feeling of excitement swept over me as I drove along Lake Winnipesaukee. I opened my car window to let in the warm July breeze. In the distance I could hear the distinctive calls of the loons, those peculiar-looking birds with their white breasts and black-flecked feathers that lived on the lake.

The lake was awash with small boats, their passengers enjoying the brilliant sunshine. There were lots of visitors at this time of year, enjoying the spectacular scenery and fine weather. I passed some antique and souvenir shops and a second-hand bookshop with its merchandise piled up outside.

As I drove up to the main entrance of the Manor, I had a feeling my aunt would be outdoors. More than eighty per cent of New Hampshire is covered with forest and the Thornhill Estate is no exception. Aunt Elizabeth liked to sit in the garden in the afternoon, under the shade of one of the maple trees. As well as maple trees, we also had beech, elm and oak.

"Victoria, how was your morning?" she greeted me, beckoning me to sit beside her on the other chair.

"Fine, I went to the library in Moultonborough to do some research for my book." I decided to tell my aunt about my visit to the library just in case Simon mentioned it to her later. I wanted to make it sound like a normal event and didn't want to arouse any suspicion.

"Are you hungry? Mrs. Winton made a nice chicken soup today. I can ask her to bring you some."

"It's okay, Aunt Elizabeth, I've eaten already. I think I'll do some work on my book this afternoon. I'll see you later."

The following day, after a hurried breakfast, I told my aunt that I had more research to do in Moultonborough. I hit the main Highway 109 and then Route 3 and arrived in Laconia just before ten. It was market day, so it was busier than usual. I eventually found a parking place not too far from the *Herald*'s office. I opened the door and Jim Houghton was sitting at the News Desk on the phone.

"Yeah, that'll be fine. Just give me a call when you get more details. See ya, Bill," he said, as he put down the phone. "Miss Green, please take a seat. I'll be with you in a moment." Houghton grabbed a file on his desk, took the pencil from behind his ear, made some notes, and stood up.

"Right then, I'll show you to our archives." He moved towards the staircase. The overpowering smell of dusty old files hit me as I followed him down a rickety wooden staircase. There were no windows, just a couple of flickering light bulbs and lots of cobwebs. Houghton took me into a small room with some filing cabinets and a desk piled high with files.

"The files for the years 1924 through to 1926 are in this room," he said. "Jason Bridge left most of his files here when he retired, but he may still have some himself."

"What do you mean?" I turned around to look at Houghton. "Is he still alive?" I asked, somewhat incredulous. I couldn't believe my luck. What better way to find out about a story than speaking to the writer.

"Yes he is, but as you can imagine, he's getting on a bit, but his mind is still as sharp as a pin," Houghton said, smiling proudly, revealing yellowed teeth. "Here are the files. Let me know if you find anything or if you need anything else," he said, and headed back upstairs.

"Thanks. I'll get started right away." To be honest, I didn't really know where to start. I was gripped by a mixture of excitement and fear. I pulled out one of the filing drawers and quickly scanned the files. January 1924, June 1924 etc. I opened another drawer. February 1925, a little warmer. I opened another one and saw the date November 1925 looming from the file pocket. I reached inside and took out the file. It was huge and I practically staggered to a chair next to the table covered with a mountain of other files. I made a small space amongst the other papers and started to sift through the information.

Laconia tennis tournament cancelled, fire at a house in Meredith kills two young children. I turned the pages, and then saw the article. It was the same article I'd seen in the library's database. No surprise there. I quickly looked through the rest of the file and then another article caught my eye:

THE LACONIA HERALD

April 1926
Inquest on Heiress
Court rules death by misadventure

By Jason Bridge

The Inquest into the death last November of Emily Thornhill concluded that the twenty-five year old died from injuries as a result of a fall from her horse at her uncle's estate. Despite persistent rumours, no evidence of foul play has been found by the Lawyer acting for the Thornhill family.

Sources close to the Herald reveal that on the night of the accident, some of the staff were sworn to secrecy as to the events surrounding it. Attempts by this reporter to get to the bottom of the affair have met with a wall of silence.

If I had any doubts about my interest in this case, they just went out of the window. I was even more curious about this story and my interest was developing hour by hour. For the next hour I quickly went through the filing pockets and only found files for other stories, but nothing for the Thornhill case. The remaining cabinets housed files for up to the year 1927. I sat down and then looked at the mound of files on the table. I wonder whether there is anything in that pile, I thought. Dreading the idea of having to look through it all, but in the interest of research—a saying I often used between myself and my publisher if a point needed developing—I decided to ask Houghton whether there was anything for the years 1926 or 1927 in the pile before I undertook the mammoth task of sifting through it. I felt as if I was preparing to run the New York marathon.

I made my way along the corridor, trying to avoid the cobwebs and spiders, and went upstairs to Houghton's office.

"Hi there, any luck?" His eyes grew wide as he put his coffee cup on the table.

"Well, just one new article that I didn't see at the library yesterday."

"Coffee's hot, would you like some?"

"Great, love some." I was quite thirsty with all that dust. He took one of the Styrofoam cups from the stack near the coffee machine and poured a cup of the hot steaming liquid.

I glanced at the clock on the wall and noticed it was twelve thirty five. Houghton would be closing his doors for lunch soon. He was a creature of habit.

"Do you know if those files on the desk downstairs are for the years 1925 or 1926?"

"I'm not sure. They've been there a long time. Always been meaning to clear that desk, get some order in the place, but, just never got around to it," he shrugged.

"Can I look through the files and I'll take a note of the years and maybe that will help you with your records?" I hoped the offer to act as Filing Clerk to at least identify the years might be a softener into his letting me see the files.

"That's fine, but I'm closing up for lunch now." Surprise, surprise; I tried not to smile. "Can you come back around two o'clock?"

I agreed to go come back at two and the rumblings in my stomach told me it was time I had some lunch. I decided to try Frankie's Diner again. When I got there I found it was heaving with people and I was just about to turn round and go out again when I heard a familiar voice.

"Hi, you decided to give us another try." It was the waitress who had served me yesterday. "Just a minute, there's someone leaving over there. I'll clear the table and then it's all yours." I looked down at her name badge and smiled.

"Thanks, Cindy." I made my way over to the booth and she came over to take my order.

"What can I get you today?"

"A large gin and tonic on the rocks," I said, and let out a sigh.

"Wow, one of those days, hey."

"Yes, you could say that. Actually make it a sparkling mineral water and a Caesar salad."

Cindy scribbled on her notepad and came back a couple of minutes later with the water. The salad appeared about ten minutes later. It didn't take me long to devour it.

"Can I get you anything else, Honey?"

"Yes please, a cappuccino and I'll have the check." She came back with both, placing the check under the salt cellar.

"Are you from Laconia, Cindy?"

"Sure am. Born just down the road."

"So you probably know most of the residents. It seems to me like a close-knit community?"

"Yes, I do. Most of them come in here. We always know when there's a visitor, even though we get some tourists in the summer. You can always spot a tourist though, cameras, shorts, baseball caps. I wouldn't say you were a tourist." Cindy looked at me.

"Well, I am and I'm not. I'm staying with family here in Moultonborough." I quickly changed the subject as I didn't want to give out too much information. "It looks as if the lunch crowd has gone," I said, smiling.

"Yes, some of them work in town and they don't have much time for their lunch break." Cindy started to clear the table next to me.

"Do you know the Bridge family Cindy?" Cindy looked a little surprised at the question, but then smiled.

"Yes, I went to school with Annie Bridge, or Annie Farlow as she is called now. I see her from time to time in town, at the gas station, the pharmacy," Cindy replied and continued wiping the tables. *Was Annie Jason Bridge's daughter?,* I wondered.

"And Mr. Jason Bridge?"

"Oh, that's Annie's Uncle Jason. He must be in his nineties now. He used to be our resident reporter until he retired. Must be about thirty years ago. He lives with Annie and her family at the Millstone Farm, east of Wolfeboro. Hey, why all the interest in the Bridge's?" Cindy stared at me.

"His name came up after I read one of his articles in an old issue of the *Herald*." I prayed that would be a satisfactory explanation, paid the check and made my way out of the Diner.

———————

Cindy walked over to the payphone and dialled the number.

"Annie hi, It's Cindy how ya doing?"

"Hello Cindy, I'm fine; this is a nice surprise." Annie Farlow put down her hand towel. She had just made a vegetable pie and some scones when the phone rang. They chatted for a while and then Cindy decided she should mention the customer's interest in her and her uncle.

"There was young lady in here today asking about you and your uncle. She was in here yesterday asking for directions to the *Herald's* office."

"I wonder who she is?" Annie asked, but Cindy didn't have the answer; she didn't get the young woman's name, but she was staying with family in Moultonborough. Anne heard a noise behind her as she said her goodbyes to Cindy and turned to see her uncle in the doorway sitting in his wheelchair.

"Uncle Jason, I thought you were watching TV."

"No, I heard the telephone and I also smelled that lovely pie." He laughed as he wheeled himself over to the table. Annie wasn't sure whether to mention anything to him. After all, he was retired from the business. A very stressful and sometimes dangerous business. She didn't want to burden him with anything.

"Who was it on the phone?" Annie told him it was Cindy from Frankie's Diner. She decided not to tell her Uncle about the inquisitive young woman.

"Now then, how about a piece of my vegetable pie before the others come in from work?"

I arrived back at the Newspaper office just after two to find Houghton staring at the computer screen. He grinned as I came through the door showing those awful yellowy teeth.

"Ready for your next excavation exercise down in the dungeon?"

"As ready as I'll ever be," I said, laughing. I was enthusiastic to find out information on the case, but not so happy about sifting through those files. I made my way down the stairs, switching on the light and walking hurriedly down the corridor. I got to the archive room and the table of files stood to attention on the table. As I picked up the first one, a cloud of dust rose into the air like a mini atom bomb, making me cough and then, a few seconds later, sneeze. After I was able to see again, I saw the date. It said 1924. I put the file on the floor in the corner. I made a stack of files for each year. The next file I came to was dated 1925. When I looked inside it was filled with press cuttings and some handwritten notes, but nothing referring to the Thornhill case. I got through half of the files on the desk and had made several piles behind me on the floor. The next file I picked up didn't have a year on it. I looked inside and the first article was dated July 1925. I leafed through the mixture of articles and notes and then came to one:

November 27th 1925
The Manor House,
Horse riding accident??
Servants nervous

I looked at the note. Had Bridge written it? November 27th was two days after Emily's death. Why was there a question mark after the reference to horse riding accident? The more time I spent on this, the more intriguing it became. I took out my notebook and copied the details on the handwritten note into the book. I continued to look at the file, but couldn't find anything else.

I managed to look at all the files in total on the desk. After a quick count, I put thirty two files into a neat stack. *Houghton should be pleased with my filing efforts*, I thought, as I went back upstairs to the main office. The clock on the wall told me it was ten past six. I hadn't realised that it was so late. I hoped my aunt wasn't worried about me.

"Well, I've put all the files in bundles according to year. Thanks for letting me look through them. I didn't really find a lot," I lied as I didn't know if I could trust Houghton and I didn't want to stir up a hornet's nest. Perhaps it was nothing and Emily did have an accident and it was just some gossip. Small village, close-knit community, rumours fly. However, there's no smoke without fire. Houghton was poring over some articles on his desk.

"I was wondering if I could speak with Mr. Bridge."

"And why do you want to do that?"

"Perhaps he has some of his own files on Emily Thornhill's case and he could share his knowledge."

"Well, you know he is retired. Um." Houghton hesitated, took off his glasses and rubbed his nose. He sighed, rubbing his right hand across his chin. He sat there thinking for what seemed like an eternity.

"He lives with his niece. He never married. I'd prefer to call her and let her know that you want to speak to her uncle. She'll have to check with him." I agreed and he said he'd call me in the morning with the answer.

I hurried towards my car filled with the excitement of a special find. I loved digging for information.

I arrived back at the Manor around seven. My aunt came to meet me at the front door. She looked tense.

"Victoria my dear, where were you? I mislaid your cell phone number and Mrs. Winton suggested we call the library to find out what time you would be home. When we spoke to the Librarian she said that you hadn't been in there today?" she said searchingly.

"I decided to go to the library in Laconia. Sorry for worrying you. It was one of those last-minute decisions, you know how it is with us women," I laughed nervously.

We walked arm in arm towards the dining room to one of Mrs. Winton's delicious roast dinners.

As soon as Victoria left the office, Houghton picked up the phone and dialled Annie Farlow's number. She answered it after three rings.

"Annie, it's Jim Houghton."

"Hello, Jim, how are things at the newspaper?" she said cheerily.

"Everything's fine. Busy few days, but coping. How are you all doing?"

"We're all fine. Uncle Jason is in top form," she laughed.

"Annie, I have something to ask you." Houghton hesitated, but Annie knew what was coming next.

"There's a lady up here from New York. Nice young woman who is interested in a story covered by Jason in 1925."

"Wow, that's a long time ago. Why would she be interested in a story back then?" Jason was sitting at the dining room table listening to a one-sided conversation that didn't make any sense to him.

"Well, it seems one of her relatives was involved in a so-called accident up in Moultonborough and according to the article by Jason it may not have been an accident. Anyway, she wants to come over and speak to Jason. Try to shed some light on it, you know."

"Who is she?" Annie asked. Jason shifted in his chair.

"Her name's Victoria Green.

"Green. That name doesn't ring a bell." Annie tried to recall it.

"She's one of the Thornhill's. Looking into her family tree."

"Thornhill, oh, as in Thornhill Manor?" Jason wheeled himself across to where Annie was standing and tried to catch her attention.

"Yes, she's the great niece of Emily Thornhill, a twenty-five year old heiress who died in November 1925 after allegedly falling from a horse. Annie, I need to speak to Jason. Is he there?" Annie looked at her uncle.

"Jim, yes he is, just a moment. He wants to talk to you about the Emily Thornhill case of 1925," Annie said, placing the phone in his frail hands.

These new-fangled things with all these buttons. Too god damn heavy for my liking, thought Bridge as he placed the phone to his ear.

"Hey Jim, how ya doing old buddy." Although they had only worked briefly together for a few years in the seventies, Houghton had fond memories of this man. A great newspaper reporter if ever there was one.

"Annie tells me there's something cooking on the Thornhill case I covered a few moons ago. What do you have?"

"Well, I don't have anything," Houghton told him. *He must think the newspaper is reopening the story*, he realised. "The great niece of Emily Thornhill saw an article you wrote back in 1925. She was especially interested in the rumours that it wasn't an accident. She's spent practically all day here digging around in our archives, but didn't find that much."

"What's she going to do now?" Jason asked, intrigued.

"She wants to come to see you to talk about the case." Houghton waited for the response. Knowing Jason, it wasn't the one he was expecting.

"No, Jim." Houghton could hear something in his old colleague's voice, but couldn't quite pinpoint it. "It's best left alone. No use raking up the past like that. Tell the young woman I don't have visitors anymore. So long Jim." Jason hung up.

Houghton sat drumming his fingers on his desk. *I wonder what's eating him*, he wondered.

———◆———

I said goodnight to my aunt. I felt tired as I made my way back to my room. It was probably a combination of dust-filled surroundings, excitement and sheer exhaustion. I checked my cell phone. I noticed that Houghton had tried to call me just before eight o'clock and again shortly after nine. He wasn't supposed to call me until tomorrow.

I was glad to slip into my nightdress, climb under the duvet and switch off the light. I was awakened by the sound of my cell phone. Who's calling me in the middle of the night?, I wondered. Perhaps someone was calling from England about my upcoming book. I switched on the light and noticed it was only half past ten.

"Miss Green." It was Houghton. "Sorry for calling you at this hour. I tried earlier, but all I got was your voice mail."

"Sorry I couldn't take your call, Mr. Houghton. I switched off my phone during dinner. My aunt hates the things." I shook away the irascibility that comes with broken sleep. I still felt tired from the day and the effects of the Cabernet Sauvignon at dinner.

"Well, I thought you'd like to know that Jason Bridge is not interested in speaking to you about his report on your relative's accident."

"Why not, Mr. Houghton?" I was puzzled. Usually older people loved to chat about old times, old experiences.

"I've no idea. When I spoke to him on the phone this evening, he sounded okay one minute and withdrawn the next. Sorry I couldn't help you."

"Sure. Thanks again for taking the time to call." I climbed back into bed, somewhat disappointed. I lay there in the dark thinking of the day's events. I drifted off into a deep sleep dreaming of files, handwritten notes and the niggling question, how do I find a way to speak to Jason Bridge?

————•————

The next morning I dressed in my riding gear. Although I didn't ride that much these days, I always brought my jodhpurs, boots and hat to the Manor. Force of habit, I think. Horses were very much a part of life here. I set off towards the breakfast room, as I had time to grab a quick bite and a coffee before meeting Simon for our ride.

Mrs. Winton was setting the breakfast table when I walked into the room. The window was open and a welcoming cool breeze drifted through the room.

"Good morning Victoria. You're going riding, I see."

"Yes. I'm meeting Mr. Flynn. I thought I would just have a coffee and some toast this morning, Mrs. Winton." I sat down at the table and poured some coffee.

"He's a nice young man. He is such an asset to your aunt. I really don't know what she would do without him." The housekeeper finished setting the table and left the room.

I sat drinking my coffee and thought about my visit to the *Herald's* office and the conversation with Jim Houghton the night before.

"Hello my dear." I didn't see my aunt come into the room.

"Morning, Aunt Elizabeth. Can I get you some tea?"

"Yes, that would be nice, Dear." I poured the tea into the cup and added a slice of lemon.

"What's wrong, Victoria? You look worried." She said taking the cup and saucer and setting it down on the table. When I was deep in thought I looked quite serious.

"Oh, nothing really," I laughed, but I didn't manage to convince the intuitive Elizabeth Thornhill.

"There's something on your mind, Victoria. I can tell. Is it your book? Are the publishers giving you any problems?" Aunt Elizabeth tried to get me to talk about whatever was on my mind.

"Aunt Elizabeth. I found Aunt Emily's journal."

My aunt looked at me, her face full of concern. "Where did you find it?"

"It was at the back of the bookcase in my bedroom. It was inside a box with a Japanese scene on the front of it. The box was locked when I found it, but the key was inside the shoe box you gave me. The one with the poetry." I looked at my aunt. She leaned back in her chair and sighed.

"I remember it was Christmas 1924 when Uncle Todd gave her the journal. I always saw her writing in it. She once told me that although she loved writing she had never kept a journal before. She used to put ideas for her stories and her poetry in a notebook. I always wondered what had happened to it. Aunt Eleanor and Uncle Todd had put most of Emily's things in storage and I just assumed that the journal was part of the effects. Have you read the journal, Victoria?"

"Only small parts of it." I imagined that she'd want to read it at some stage.

We sat there in silence as I waited for her reaction.

"Is there anything interesting in it?"

"Well, she talks a lot about James Flynn," I said, finding my voice.

"Oh him. Uncle Todd and Aunt Eleanor didn't approve." She looked at me over the rim of her glasses.

"Why didn't they approve?" I looked at my aunt with a quizzical look.

"He was quite charming, handsome, but a terrible womaniser. They thought he was taking advantage of Emily." I didn't want to press her anymore, especially about the subject of Emily's death. I needed to tread carefully.

At that moment, I thought I heard something outside. I instinctively looked over at the window. The net curtains fluttered in the wind. My eyes wandered over to the grandfather clock. It was a couple of minutes after nine.

"Oh, I'll have to hurry. I'm meeting Simon for a riding lesson," I said, raising my eyes to the ceiling. I knew I would get some kind of reaction from my aunt.

"You don't need a riding lesson, my dear. You ride perfectly well." A warm smile spread across her face. She'd relaxed a little after our conversation about Emily and Flynn.

"Oh, I almost forgot. I also found the most exquisite pair of pearl-drop earrings in Emily's box.

"That's strange my dear. I wasn't aware that Emily ever owned a pair of pearl-drop earrings. I wonder how they got there."

"I've no idea. Well I must run now. I'll see you at lunch." I kissed her and walked out of the door. As I walked towards the stables, another niggling question crossed my mind. If the earrings didn't belong to Emily, then who did they belong to?

————•————

The person standing outside of the window had heard every word of the conversation between Victoria and her aunt and quickly hurried through the trees. *Just what was that little minx up to? She's here five minutes and now she wants to rake up the past. She's found the journal and the earrings. She'll probably tell Elizabeth Thornhill everything. Some things are best left alone, Victoria. You will have to be silenced.*

CHAPTER EIGHT

The stable block was very close to the house. Simon was waiting. As I approached him I couldn't help noticing how tall and handsome he was, especially in his riding breeches and boots. Every time I see his face, I think of his remarkable resemblance to his grandfather James.

"Hi Simon. How are you?" I smiled as we walked to the stalls.

"Fine thanks, Victoria, and how are you today?"

"Okay. It should be a nice morning for riding." He was looking at my outfit.

"A perfect fit." He grinned. "Looks like someone else is your size."

"Well, I know riding and horses are an important part of the estate, so each time I visit I bring some things." I was teasing him.

"I've chosen a gentle horse for you." He said stopping at one of the stalls. "Victoria meet Winston." The horse was slate grey with little flecks of white in his coat. His ears pricked up at the sound of his name.

"Hey Winston, how ya doing boy." I scratched his forehead and then gently opened the door. "There now isn't it nice to be outside." I regretted not bringing some sugar lumps from the breakfast table.

"Let's see how you handle him." Simon said as a mischievous smile spread across his face.

I put my foot in the stirrup and Simon helped me into the saddle. I picked up the reins and turned Winston towards Simon and his mount.

"Ready then?" Simon enquired.

"Sure thing." We trotted out of the stable block and then set off at a brisk pace down one of the estate roads. It was a beautiful sunny morning, cooled by a light breeze and the smell of pine filled the air as I tried to keep up with Simon.

"I should do more riding Simon. I can feel muscles I didn't even know I had."

He laughed. "I know it happens. I always feel the same when I play tennis after a few months break." For the next five minutes, we rode in silence enjoying the fresh air and the gentle birdsong floating around us.

"How's your book coming along?"

"Oh, so-so. The research takes some time, but I'm getting there."

"I hear you visited the *Laconia Herald* the other day." I tried not to look too surprised. How did he know I went to the newspaper office?

"News travels fast in these parts. I was doing some research on a future book." I hoped it sounded convincing. No need for Simon to know about my interest in Emily's death even if she had been involved with his grandfather.

"We live in a small community," he said. "I saw Jim Houghton the other day in town and he mentioned you were coming back to see him to look at some old archives." I suddenly had a feeling that Simon was getting a little bit too curious for my liking. *How much had Houghton told him*? I wondered.

"Yes, it is a small place." I hoped my forced laugh didn't show. "I was just following up on a possible lead for a future book. I'm always looking at new material." I pulled up just by an opening at a fence and I could see the lake glistening below.

"Oh, just look at that." I said changing the subject. "Lake Winnipesaukee is so beautiful. I always forget how much, what with living in New York."

"Yes, it is. Do you like living there?"

"Yes and No. I love the hustle and bustle, but I like to get away now and then."

"Your boyfriend doesn't mind you leaving him in the big city, then, while you take in the country air?"

I wondered how Simon could have known that I had a love interest. Or rather had, past tense.

"There's no one at the moment," I said, finding myself a bit miffed that I had to explain to a practical stranger that I no longer had a man in my life. "And even if there was, I think it's important to any relationship to spend some time away from each other." So there, I wanted to shout. "The only complaint my absence might provoke is from my cat. When I travel she hates being left with my friend. I can always see the change in her when I get back. Walking around my apartment as if I don't exist, except when she wants feeding."

"Yes, animals don't hesitate to let you know how they feel. We had a dog once and had to put him in the kennels for two weeks when we went skiing in Canada. When we got back and picked him up he gave us such a look as if to say hey you two left me in that place. Why did you do that?" I couldn't help smiling at Simon's recollection of him and his sulking dog. As he was telling me the story, I suddenly remembered that his wife had been killed in a car crash.

"Let's take this bridle path." Simon suggested. By this time I was aching all over. I thought longingly of a nice soothing bath back at the manor. As we reached the clearing the horses seemed to recognise the terrain and their ears pricked up. We set off again on a brisk trot and arrived back at the stables around noon.

My bath would have to wait and I settled for a quick shower. I remembered that I wanted to show the pearl-drop earrings to my aunt, so I retrieved them from the Japanese Box and made my way to the dining room to join her for lunch. She was already seated at the table.

"How was your ride, Victoria?" I sat down and helped myself to some bread.

"Wonderful. I forgot how nice it could be here." My aches were subsiding, but I would probably feel as if I'd been hit by a train tomorrow. Always happens to me after I do exercise, the next two or three days I suffer.

"The estate is beautiful and Simon certainly knows his stuff." I'd been impressed by Flynn's knowledge of the estate and decided he was a nice man, a bit reserved in some ways, but nice company.

"Aunt Elizabeth, here are earrings that I found in Emily's box." I laid them on the table. My aunt had a puzzled expression on her face.

"Well, like I said this morning Victoria, to the best of my knowledge these are not Emily's earrings. You say you found them with the journal?"

"Yes, in the same box."

"This is very strange. I have absolutely no idea how they got there. Perhaps Flynn bought them for her and she didn't say anything to Uncle Todd and Aunt Eleanor." I was as perplexed as she was.

"Can I hold onto them for the moment?" I thought if I had a chance to speak to Bridge I could ask him about the earrings.

"Of course, Dear. We'll have to find out who they belong too. Now what are you doing for the rest of the day?"

"I think I'll sit in the garden and do some writing. I'll find a nice shaded place. It's too nice to stay indoors."

"That's a good compromise, Victoria. Have a nice afternoon. I'm going to work in my study and then Simon is taking me into town. I have a meeting with some members of the Conservation Committee at the Town Hall."

"Have a nice time, Aunt Elizabeth. I'll see you later." I got up from the table and went back to my room. I grabbed my laptop and then made my way to the garden. I found a spot under one of the oak trees. In the distance, I could see the mountains and the lake. This was a perfect place to write. I just hoped my creative juices would flow and that I wouldn't get too distracted and end up daydreaming.

I sat there for a few minutes, just taking in the view. I then closed my eyes. Was that a rustling in the trees or just the breeze? I wasn't sure, but I had the same feeling I'd had that morning at breakfast. As if someone was watching me. I turned around quickly, but I couldn't see anything. I know a writer has to have an imagination, I thought, but mine is on overdrive at the moment.

I sat back and before long I was caught up in the intrigue and events at Hampton Court. The Palace had a new occupant, none other than Anne Boleyn, Henry VIII's new wife. Katherine of Aragon had been cast aside like an old shoe, to the cold and windy Kimbolton Castle. I pounded away at the keyboard and made notes in my journal of further research I needed to do. I heard a car in the distance. My aunt on her way into town for her meeting.

I looked at my watch and hadn't realised that it was almost half past five. I heard a sound on the terrace and looked up to see Mrs. Winton carrying a tray.

"That looks heavy, let me take it," I said, standing up as the housekeeper walked towards me.

"Thought you'd like some lemonade," Mrs. Winton smiled.

"Thank you. I'd love some." I poured myself a glass. It was delicious and after a busy few hours of writing, I welcomed its coolness.

"Your aunt said that she'll stay in town and have dinner with the other Committee Members. Shall I fix you something later?"

"Yes, okay. An omelette and salad will be just fine. Around half past seven."

"Would you like to eat outside this evening, Victoria?"

"Yes, it would be nice to have dinner on the terrace. I'll be able to see the sun go down."

"Okay. I'll set everything up for half past seven then." Mrs. Winton made her way back to the house.

I was staring at the screen on my laptop when my cell phone rang. It was a Laconia number.

"Hello, Victoria Green."

"Miss Green, Jim Houghton here at the *Herald*. Look, I'm sorry for my late call last night. Have you decided on your next step?" I thought it was strange that Houghton should call again so soon. However, the subject was still at the back of my mind and it was nice to talk to someone.

"Mr. Houghton, I'm not sure. I'd love to speak to Jason Bridge. I'm sure he has something to tell me. He must have spoken to witnesses at the time."

"Yes, I gather he was on this story like a dog with a bone. Wouldn't leave it alone, you know. That might tell you something." I thought for a minute and knew Houghton had a point. From my search in the bowels of the *Herald* building, I pretty much got the same feeling that Bridge was onto something. It made me all the more determined to find out.

"Do you think I could speak directly to Mr. Bridge or his niece on the phone? Would it help?"

"Well, you can try. He might change his mind. You know he was an easy-going guy and I can't understand why he doesn't want to talk to you about it. He understands how journalists work. He's used to fishing for information himself. A couple of years ago, all we got out of him was Emily Thornhill this, Emily Thornhill that." I also thought it was strange.

"His number's Laconia 56 75 12. Good luck. Let me know how you get on."

"I will. Oh, by the way. I don't want to mention my search to anyone. So let's just keep it to ourselves. If that's possible in such a small town."

"Fine with me," he replied. I hung up and sat back in my chair, finishing off the last drops of lemonade. I packed away the laptop and walked back to the house. When I got back to my room, I suddenly felt nervous. I said a silent prayer that Bridge would speak to me. I took a deep breath and dialled the number. After three rings it was picked up.

"Hello." I guessed correctly that it was Bridge's niece.

"Hello, Mrs. Farlow. I'd like to speak to Mr. Bridge, please."

"Yes, who is it speaking?"

I tried to calm myself and sound warm and friendly. "Victoria Green. I wanted to speak to Mr. Bridge about a story he did some years back about my great aunt Emily."

"He's not here now. He's at the Town Hall. He won't be back until about nine."

When I heard Annie Farlow mention the Town Hall, I made the connection—the Conservation Committee. He must be attending the same meeting and having dinner with my aunt and the other Committee Members.

"Oh, my aunt's at the Town Hall today. It seems to be a popular place." I was fishing for information, but Bridge's niece went on the defensive.

"Well, I wouldn't know about that. He'll be back later, but I'm not sure he wants to speak to you."

"Why not, Mrs. Farlow? I don't know your uncle, but I heard he had an excellent reputation as a journalist and was highly respected. I just want to speak to him about his research." I tried to sound sympathetic. I heard a sigh on the phone line.

"Is your interest personal or professional? You say you're a Thornhill. Why do you want to know?"

"I'm writing a book and the story interests me." I thought this excuse might get me a foot in the door.

"Oh, you're a writer too." She hesitated. "I'll tell him you called. That's all I can do, Miss Green. My uncle is his own man and he makes up his own mind." I gave her my phone number and she hung up. I was even more intrigued. Was Bridge on the Conservation Committee? Should I mention his name to my aunt? I thought about this as I sat in the armchair overlooking the garden.

———◆———

I got to the terrace just after half past seven and helped myself to a glass of Californian Chardonnay. I sat looking into the glass, swirling the wine around. I heard a noise coming from the trees. Simon was walking towards me.

"Hello Victoria. How was your afternoon? May I?" He pointed to a chair and sat down.

"Hi Simon. Well, I caught up on some writing this afternoon. It was nice to sit in the garden. Would you like a glass of wine?"

"Sure, that would be nice." I walked over to the cupboard next to the window and took a glass. I poured some wine into it and handed it to Simon.

"What do you do when you're not working, Simon? Any hobbies?" Despite our ride that morning, I still felt he was a bit elusive.

"I like swimming, but I don't get much chance during the day. Sometimes I go to the pool at Laconia. My grandfather won several competitions there when he was young." Here was my chance to ask him some questions about James Flynn, Emily's paramour.

"That's interesting. The talent must run in the family." I laughed. "Did your grandfather live on the estate?"

"Not all the time. He did visit from time to time with my grandmother. He was a journalist and spent most of his time in New York. I never knew him. He died before I was born."

I had assumed Flynn died of old age, but the way things were happening around here, I should never assume anything. "How did he die?"

"He was killed in a hit and run accident in 1946. Someone mowed him down near Madison Avenue, just as he was coming out of his office building."

"Did they find out who did it?" I couldn't believe what I'd just heard.

"No, the driver was never found. The police said later that there would have been a lot of blood on the car bumper. They got a make on the car from an eye witness, but no leads. The case was closed a couple of years after it happened. I guess the person who did it would be dead now." Simon took a sip of his wine. "It was hard on my grandmother. They'd only been married a few years and she had to raise my father on her own. The Thornhill family were quite kind though, because she took over Flynn cottage on the estate when her father-in-law died. My father became one of the estate workers when he was twenty."

"What happened to your mother, Simon?"

"She died five years ago. Cancer." He looked pained as he finished his wine and put the glass on the table. "Well, enough of my family history, I must get back to the cottage. I've got a mountain of paperwork to do. I always leave it until it's piled high on my desk."

I thought about what Simon had told me about his grandfather. In some ways, it seemed sad that James should die in tragic circumstances. I noticed some inky black clouds lurking on the horizon. We're going to have a storm, I thought, as I sipped the cool white wine.

I heard a taxi pull up around ten. It was my aunt returning from the Conservation Committee. I could hardly wait to speak to her, as I wanted to know if Jason Bridge had been there tonight.

"Hello Aunt Elizabeth. Did you have a nice evening?" I kissed her and helped her remove her coat.

"Yes, it was a lovely evening," she said, smiling. "It's always nice to see old friends and have the chance to discuss issues close to all our hearts. Let's go into the library. I have something to tell you. Mrs. Winton will bring us some brandies."

The fire had been lit and it gave the room a feeling of intimacy and warmth. I felt a chill in the air as we sat sipping our drinks, I stared at her, anxious to hear what she had to tell me.

"I saw Jason Bridge tonight. He told me you were asking about his stories on Emily's accident." She put her glass down on the small table beside her armchair. She sighed and sat with one hand covering the other.

"Yes, I came across an article in the library and I thought I would do some follow-up." I was now racked with guilt that I'd kept this from her, but at the beginning it seemed the right thing to do.

"It might be best to leave things alone. It was such a terrible time for all of us, Victoria." She looked at me with a pained look on her face. "I need to tell you something. So you'll understand the situation. Emily was a carefree young woman. A lot of men were in love with her. Apart from James Flynn, there was another young man who was in love with her." I looked at her and wondered who the other suitor could have been.

"A young journalist." My aunt was drip feeding the information and she could see the surprise on my face.

"You mean Jason Bridge." I was startled to hear this news. "That probably explains why he doesn't want to talk to me."

"Yes, Jason. We've been friends for years. We were both so shocked when Emily died. Out of his love for Emily, he felt he had to get to the bottom of exactly what happened to her. He couldn't accept that she had died accidentally."

"Did he blame anyone in particular?" I asked.

"Well, naturally he suspected James Flynn, but he couldn't say so publicly. He had no proof, but he knew there was something not right.

"The rivalry between Jason and James hit fever pitch one evening in 1946, when I was having dinner with Uncle Todd and Aunt Eleanor at the 21 Club in New York."

———————

"Evening, Sir, what can I get you?" The bartender said, placing a coaster in front of his next client.

"Scotch on the rocks." James took a cigarette from the gold-embossed case. She'd given him that case 20 years before. Even though he was now married with a young son, he still thought of her. He stood at the bar. The place was teeming with people. A sense of jubilation filled the air; the War was over, time to celebrate. He polished off his drink in one gulp.

"Same again." He said slamming the glass on the bar.

"Coming right up Sir." The bartender filled the glass. The amber liquid seemed brighter this time. He couldn't hold his booze like he used to. *Even during Prohibition, we could always get a few bottles,* he remembered. *The real McCoy and not some crap that someone had made in their backyard.*

"Bartender, any chance of getting a table tonight?"

"No Sir. We've got a large party in tonight and we've been booked solid for the past three weeks. Now that the War's over, well, everyone wants to celebrate," he said, wiping down the bar. "You can always check with the Maitre d'; perhaps he's had a cancellation."

"How many are in your party, Sir?" the man in the evening suit and clutching a menu enquired.

"Just the one. Any chance of a table? I hear you're pretty busy, but if you can find me something." He pulled a crisp $100 bill from his wallet. The Maitre d's eyes lit up like a cat's on a dark night.

"Come this way, Sir." They entered the main dining room.

"Well, what do we have here? A little family gathering. Ain't that nice," Flynn said sarcastically. Seated in a booth were Todd and Eleanor Thornhill, their Niece Elizabeth and Jason Bridge.

Jason stood up. "Flynn, you've had too much to drink. Don't start causing a scene."

"Who the hell asked you to speak? Always sticking your nose into things where it doesn't belong." Flynn pushed Jason back into his seat.

"You'd better leave, Flynn. Go and cool off somewhere."

"Bridge, if I want to cool off I'll go and sit next to the ice box."

Todd Thornhill had been clenching his fists, his knuckles growing whiter by the minute. He suddenly jumped up and grabbed Flynn around the neck.

"I'll kill you, Flynn, if you ever come near my family again. You hear me?" It took two waiters and Jason to haul him away from Flynn.

In 1946, the offices of the *New York Chronicle* took up a whole block near Madison Avenue. James Flynn was fortunate that he had a corner office. He'd been its Editorial Desk Chief for the past five years. He'd been determined to learn the newspaper business the hard way.

Life was better for him here in New York than it would have been at Thornhill Manor. He really had no time for ploughing fields and getting cow dung all over his boots. He'd met another young reporter a couple of years ago and they now had a young son.

"You know, I can't run this story, Sam. That Senator from Washington had a wife and two kids. What kind of a paper do you think we have here? It's not some rag. Sure, I know. News is news, but find me something else." No sooner had he put the phone down when it rang again.

"Flynn here. Yes, hello." There was no sound.

"Hello is anyone there?" He heard a click and then the dialling tone. He buzzed his secretary.

"Miss Forsythe, did you put a call through to me? The line just went dead."

"No Sir. It must have come straight through on your private line. I didn't handle it."

"Well, never mind. They'll call back if they want me. I'm going to lunch now and I'll be back around two thirty. Oh and Miss Forsythe, can you leave the Saunders file on my desk. I want to take another look at that story.

"Yes Sir."

He took the elevator to the ground floor and emerged into the sunshine ready to join New York's lunch mob. As he stood at the side of the road he removed a cigarette from his case. It was his last one. He squinted in the sun, cursing himself because he'd left his sunglasses in his car. A couple of cars passed him and then he saw a gap in the traffic. He took a puff of his cigarette as he crossed the road, eyeing the diner in the distance where he liked to order his steak, fries and salad.

Suddenly out of nowhere, a car sped towards him. He stared at the driver in disbelief. His body hit the bonnet and he was tossed up into the air like a rag doll. The car swerved to avoid another pedestrian and sped away amidst a cloud of smoke and screeching tyres. James Flynn had seen the driver's face. The eyes cold and unforgiving. He could hear screams as he slowly slipped into unconsciousness.

———•———

"Aunt Elizabeth. I really want to talk to Jason Bridge. Can you contact him and ask him if he'll speak to me? Please." She sighed and I could see it pained her to think of the events surrounding Emily's death. I now had a strong feeling I was opening a can of worms, but I needed to get to the bottom of this. This seemed to be the best way forward. My aunt was an old friend and if she couldn't persuade Bridge to see me, nobody could.

"I'll call him in the morning." She smiled and we said goodnight to each other.

I tried to get some sleep in spite of the storm that raged over the estate that night. I fell into a deep slumber, satisfied that there was a strong chance I would be speaking to Jason Bridge very soon.

———•———

The next morning I woke up to bright sunshine. It was just after half past nine. I couldn't believe that I'd slept so late. I made my way into the bathroom. As I pulled one of the towels from the cupboard to put onto the heated towel rack, I heard voices in the garden.

"Oh what's happening? This is terrible." It was my aunt talking to Mrs. Winton. From the anxiety in their voices I could sense something was wrong. I looked out of the window. My aunt and the housekeeper were standing on the terrace. Mrs. Winton had her arm around my aunt's shoulders.

I went back into my bedroom and hurriedly put on a pair of jogging pants, t-shirt and pumps. I threw open the French windows and quickly joined them on the terrace.

"What is it?" I looked at Aunt Elizabeth and then Mrs. Winton. They both stood there with haunted expressions on their faces. The silence was deafening and time seemed to pass, but it was only a matter of seconds before my aunt spoke.

"It's Jason Bridge. He was found dead this morning." Aunt Elizabeth started to cry. I stood there dumbfounded. I couldn't believe my ears.

Through her tears Elizabeth told me that she had telephoned Jason that morning as promised to ask him to speak to me. Instead she received the news that he had died during the night.

"Oh my god. This is terrible news." I said putting my arms around her. I had a terrible feeling about all this. As I tried to comfort my aunt, the telephone rang and Mrs. Winton hurried inside to answer it.

"Victoria, it's Jim Houghton from the *Laconia Herald*. He says it's urgent."

"Thank you Mrs. Winton, I'll take it in the library." I made my way to the library and picked up the phone.

"Hello, Mr. Houghton." I tried to remain calm recalling all the yoga sessions I'd had over the years, deep breathing and all that.

"Hello, Miss Green. I have some bad news I'm afraid. Old Jason Bridge died last night. Thought you'd like to know."

"Yes, I heard the news this morning. My aunt saw him last night at a Conservation Committee and then they had dinner together with a couple of old friends. I really can't believe it."

"Well, I'm sorry you didn't get a chance to speak to him. What are you going to do now?" I hadn't had a chance to think about my next move, if I had a next move. I was still reeling from this shocking news.

"I don't know. Maybe I'll speak to his niece in the coming days. Perhaps she'll let me look through his records. I'm really not sure." I didn't feel in the mood to answer any more of his questions.

"Well, if there's anything else I can do, give me a call."

"I'll do that thanks." I hung up. Something just wasn't right. Bridge conveniently dies just as I have a chance to speak to him about the events of 1925. Too much of a coincidence, if you ask me.

I returned to the terrace. My aunt wasn't there. I sat down in one of the garden chairs. Just what was I going to do now?

———•———

I wasn't sure exactly what made me think that Jason Bridge's death was not an accident. Was it instinct or was I just overreacting? I decided to go into Laconia and see if I could find out how he died. I wanted to speak to his niece, but not now. It just wasn't right to impose on the family at this time. I'd try to speak to the police, but whether they would speak to me was another matter. I hadn't experienced any problems getting information from the police when it came to research for my books. This might prove to be a bit tricky, though. They would ask what my motive was.

I drove down to Frankie's Diner on Main Street. I hoped that Cindy, the loquacious waitress, might be at work today. She might be able to fill me in on what was happening in town. I was sure she probably picked up little snippets of conversations in the Diner. I walked in and found a booth near the main counter. I looked around and saw it was not so full. Cindy rushed through the swing door from the kitchen carrying two plates of piping hot food and made her way over to a young couple sitting at a table on the far side of the room. She spotted me as she made her way back to the counter.

"Hi there, how ya doing? She smiled.

"Hi Cindy. I'm fine," I said, sitting at one of the booths.

"You're becoming quite a regular in here." She smiled again.

"I know. I just can't keep away." I hoped she wouldn't suspect that I wasn't just here for the food, which actually wasn't all that bad.

"What can I get you today?" Cindy took the pencil from behind her ear ready to scribble my order on her notepad.

"I'll have a BLT and a large cappuccino, please," I said placing the menu back in its holder.

"Sure, coming right up." Cindy brought the order about fifteen minutes later.

"Cindy, did you hear about Jason Bridge?" I was pretty certain that she had. The whole town probably knew by now. I was just testing the water. I didn't want to sound too nosey.

"Yes I did. Oh, you know it's so sad. I feel really sorry for Annie. She found him."

"Did she? Still it must have been a shock finding him dead in bed like that."

"Oh, didn't you know? She found him at the foot of the stairs."

"I'd assumed that he had died in his sleep. How the hell did he get there?"

"She thinks he tried to go to the bathroom."

"Cindy, can I have the check please. I'm sorry, I have to go." I grabbed my jacket as Cindy gave me the check with a quizzical look on her face. I placed a $20 bill on the table and rushed out of the diner.

I walked the few blocks to the *Laconia Herald*. I had to speak to Houghton. It was strange that he didn't say anything on the phone this morning. Did he know something and was not letting on?

"Yes, come in," Houghton shouted as I knocked on the door. The window blind on the door clattered against the glass as I stepped inside.

"Ah, Miss Green. I've just left a message for you up at the Manor." Houghton was sitting at his desk surrounded by newspapers.

"Oh, I've been out for a while. What did you want to tell me?" I sat down in the chair facing his desk and stared at him.

"Bridge was found at the foot of his stairs. Seems like there's something not quite right." Houghton folded some papers on his desk.

News does travel fast in this town, I thought. An old hack like Houghton would probably have an informant at the police station.

"Oh, really. I assumed he died in his sleep." I didn't tell him I already knew where he was found.

"I'm covering the story for the *Herald*. I had a chance to speak to the police early this morning. They couldn't understand how Bridge had got out of bed and into his wheelchair." Houghton walked over to the hotplate and poured two cups of coffee. He set one down in front of me.

"Was he completely disabled or could he walk a little?"

"Well, I thought he was completely disabled. He had arthritis and over the years it was becoming increasingly difficult for him to get around. You never know, maybe he could walk a little." Houghton took a gulp of coffee.

"I'd like to speak to the police, if they'll speak to me." I was hopeful.

"I'm not so sure they will. They've been a bit reluctant to say much to me, but then again I'm covering the story and they're not so happy about talking to journalists." I thought about it for a while and then decided to give it a try. The worst thing they could tell me to do was to get lost.

"I'll be in touch, Mr. Houghton. Let me know if you find out anything."

As I walked the few blocks to Laconia Police Headquarters, I noticed a car drive slowly past me. I couldn't see anyone inside because the windows were blacked out. Something made me feel uneasy about it.

As I walked through a set of revolving doors at Police Headquarters, I saw a young man at the reception desk.

"Can I help you, Ma'am?"

"Hello, I'd like to speak to someone about the death of Jason Bridge." He looked at me suspiciously.

"What's the name?"

"Victoria Green."

"Are you Victoria Green the writer?" he asked, with a hint of recognition on his face.

"Yes I am." I gave him my best smile.

"Ah, I really enjoyed your last book, the one about the early life of King Henry VIII. I completed my Masters in English History last year and your book really helped fill in a few gaps," he said, laughing.

"I'm glad you enjoyed it." Normally, I'd be happy to chat all day long about the English King and why this young man was working on a reception desk, but I was anxious to talk to someone about the Bridge case.

"So do you think I'll be able to speak to someone?" I smiled not wanting to sound rude.

"Oh yes, sorry just a minute." He made a brief call and then he told me to go to third floor.

"Thanks for your help." I hurried towards the elevator before he could ask for my autograph.

———•———

Detective William Rainer—Bill to his friends and family—had been born in Antigua. He had moved to Laconia with his parents when he was fifteen-years old and they had opened a small hotel in the area.

Bill's parents had been in the hotel business for the best part of their lives. His dad had been a manager at one of the hotels on Antigua when he had the chance to take over a place in New Hampshire. They were now enjoying their well-earned retirement at their house overlooking Squam Lake.

Bill, their only son was a tall bear-like man, now in his fiftieth year and looking forward to an early retirement. *Just five more years to go*, Bill thought, as he sat at his desk surrounded by files from several cases. *There's some good fishing to be had in Maine.* He leaned back in his chair.

His thoughts wondered back to the time he worked in Homicide in New York. The big melting pot where you never knew if you would get a bullet in the back or one between the eyes. When the opportunity to move to New Hampshire had come up, he'd jumped at the chance and Sheila, his wife of twenty-five years was relieved. He'd miss his two kids, the eldest was at Colombia studying law and the youngest was working for the United Nations as an interpreter. He was proud of them and thought back to his humble upbringing on that sunny Caribbean island.

Bill laughed to himself recalling the last time he'd seen his parents a few weeks ago. The conversation always turned to the grandchildren and at some point whether there was any possibility of any great-grandchildren.

Bill pictured himself on his boat, the proud Grandpa teaching his grandson how to fish. Of course, he'd be only too happy to take along a granddaughter. He could teach her how to water ski.

The ringing of the phone interrupted his thoughts.

The officer at the front desk told him that a Miss Green wanted to speak to him in connection with the Jason Bridge case.

"Miss Green. I don't know her, what does she want? Oh, I see a journalist, New York, Thornhill Manor. Okay, send her up." He replaced the receiver in its cradle. He stood up and cleared some files off a chair and placed a chair in front of his desk.

———•———

I turned right when I got out of the elevator and walked down a long corridor. I stood outside office 3057 and knocked on the door.

"Come in," a voice shouted from inside. I opened the door and walked in.

"Good afternoon. I'm Detective Rainer." We shook hands and he offered me a seat.

"Good afternoon, Detective. Victoria Green." I sat down and my eyes swept the room. It was a small office and the desk was piled high with papers. Not quite as chaotic as Houghton's archives though. An ashtray crammed full of cigarette butts had pride of place next to his telephone. In one corner there was another table full of files, next to that was a water cooler and a small cabinet with a decrepit-looking fan on it.

"I understand you have some information concerning the Jason Bridge case?" Rainer said, as he opened his desk and reached for a pack of cigarettes. He offered one to me, but I refused. I had smoked at Yale, but gave up when I met my last boyfriend. He complained about my breath. It's like kissing an ashtray, he used to say. It still amazes me how quickly I gave up. Just like that. Well, the things you'll do when you're madly in love, one of my friends had remarked at the time.

I took a deep breath before answering him.

"Yes, I have." I knew that I needed a good excuse to speak to the police. I was just searching for one. Rainer looked at me.

"Mind if I smoke?" Rainer had the cigarette between his lips with a lighter poised ready to flick it into action.

"No, of course not." *Another nail in your coffin,* I thought. Despite my earlier encounters with cigarettes, I now detested the smell of cigarette smoke, but I was on his territory so I had little choice but to put up with it. I quickly dismissed thoughts of secondary smoke inhalation.

"You were saying, Miss Green?" Rainer took a drag of the cigarette, the smoke emanating from his nostrils; the rest came out of his mouth.

"I was looking for some information concerning the death of a relative of mine, Detective, and discovered an article written by Jason Bridge in 1925. I had wanted to speak to him about his research, but never got the chance. He wasn't interested in speaking to me. I persuaded my great aunt, who's a friend of his, to contact him directly and ask for an interview on my behalf. The next thing, we get a call to say he's dead." Rainer looked at me.

"So what's this got to do with his death?"

"It seems a coincidence that he's dead, just when I'm trying to find out the events surrounding my relative's death." Did my excuse sound corny or what? Maybe I was overreacting after all.

"Miss Green, people die all the time in this town. The guy was in his nineties. He wasn't gonna live forever." I looked puzzled because of the information Cindy and Houghton had given me. Bridge was found at the bottom of the stairs.

"Do you think that his death wasn't natural, Miss Green?" *Here we go*, I thought, *he's fishing.*

"Perhaps. I very much wanted to speak to him. I did hear from a friend of the family that he was found at the bottom of the stairs." Rainer probably knew that news, good or bad, spreads faster than a bush fire in a small town.

"Yes, he was. We can't quite figure out how he got there."

"What did his niece say, Detective?" Rainer stubbed out his cigarette. The butt lay in the ashtray as a trail of smoke rose into the air.

"She awoke around six thirty to go to the bathroom. She looked into his room to see if he was okay, but he wasn't in his bed and his wheelchair had gone. She got about halfway down the stairs when she saw her uncle lying at the bottom. She screamed and her husband came running. They both checked the body for any vital signs, but he was as dead as a doornail. Soon after, they called the family doctor then the police. The local doc put the time of death at between ten and half past midnight."

"Does the doctor know what killed him?"

"We're waiting for the autopsy results. I should have them later this afternoon." Rainer got up and looked out of the window. He was standing with his back to me.

"Do you suspect foul play, Detective?"

"What makes you say a thing like that?" He swung around.

"Well, he suffered from arthritis. How easy would it have been for him to get out of bed into his wheelchair?"

"Good question. We know that he could walk a little and the wheelchair was still at the top of the stairs. Maybe he thought he'd go downstairs for something. We don't know. It's all speculation at the moment." Rainer sat down again and lit up another cigarette.

"You said that a relative of yours died in 1925. Who was that?" Rainer leaned back in his chair, the smoke lingering above him like a big white cloud.

"My great aunt, Emily Thornhill. They said it was a riding accident, but I believe Bridge knew something that implied it wasn't an accident. Hence my reason for wanting to meet with him and my interest in the case."

"I see. Well, forensics are still going over Bridge's home, so we'll see what happens when we get those results." If Rainer knew more, he wasn't going to admit it.

"Detective, thank you for your time. Please call me if anything else comes up or if I can be of any use." I left his office and walked back to my car, which was still parked outside Frankie's Diner.

———•———

She's a proper little Sherlock Holmes, the person thought, watching from the doorway across the road. *You couldn't see me in my car as I drove past Victoria, but I could see you. Oh yes, and I'm watching every little move you make.*

———•———

Jason Bridge's funeral would not take place for a while yet. After the autopsy, the police had to be satisfied that they didn't need the body anymore and then they could release it for burial. I was growing impatient and decided to go ahead and call Annie Farlow to see if I could look through Jason's files.

"Hello, Mrs. Farlow, it's Victoria Green. I'm so sorry for your loss." I knew that Aunt Elizabeth had already called her and sent flowers on behalf of the Thornhill Family. Another message from the Conservation Committee had quickly followed.

"Thank you. It's been a terrible shock for all of us. I still can't believe it." I could hear the anguish in her voice. We chatted for a few minutes about the police enquiry and then I thought there was no time like the present to ask her if I could come over.

"Mrs. Farlow, do you think I could come over some time to look at your uncle's papers? You know he may have some information on my great aunt. I'm sorry to ask you this at this time." I secretly crossed my fingers. Was I being inconsiderate at a time like this? Should I have waited a few more days?

"I don't know. The police have been crawling all over the place. I'm not sure they would want someone else looking through them." Annie Farlow hesitated. "I don't know if they've finished up in his office. I'll have to check with them and call you back."

"Of course. I understand. Looking forward to your call Mrs. Farlow." I was hopeful I'd get a positive response later that afternoon.

I was catching up on some writing when she called me back later that afternoon.

"Miss Green. The police have finished up here at my home. Do you want to come over tomorrow morning?"

I would have liked to have gone over there and then, but thought it prudent to wait just a couple of hours longer. The following morning would have to do.

"Tomorrow morning is just fine. Thank you very much Mrs. Farlow."

We arranged to meet at ten o'clock. I was thrilled. I rushed down to the library to find Aunt Elizabeth. She was dozing peacefully in one of the armchairs next to the fireplace. It was pouring with rain today, so her usual spot under one of the trees in the garden was out of the question.

She stirred as I crept out of the library. I'd decided my news could wait until dinner, but then my aunt opened her eyes. I could see she'd been crying, but that didn't surprise me. After all, she'd lost an old friend.

"Hello, Dear." She smiled at me. I knelt beside her and took her hand.

"Aunt Elizabeth, I've spoken to Annie Farlow, and she's agreed to let me look through Jason's things."

"Oh, that's good news for you, my dear. I only hope we can find something that might put our minds at rest." She sighed and pulled the cord at the side of the fireplace.

"Let's have some tea, shall we?" Mrs. Winton almost on cue walked through the door a few minutes later with a tea tray and slices of her homemade fruit cake.

"When are you visiting Annie?" my aunt asked me as we sipped our tea.

"Tomorrow morning at ten. I can't wait to take a look at his files. I must tell Houghton over at the *Herald*. He's been following my progress on this." We both laughed.

CHAPTER NINE

I arrived at Millstone Farm a couple of minutes before ten.

I parked my car outside the quaint pale yellow farmhouse, where chickens ran around in a pen near the main door. As I knocked at the door, I noticed the garden was well stocked with cabbages, lettuces and tomatoes. I could see plenty of apple and cherry trees. When Annie Farlow opened the door I caught a faint whiff of baked apples and cinnamon.

"Hello Miss Green, please come in," she said, wiping her floured hands on her apron. "I've just made a batch of apple and cherry pies. I supply the local diner and I'm never short of orders."

Annie Farlow was in her fifties, a small woman with dyed blond hair tied back in a ponytail, warm blue eyes and a large mouth. I noticed that her hands, now flour free, were hardworking and wrinkled.

"That sounds great. I don't do much cooking myself. I tend to eat out a lot in New York. Our kitchens are so small." We both laughed at my feeble excuse and it seemed to break the ice. When she mentioned the local diner, I assumed that it was Frankie's.

"Is that Frankie's Diner that you cook for, Mrs. Farlow?" I asked.

"Yes, it is. Their other supplier let them down a few months ago and they asked me if I could help them out. It's nice to know I can."

Although the house had a lot of land, inside was small and cosy. She led me into the living room just off the main door and we sat down on the floral-covered sofa. There was a small fireplace in the room, some bookshelves and a coffee table. I immediately thought it had the feel of a country cottage about it.

"Would you like some tea or coffee, and perhaps a slice of homemade chocolate cake, Miss Green?" I have rather a sweet tooth and gladly accepted the offer. Annie retreated to the kitchen. I stood up and looked at the pictures over the fireplace. A little girl who looked about ten or eleven years old with long blond hair—perhaps this was Annie. She was standing next to an older man, perhaps her father or even Jason for that matter. There was another picture of a young man in an army uniform. He was handsome, with tall swarthy looks. I guessed this was Jason Bridge, but couldn't be sure. I sat down again on the sofa and could still smell the aroma of baking pies coming from the kitchen. Annie returned with a tray bearing two mugs of steaming coffee and a plateful of delicious-looking chocolate cake.

"Thank you Mrs. Farlow, this looks delicious." It tasted even better. I wished I could cook like this. Whenever I had friends over to my New York apartment, we always ordered in. I must have just about every take-away menu that exists in New York.

"Please call me Annie." She smiled at me.

"Annie it is and I'm Victoria."

"It was nice of your aunt to call me. That meant a lot to us." She looked at me as tears welled up in her eyes. "I know she was deeply saddened at my uncle's death. They go back a few years."

I felt sorry for the lady sitting opposite me. She seemed like a nice, down-to-earth woman who had loved her uncle dearly.

"Time goes by so fast," she said. "Uncle Jason often spoke of your aunt. They enjoyed their time together over the years and had renewed their friendship recently with a shared passion for the environment."

I nodded.

Annie Farlow picked up her coffee mug and took a sip. "The police don't think it was an accident."

The statement came out of her mouth like a thunderbolt and I didn't know how to react to it, even after my attention-grabbing meeting with Detective Rainer the day before.

"What did they say to you?" I gripped my coffee mug as I listened.

"The police couldn't understand how Uncle Jason had gotten out of bed and into his wheelchair. Some days were good, some bad. If you know what I mean."

Even for someone as healthy as myself, I imagined if you had an illness like arthritis it was not so bad one day and hell the next.

Annie continued. "They think that someone broke into the house. We are not absolutely sure how they did that, as there doesn't appear to be any sign of forced entry, according to the Police. Anyway, whoever got in then put my uncle into his wheelchair, pushed it to top of the stairs and then tipped him out of it."

Detective Rainer had been careful not to reveal everything, but Annie Farlow spoke openly. Of course Rainer wasn't going to admit anything to a total stranger. I also wondered if Bridge had had the chance to put up a struggle.

"That's terrible. Who would do such a thing?" I couldn't believe it.

"I don't know. My uncle was a good man, but he was in a tough business. He had touched a couple of raw nerves over the years. Maybe he had made some enemies, but if he did, why wait till now to hurt him? It doesn't make sense." Annie started to cry and reached for a handkerchief in her apron pocket.

"Let's not speculate too much, Annie," I said putting my arm around her. "Let the police do their job and see what they come up with." She dabbed her eyes.

"Come now, let me show you my uncle's old study. We walked down the hall and passed the kitchen. Then I stopped. I glanced quickly at the staircase where Jason had fallen or, if the rumours were correct, where he'd landed after being pushed. I tried not to look too shocked, but it was difficult not to show any emotion.

We walked down the hall and came to a room. It had the sign *newsroom* painted onto a piece of wood in black letters. Annie showed me into the room. It contained framed cover pages of newspapers over the years and a couple of photos of Jason and people who he'd met including President J.F. Kennedy, The Beatles and Truman Capote. There were several book cases, filing cabinets and a desk with an old leather chair with cracked upholstery. To say it was well worn or well sat on was an understatement.

"I'll leave you here for a while. Take your time. Would you like another coffee?"

"Yes, please. That would be nice."

It was a nice bright room that overlooked the rear of the property and the surrounding mountains. *Just the place to work*, I thought.

The desk was tidy. It had an ink blotter pad on the top, a table lamp and a mug containing pencils and pens. I could see a typewriter tucked away in the corner. I peeked under the cover and saw an IBM golf ball typewriter. I suppose it could have been worse. It could have been a manual.

I saw the four grey filing cabinets standing to attention on the far wall. I opened the first drawer of the first cabinet. I quickly looked through the file labels to get an idea of the dates etc. This section read—*1920s*. I removed a large manila file out of the drawer and saw the label on the front: *hot news items*. Too early, I thought. I replaced the file and took another one behind it—*1923*—a little closer. I picked up another—1925. I opened the buff-coloured file. There were quite a lot of loose clippings in it.

I walked over to the desk and placed the file on top of it. I came across the two articles that I'd seen in the *Herald's* office. There were several other articles about Emily's accident from various newspapers: *The New Hampshire Times*, the *Boston Observer*. I was disappointed. This isn't the file I want. Bridge must have a record of his interviews with witnesses at the time. I closed the file and put it back in the cabinet.

I sat down at Bridge's desk and closed my eyes. I was lost in thought when I heard the door slowly opening. It was Annie with her tray of coffee.

"Here's your coffee. Thought you'd like a slice of apple pie too." I was grateful for the coffee and the pie.

"Thank you."

"Found anything of interest yet?" Annie stood beside the filing cabinets.

"No, nothing yet." I felt sure that I would put my hands on something, but it was trying to find it.

"Would you like to join me for lunch, Victoria? I'm just gonna prepare some salad and I have some roast chicken from yesterday. My husband is out all day, so I'd appreciate the company."

"Sure. I'd love to." I was glad that I'd get the chance to stay a bit longer at the farm.

"That's settled then. I'll prepare everything for one o'clock. See you later." Annie went out of the study and I leaned back in the chair.

My eyes fixed on the desk. It had two drawers either side. I opened the right-hand drawer and looked inside. A couple of pencils, some paper clips, an eraser, some file tabs, elastic bands; the usual things, nothing out of the ordinary.

I opened the second right-hand drawer. Inside was a large notepad. I opened it, but it was empty. I then tried to close the drawer, but it wouldn't close. I moved it from left to right and tried to push it forward. Something was blocking it. I then heard something drop at the back. I took the whole drawer out and peered into the gap. I reached inside and felt around. Yes, there was something inside. It had lodged at the back of a small ledge behind where the drawer had been. I reached inside again and stretched as far as I could. I pulled out a small packet. From the feel and shape, I knew instantly that it was an audiocassette tape.

I took the cassette out of the envelope and placed it on the table. In black ink, Bridge had written: *The Thornhill Secret*. Whatever could that mean? I looked around the room for a tape machine. Nothing in the two left-hand drawers. I looked in the large drawer under the typewriter, but there was nothing. I popped the cassette in my bag. I'd have to listen to it later in the car.

I opened up the last filing cabinet. I sifted through some of the files and then found one marked: Interviews, *Thornhill Estate*. I looked through them and found several batches of A4-size pages with handwritten notes. Jason Bridge's handwriting was clear. I could hardly contain my excitement at my find. I flicked through the pages and came across some notes from an interview Bridge had had with Mary Riley, Eleanor Thornhill's maid on Thursday November 26th, 1925. It was the day after Emily died.

———•———

"Miss Riley, how long have you worked here at Thornhill Manor?" Jason Bridge sat opposite Mary in the Manor's staff dining room.

"Only two years, Sir." Mary Riley sat bolt upright with her hands folded on her lap. She wore a calf-length black dress with black lace-up shoes, a white apron and a white cap, which was trying to do its best to cover up her mop of fiery red hair.

"Did you have a lot of contact with Miss Emily Thornhill?"

"Sometimes, but I work mostly for Mrs. Thornhill." Mary stared nervously at Bridge.

"What can you tell me about the day of Miss Emily's accident?"

Mary sighed. "Well, I'd finished the ironing and then I had to take some fresh linen up to Mrs. Thornhill's room. I left the laundry room and walked along the corridor towards the staircase on my way up to Mrs. Thornhill's room. As I mounted the stairs, I heard raised voices coming from the library."

"Whose voices?" Bridge was scribbling on his notepad.

"Miss Emily and a man's voice."

"A man's voice. Could you identify it?"

"I'm not sure, Sir. I think it might have been her boyfriend, Mr. Flynn."

"And what time was this?"

"Just after one o'clock Sir."

"Could you hear what they were saying?"

"Well, I stood at the bottom of the stairs. I didn't want to listen at the door. I got told off for doing that a few weeks ago."

"I see." Bridge tried not to smile.

"I didn't catch all the conversation, but I know Miss Emily was crying. Mr. Flynn was pleading with her to stop. I heard him say something like "You can't do that Emily. It's ridiculous.""

"What do you think he meant by this?" Bridge sat with his pencil poised ready to scribble on the notepad.

"I don't know, Sir. I had to go back upstairs. Mrs. Banbury came along just then and asked me why I was dawdling. She told me to hurry along, that I had work to do."

———•———

Bridge drummed his fingers on the kitchen table as he waited for Thora Banbury to come downstairs. One of the maids had told him she'd taken Mrs. Thornhill her lunch in her room and would he kindly wait in the kitchen. He could help himself to some tea and a scone.

"I don't much like talking to reporters," Thora said, wiping her hands on her apron.

"Mrs. Banbury, a lot of speculation is sweeping through Laconia and we would like to set the record straight if we can."

She sighed. "Well, I'll tell you what I can, but I don't want any trouble."

Bridge sat next to her and opened his notebook.

"Can you tell me where you were yesterday afternoon between one and three?"

"I was putting some flowers in baskets, ready to put around the house. I was on my way along the corridor to replace the fresh flowers in the hallway and library."

"Did you see anybody around that time?" Thora's expression turned to disgust. She pinched her mouth, thought for a few seconds and said she had seen Mary Riley hovering near the main staircase.

"Probably eavesdropping. I don't know the number of times I've had to light a fire under that girl. Bone idle. I told her to go upstairs and finish her duties."

"Yes, yes, anything else." Bridge wasn't in the least bit interested in Mrs. Banbury's problems with the housemaid. He wanted information on Emily and Flynn.

"I heard a commotion a few minutes later. James Flynn ran out of the library. Almost knocked me over he did." Banbury was not amused.

"Where did he go?"

"He ran out of the front door. The next thing, Miss Emily was running after him in floods of tears."

———————

I noticed that Bridge had written in red pen *where did they go next*—good question, I thought. The sun streamed through the window of Bridge's study and I felt a pang of sadness for him. He was in love in Emily and it must have been hard for him, but was his interest in the case purely because of his love of Emily or just the normal journalistic one? Whatever it was, he seemed like a determined sort of reporter, who wanted to get to the bottom of the mystery surrounding Emily's death.

At around one o'clock, I joined Annie in her garden for lunch. We chatted about the farm and she told me her husband was over in Meredith at a cattle auction.

After lunch I went back to the study. As I sat at the desk again I thought of the label on the cassette. What kind of Secret was Bridge referring to? I had decided to tell Annie about the cassette and she'd agreed that I could take it and see what it contained. Although I wanted to listen to it, I knew that there were probably more bits of information here in the study. I had to carry on here while I had the chance.

In the file, I came across a note written by Bridge: *Lady of the house would not speak to me*. I'd heard various little snippets of information about my relative Eleanor Thornhill. I thought about the painting of her that hung at the top of the stairs at Thornhill Manor. She must have been in her mid-twenties and recently married when it was taken. I recalled something that Aunt Elizabeth had said to me earlier.

"She was a very unhappy woman. I think she put up with a lot from Uncle Todd and his womanising. My aunt and uncle were constantly arguing. I overheard one of their arguments one day," Elizabeth had told me.

"You're nothing but a scoundrel and you've brought shame to our name. I'll never forgive you for this, Todd. I'm sick and tired of all your womanising. I've had enough; I'm packing my bags and leaving. I won't stay another minute in this house with a man who betrays his wife and family like this. How could you do such a thing?"

"Eleanor, I'm sorry. Please don't go. You know I wouldn't do anything to hurt you or the girls."

"I don't know what to think anymore, Todd. I don't think you care about us."

"But I do Eleanor, believe me."

"You care about three things Todd, women, money and guns. Get out of my room. Get out," she shrieked.

The vase of flowers came hurtling towards him and smashed into a dozen pieces against the door.

Yes, it wasn't easy for Eleanor, but according to Aunt Elizabeth, they remained married until Todd's death in 1955. Eleanor died two years later.

I put the file to one side. I'd look at it again up at the Manor. I looked inside another cabinet and saw a file pocket, marked *photographs*. Inside, I found the picture of Emily and James taken at Oakwood House in November 1925. Another picture showed Thornhill Manor. It hadn't changed in all those years. There was a family photo of Todd, Eleanor, Emily, Elizabeth and my Grandmother Mary. They all looked so sombre, but that was how they did things then. I put the packet of photos in the pile to take with me.

I said my goodbyes to Annie Farlow and thanked her for letting me look through her uncle's things. I promised to return them after I'd had a chance to look through them more carefully.

———•———

As Victoria drove through the main gates of Millstone Farm, the black car parked on the far side of the road slowly edged out onto the highway. The driver could see Victoria's car up ahead, but didn't get too close. *No need to arouse too much suspicion*, the driver thought opening the window slightly.

———•———

As I headed back to Thornhill Manor, I put the radio on for the latest weather. I'm one of these people who start listening to the weather and by the time they come to my area, I've lost interest. I then upbraid myself for not listening. Well, this time wasn't any different. My mind wandered to the tape. I'll wait until I'm inside the estate grounds before I stop to listen to it, I thought. I keyed in the code and the main gates swung open. I drove for a few minutes and then pulled into a small clearing. I reached into my handbag, grabbed the tape and put it into the machine. I felt a little nervous not knowing what to expect:

"This is Jason Bridge of Millstone Farm and it's Friday the 26th."

That was three days before he died and the day after I wanted to speak to him. It looked like he had a change of mind. Had he intended to send me the tape?

"I need to put some things on the record about the events of November 1925. I was a young reporter back then. You could say cocky with an air of confidence, but I felt I knew my stuff. I was also in love at the time. The focus of my attention, well, one of the loveliest girls in these parts. Her name was Emily. We had a few laughs together, but I knew all along she was in love with that crook James Flynn." I sat back in my seat as Bridge continued. Nothing new here, I thought.

"What does this tape have to do with Emily's death?" Bridge continued *"Well, I can't prove it, but I think he killed her. It was made to look like an accident, like she fell from her horse. Emily was one of the best riders I knew. What she didn't know about horses wasn't worth knowing."*

I noticed that Bridge hesitated slightly before continuing. Despite the various revelations of the day, I wasn't prepared for what came next.

"Flynn had another woman who was pregnant. Emily had found out and was threatening to spill the beans. She confided in me one day. She didn't know what to do."

I assumed it was Mary Riley who Flynn had gotten pregnant. Was she still alive today? What happened to the child? My mind was working overtime.

"Victoria." The tap on the window made me nearly jump through the roof. I looked up to see Simon Flynn peering at me. I quickly pressed the stop button and rolled down the window.

"Hi. I didn't hear you."

"Are you okay? Are you having car problems?" He looked at me with a quizzical look on his face.

"Fine, no problem. Thought I saw a red light on the dash board a few miles back, but everything seems to be OK now." I managed a laugh in spite of my nervousness.

"This is quite a secluded part of the estate. I was just checking some fences back there and noticed your car."

"Well like I said everything is fine. I must get back to the Manor. I need to freshen up and change for dinner. My aunt worries if I'm not back on time."

"OK, see you around." He stood there with a puzzled look on his face as I drove off, his shape getting smaller and smaller in my rear view mirror.

———•———

It had been a long day and all I wanted was a shower and a change of clothes. I was still on a high with all my discoveries—the files, the photos, the tape plus the shock of seeing Simon peering at me through the car window. I wanted to pour myself a stiff drink, but thought better of it.

I bumped into Mrs. Winton as I came through the front door.

"Hello Miss Victoria. Dinner will be served on the terrace at half past seven."

"Thanks, Mrs. Winton." I got to my room and dropped my bag with all my goodies onto the bed. I got into the shower and stood there with a lathery mass on top of my head. It felt relaxing to feel the soap and water wash over my body.

Oh my god, I thought, as I rinsed the soap off my hair, I've left the tape in the car. I quickly stepped out of the shower, towelled myself dry and dressed hurriedly. It was almost half past seven. My aunt was a stickler for punctuality. I just had enough time to get to the car, take the tape and make my way into dinner.

The quickest way to the car without being seen was via my terrace and through the rose garden. I went out through the French windows and jogged through the rose garden. My car was parked a few yards from the main door. I opened the door and then pushed the button on the cassette machine and quickly pulled out the tape. I slipped it into the pocket of my dress and closed the car door. I walked around the side of the house towards the terrace and dinner.

CHAPTER TEN

The next morning, I was sitting in the rose garden working on my laptop. It was a bright sunny day, the roses were in full bloom and the colours were stunning, so it wasn't easy to focus on my book, I can tell you. I would have been happy to just stare into space or even close my eyes and breathe in the heady scent of the roses. I was soon jolted out of my reverie when my cell phone rang. I looked at the number, but I didn't recognise it.

"Hello, Victoria Green speaking."

"Miss Green. Bill Rainer here. I've got a piece of news for you regarding Jason Bridge's death." I was surprised to hear from him.

"Our forensics team has just come back with the results of their analysis. Miss Green, we believe that Jason Bridge was murdered." I almost dropped the phone.

"Miss Green, are you still there?"

"Yes Detective." I could hardly speak. I thought immediately about how my aunt would react to this news.

"Detective, this is a shock. Can you give me any more details?"

"Well, it looks like someone got into the house by an open window, and made their way up to Bridge's room. They forced him into his wheelchair, pushed him to the top of the stairs and tipped him over." I listened to Rainer. Who would want to kill Bridge?

"Wouldn't there be a lot of noise? Some kind of struggle? How is it that Annie Farlow and her husband didn't hear anything?'

"It seems Mrs. Farlow and her husband had had a little bit too much to drink that night. They'd had some friends over and polished off a couple of bottles of wine between them. Put it this way, if a herd of buffalo had run past their window that night, they wouldn't have heard them."

"Do you have any leads?" I knew that even if he had he wouldn't reveal them. He was probably only telling me things that would be reported in the papers.

"No, but we're going over all our evidence. We'll be interviewing some of the last people who saw Bridge alive." When he said this, I thought of Aunt Elizabeth. She'd had dinner with him and some other friends on the night he was murdered.

"Detective, many thanks for calling me. I have to go and tell my aunt. Please keep me posted." I switched off my cell phone. I leaned back in the chair hardly able to believe what he had told me. I picked up my laptop and walked towards the house. My aunt was standing in the hallway with her back to me.

"Thank you, Jim. I can't believe it. Who would want to do such a thing?" I knew instantly that she was talking to Houghton at the *Herald*. He must have broken the news to her.

My aunt turned around as she heard my footsteps. She managed a smile, but I could see the pain on her face. Not only had she lost a dear friend, but in terrible circumstances. If I didn't feel guilty before, I sure enough felt like a death row prisoner now.

"Jim, Victoria's just come in. Just a minute." My aunt handed the phone to me. As I took the receiver, I could see tears in her eyes. She walked towards the library and I heard the door close as I heard Houghton's voice come on the line.

"Miss Green, Detective Rainer told me he would call you with the news of Bridge. We don't know what to make of it." *Join the club*, I wanted to say. I was as baffled as he was.

"Maybe he made some enemies over the years. You know, journalism is a tough business."

"Yes it is, but how many people are murdered because of it?" Houghton told me about his article that would appear in a special late edition. I made a mental note to drop by the store later to pick up a copy. I had absolutely no idea who could have wanted Bridge dead. I had a hunch that it was connected with the so-called *Thornhill Secret*. I had to find out just exactly what this secret was and I had a feeling this would lead me to Jason Bridge's killer. I decided to go and listen to the remaining part of the tape. The *Thornhill Secret* was just too irresistible not to follow up on. I knew from my writing that every family has its secrets and its fair share of black sheep. My family was no exception.

When I got back to my room, I took the tape from my bedside table where I'd left it the night before. I'd borrowed an old tape recorder with a cassette deck and play-back facility from Mrs. Winton. I decided it was too risky to use the machine in the car. I couldn't be certain that I'd be left in peace to listen to the tape. Simon had a habit of appearing out of nowhere. I had a strong feeling that he was mixed up in all of this, but I couldn't be one hundred per cent sure. That left Mrs. Winton and my aunt. Then of course there was Houghton from the *Herald*, but what motives did he have. My mind was full of all kinds of scenarios.

I sat down on my bed and felt the warm breeze through the French doors that I'd left open. I put the cassette in the machine and pressed play.

"*. . . Emily was distraught when she found Flynn cheating on her. The final straw was finding out that his other woman was pregnant. Emily knew who it was—we all did—and she was sent off to have the baby. Emily could never forgive him. The whole thing caused such a family crisis. Old man Thornhill was gunning for Flynn. He called him into his office one day and read the riot act to him.*"

———

"Come in." Todd Thornhill took a last puff of his cigar and then stubbed it out in the ashtray. The door opened and James Flynn stood there in his riding breeches and boots. *Bloody fool hasn't even had the decency to change before he comes to see me,* he thought.

"Mr. Thornhill, Sir, you wanted to speak to me."

"Yes, sit down." Flynn sat in the chair opposite the desk with his back to the door.

"My niece means everything to me and her happiness is very important," Thornhill said. He got up and looked out of the window. "Flynn, I've heard all about the affair and my wife and I feel it best if you went away. Away from Emily, away from the estate."

"I love Emily. My affair was a mistake. I want to marry Emily, not go away from here."

"Marry my niece." Thornhill laughed. "You're not fit to wipe her shoes." The older man seethed with rage. He couldn't believe the gall of this young man. He reached in his drawer and pulled out an envelope. He threw it across the desk at Flynn.

"Here, $5,000 to stay away from my niece. You want to pursue your career in journalism, good. I've got just the job for you. An old Harvard friend of mine owes me a favour. He's the editor of the *New York Chronicle*. He's got an opening for a young rookie reporter. Looks like you've got yourself a job."

"I don't want your bribes. You think you can buy people off, Thornhill; well, you can't." Flynn met his gaze.

Todd Thornhill jumped up and lunged at Flynn, grabbing him by the neck before the young man had a chance to move.

"You piece of garbage. It'll give me great pleasure to break your neck." He slowly released his grip from Flynn's throat. Flynn slumped forward.

"Okay, but make it worth my while," he spluttered, catching his breath. "$5,000 won't go far in New York. I'll take the job, but for $10,000."

"You greedy piece of scum. You're a disgrace to the memory of your father," Thornhill said, as he sat back behind his desk.

"I hardly think my father needs to be remembered. He treated my mother appallingly," he scoffed. "Well, what's it to be?"

"You'll get $5,000 now and another $5,000 will be wired to New York when I hear that you've shown up for work. You'd better keep away from here. I never want to set eyes on you again."

"Don't worry. That ten grand will set me up nicely in New York." Flynn's mouth turned up at the edge. "I've no desire to set foot in this place again." he sneered.

"Get out of here before I throw you out," he bellowed, as James slammed the door.

———•———

I stopped the tape. It was an absolute goldmine of information. Bridge's reference to Emily's knowledge of Flynn's infidelity and the bribe that Flynn had taken from Todd was interesting. I was puzzled though. Why hadn't Bridge mentioned the name of the woman who was pregnant? Was it to protect someone? I pressed the play button.

" . . . *Emily was angry at her uncle for sending James away, but Todd Thornhill had no choice. He wanted to avoid a family scandal. We all have our secrets to keep and the Thornhill's certainly had their fair share of them. Of course, all the servants knew what had happened: the affair and then Emily's alleged accident. I don't believe for one minute that Emily fell from that horse.*" I listened intently to Bridge's words.

"*A couple of weeks after his encounter with old man Thornhill, Flynn arrived at Grand Central like the Dapper Dan he was. He reported for work at the New York Chronicle and, true to his word, old man Thornhill sent the remaining $5,000 to him. What he didn't know was that Flynn returned to Moultonborough a couple of weeks later and met Emily. They met at a hotel ten miles west of Laconia. They spent the night together and Flynn basically told her that Todd had tried to bribe him and he wasn't having any of it. He wanted to start a new life with Emily, but she seemed hesitant. It was a case of split loyalties for her aunt and uncle and her love for James. Emily went back to the estate, but it broke her heart that she would have to decide.*

So to come to the day of the so-called accident; the Thornhill family were at home relaxing after a busy few days of entertaining some important guests. Early one afternoon, Emily saddled up her horse and went out riding. She was, of course, meeting James.

What happened next is subject to conjecture. There are so many different stories. Well, the official one is that her horse reared when it heard a car approaching and Emily was thrown to the ground, sustaining a head injury. My theory goes like this . . . ."

I was listening so intensely to Bridge's commentary that I didn't hear the knocking on my bedroom door.

"Victoria, is everything alright, my dear?" It was my aunt. How long had she been there? I quickly turned off the tape, unplugged the recorder and shoved it under the bed. I walked quickly to the door and opened it.

"Victoria, I thought I heard voices." She looked at me waiting for an answer.

"Oh, I was just listening to some messages on my cell phone. These phones do all kinds of things these days," I laughed. I knew that my aunt was no fool; I would have to come clean with her on my investigations sooner or later.

"Well, I'm too old for all this technology. The television and video recorder are just about all I can manage. Anyway, let's have some lunch." I couldn't believe it when she mentioned lunch. It was almost a quarter past twelve. Where had the time gone? I told Aunt Elizabeth that I wanted to freshen up and I'd join her in the dining room in about twenty minutes. I was tempted to carry on listening to the tape, but I knew that I wouldn't have time. I quickly changed clothes, brushed my teeth and splashed some cold water on my face.

Aunt Elizabeth was waiting for me in the dining room.

"Would you like some bread?" she asked me as I sat down. She passed the basket to me and I took a bread roll.

"Victoria, I thought I heard Jason's voice in your room earlier," she said. "What's going on?" I wasn't expecting the question. My aunt was a shrewd cookie. She didn't believe all that palaver about the cell phone messages.

"Aunt Elizabeth, Jason Bridge made a tape recording of the events surrounding Emily's death."

"A tape recording? Why on earth would he do that? He never mentioned it to me."

"I've no idea. I found it in his study when I went over to see his niece a few days ago."

"You searched through his things?" My aunt was surprised.

"Yes, I want to find out the truth about Emily's death and Annie Farlow let me look through them. She knows I want to get to the bottom of this."

"Victoria. Listen to me. Whoever killed Jason could kill again. Take it from me. You are opening up a hornet's nest here." I couldn't believe what she said. It was the nearest thing to a warning that I was going to get. Well, Victoria Green does not give up a fight so easily. Looking back now, I wish I'd taken my aunt's advice.

———•———

The person standing next to Victoria's bedroom window couldn't believe it. *What was old Jason Bridge up to, talking on a tape? That bloody old fool. After all these years, still meddling in the Thornhill's affairs.* The person moved towards the French windows. The doors were open. The person crept in and looked around. *I must find that tape. Where have you hidden it, Victoria?*

———•———

I made my way back to my bedroom. The net curtains were blowing carelessly in the wind and the fragrance from the rose garden wafted through the room. I sat on my bed and thought about what my aunt had said. She had basically warned me to drop this investigation. Maybe Bridge's death happening when it did was just a coincidence. Probably some old hack getting his own back on the reporter for stealing a story. Or was it? Well, I needed to listen to Bridge's theory about Emily's death. I knelt down and pulled the cassette player out from under the bed. I put it on the table, plugged it in and pressed the play button. I couldn't hear anything so I turned up the volume. Still nothing. I pressed the rewind button and the button sprang back up. I pressed the eject button and the cartridge container shot up, but there was no tape inside. I couldn't believe it. I looked under the bed. Could it have fallen out when I shoved the machine under the bed? That was hard to believe. The only person who knew I had the tape was Aunt Elizabeth and I'd been with her for the past hour.

I felt completely washed up as I sat on the bed. Bridge was just about to tell me his version of events on the tape. I was no closer to the truth now than before I started listening to it. I would now add the tale of the missing tape to the story of the pearl-drop earrings in my growing list of unsolved mysteries.

Think, Victoria, said the little voice in my head. Maybe Bridge wrote something down and I just hadn't discovered it yet. I spent the rest of the afternoon looking through the file. My eyes hurt and my neck was stiff from sitting in the same position. I got up to look out of the window. After the nice start to the day the sky was now inky black and we were in for another storm.

As I ploughed through the file, I saw a small note in what I guessed was Bridge's handwriting. It said: *get a copy of the Coroner's report, Tel: 443 8891.*

That was it. The Coroner's report. Why didn't I think of it before? I was pretty sure that records or at least scanned or microfilmed copies of reports would be available. Maybe they might churn something up. I decided to drop by the County Coroner's Office the next day. Now though, I wanted to see what the *Laconia Herald* had said about Bridge's death. I grabbed my handbag and car keys and headed out the door.

As I headed towards Moultonborough, it started to rain. I shivered at the thought that someone had actually come into my room and taken the tape from the machine under the bed. There could be no other explanation for its disappearance. How did they know I had it and where to look for it? I can only guess that they had been listening. So my hunch was right, I was being watched. I had sensed something the other day in the garden. My prime suspect, of course, was Simon. As I drove down to the main gates of the estate, I tried to think what possible motive he could have. I know it was his grandfather who was involved, but Simon wasn't born when he died. The only other person was Mrs. Winton, but what were her motives? She hadn't been around when Emily and Elizabeth were young. I couldn't possibly accuse Aunt Elizabeth, or could I? I was tired and confused at this point as I watched the rain lash the windscreen.

I pulled into the small car park near the newsstand and grabbed the late edition. Houghton's headline leapt up from the page:

Ex-Herald Journalist murdered at Home

Jason Bridge, 92-year-old ex-journalist with this newspaper and active environmentalist was murdered at his home last night according to the police. Bridge was found at the bottom of the stairs at his home in Wolfeboro.

Bridge was an outstanding journalist who had worked for the Herald since 1923.

The rest of the article spoke of Bridge's commitment to journalism and said that police were still investigating and following up on leads. More or less what Rainer had told me.

I put the newspaper on the car seat beside me and decided to drive over to the *Laconia Herald*. I wanted to get Houghton's opinion of things. Perhaps I'd ask him if he had any contacts in the Coroner's Office.

I arrived in Laconia and parked as close to the newspaper office as I could. Some of the shops had closed so it wasn't so busy. I noticed the lights were still on as I walked over to the newspaper office. I knocked and walked in.

"Hello, Mr. Houghton. Are you there?" I sat down and waited for a few minutes. Perhaps he was in the washroom. I thought I heard something downstairs. I hesitated, but then decided to go and see if he was there. Perhaps he was doing some of that filing he said he was going to do.

I made my way down the stairs. The light was on and I peered down the corridor.

"Hello, Mr. Houghton." I walked down the corridor, avoiding the cobwebs and spiders. This place gives me the creeps, I thought.

I came to the first room, and knocked on the door. I stood outside the room where I'd been ensconced a few days earlier. Although the door was closed, I could see a light underneath it. I knocked on the door. I reached for the door handle and turned it. The door creaked as I opened it. Houghton was slumped over the desk and the files. His head was in his hands. I walked across to the desk.

"Mr. Houghton. Mr. Houghton." Either he was as dead as a dodo or was sleeping like a log. I touched his arm, but he didn't move. My god, the killer could still be in the building. Just as turned to go through the door I heard a moan. I looked back at Houghton and he moved, stretched his arms and opened his eyes.

"Wow, I must have dozed off. What are you doing here?" I could hardly speak. The fact that five minutes earlier I'd given this man up for dead scared the living daylights out of me.

"I, er, dropped by your office. I shouted a couple of times, but no answer. I'm sorry to bother you," I said, trying not to sound nervous. He got up out of the chair and we both went upstairs.

"Some coffee?" he asked. I gladly accepted, secretly wishing I could put a slug of brandy in it. I sat down opposite his desk.

"So, what can I do for you?"

"First of all, I saw your article this evening. It was a great tribute to your colleague."

"Thanks. I can't believe anyone would want to kill him. It's unbelievable. He was so well liked in the community." Houghton looked down into his coffee cup, reflecting on his contact with his friend and colleague.

"My aunt is upset. Who could do such a thing?" I added.

"I don't know. Anyway, what brings you here so late?"

"Mr. Houghton, as you know, Annie Farlow let me look through her uncle's files the other day. I also discovered that he had made a tape of the events surrounding Emily Thornhill's death. What is strange is that he had hidden the tape. It was at the back of a drawer in his study."

"Why would he want to hide something like that? Maybe it was in the drawer and it had fallen at the back. Things like that happen to me all the time."

"Well, perhaps, but what is even stranger is that the tape was stolen from my bedroom this afternoon."

"Someone stole the tape from you?" Houghton looked surprised.

"Exactly. I have no idea who could have done it. I think someone is watching me. Perhaps they were listening at my window. I don't know, but it's all very strange."

"What makes you think that someone's watching you?" He sipped his coffee.

"I just have this feeling. I saw a car here in Laconia the other day when I was coming from the Police Station. I have no idea who this car belongs to." I looked at Houghton. Did he think I was in the early stages of paranoia?

"Just because you see a familiar make of car, doesn't mean that someone's creeping around. Tell me, did you listen to the tape?"

"Well, probably half of it before it was snatched from under my nose. Bridge said that James Flynn had gotten another girl pregnant; he left Emily and was paid off by Todd Thornhill to go to New York. He mentioned the official version of the accident and he was just about to tell me what he thought when I was interrupted by my aunt to have lunch. By the time I got back to my room about an hour later, the tape was gone."

"So maybe it was someone listening. As soon as the coast was clear, he made his move."

"How do you know it was a *he*?"

"Oh, just a figure of speech."

"I also found a note that Bridge had written. It was an *aide-mémoire*. He wanted to get a copy of the Coroner's Office report into Emily's death. I'm not sure if he succeeded. I thought it would be a good idea if I went down to the records office and see if they have anything on file."

"Well, you can try, but there was a fire at the old County Coroner's Office in 1929. Whole building went up. I know they lost a lot of stuff."

Now a fire destroying the records. Was this another brick wall? My only hope was that the records for 1925/26 had survived. Failing that, I hoped and prayed that Bridge was as thorough as they said he was and that he'd managed to get a copy of the report back then. If he did, it was somewhere in his records.

"Mr. Houghton, I'll let myself out. Thanks for your time." I drained my coffee and threw the cup in the bin. I was going to pay a visit to the Coroner's Office the next day.

———•———

The following morning a heavy mist hung over the mountains. I was hoping it would be clear down in Laconia. Weather can be a bit strange in the mountains, I thought, as I made my way to the breakfast room. My aunt was sitting there reading the newspaper.

"Morning Aunt Elizabeth. How are you this morning?" I kissed her cheek and then helped myself to some coffee.

"Good morning, Dear. I'm fine." She didn't look it. I sensed she had something at the back of her mind.

"How's your book coming along, Victoria?" I had a feeling my aunt was quizzing me. She probably knew I hadn't spent as much time on it as I would have liked.

"So-so. I hope to send something to Connie at the agency in a few days. I have to go into Laconia this morning to pick up some floppy disks for my laptop."

"Oh, all this technology. I don't know one end of it from the other." We both laughed. I finished my blueberry pancake and French toast and made my way to my car. It was still very strange to me to think that someone had taken the tape from the room. Who could it have been? I decided not to tell Aunt Elizabeth about this; it would only upset her.

I was right about the mist. After driving through a cloud of thick fog, it cleared up just as I hit the main road to Laconia. There were a lot of people out and about. This was a lovely part of the country and I was glad to be here despite the events of the past few days.

I parked outside the County Coroner's Office. As I mounted the steps, I saw the date engraved into the stone *1896*. I walked through the swing doors and stopped to admire the impressive entrance hall. The marble floors, white-washed walls and high ceilings reminded me of the many buildings in London I'd visited during my book research. As I stood there, taking it all in, I saw a small group of people in the distance and then two armed security guards and a metal detection system rather like the one used at airports. I walked towards the group. It was suddenly my turn to go through.

"Please step this way, Ma'am." The guard beckoned me forward and I put my bag on the conveyor belt and watched it disappear into the x-ray machine. I walked through the metal frame, retrieved my bag and headed towards the reception desk. A smart-looking young man with blond hair and glasses was sitting there looking into his computer screen. He looked up as I approached.

"Good morning, Ma'am. Can I help you?"

"Yes, good morning. My name's Victoria Green. I'd like to see the Coroner's records for 1925/1926 please." He made a note of my name on a piece of paper.

"Do you have an appointment, Ma'am?"

"No, do I need one?"

"Well, normally we only let people see the records if they have an appointment. It depends on how busy they are in the archive section."

"I'm doing research for a book. I live in New York and I have a deadline." I gave him my best smile. "I'm sorry I didn't realise I'd need an appointment. If there's any possibility that I could get some information, I'd be most grateful." I grovelled until I could grovel no more.

"Let me check for you. Just a minute." He picked the receiver up and hit four keys.

"Hi, this is reception. I have a lady here who'd like to see the Coroner's records for 1925/1926. Any chance this morning?" I waited as he listened to his colleague.

"Oh, you don't say." He covered the receiver with his hand.

"We only have partial records for that time. We had a fire way back in 1929 and a lot of stuff was destroyed." Yes, I know, I wanted to say to him.

"Well, could I at least see what you have?"

"Can the lady see what you have down there? She's a writer from New York and has a deadline." I waited for the decision.

"Fine. I'll send her down. Her name's Miss Green. Thanks."

He replaced the receiver and I was told to take the elevator to the second basement. As I made my way into the bowels of the building, I prayed I'd find something.

Room 332 was quite large. Two women were sitting at computer terminals surrounded by filing cabinets. The floor was covered with a sickly looking orange carpet that had seen better days and there was a distinctive old musty smell. In a corner stood a fax machine and next to it was a large antiquated photocopier. I introduced myself and explained I was looking for information for the year 1926 on Emily Thornhill.

"Let me see." One of the women, a redhead with a mass of freckles, quickly punched in the information. While I waited I secretly crossed my fingers and hoped that I'd get some information.

"I'm sorry Ma'am. There's nothing in the records for 1926 on an Emily Thornhill." I asked her to try again for the years 1925 and 1927, but nothing.

"Thanks for trying." Disappointed, I grabbed my bag and walked towards the door.

"Ma'am. You might want to try the State Coroner's Office in Concord." I swung around and looked at the other woman working in the room. She had been following my exchange with her colleague.

"The State Coroner's Office in Concord. Would they keep such records?" A feeling of hope suddenly washed over me.

"Well, way back then, before all our computers, they had to send a hard copy of all reports to the State Office. The procedure wasn't always followed, but if you really want to find something, it's worth a try. Do you want me to call them?"

"Oh yes, please. That'd be great." I sat down while she made the call.

"Okay. Sure. I'll let her know." I couldn't tell from the conversation or the expression on her face if it was positive or negative.

"Ma'am. They have some records for that time. They won't reveal any details over the phone, but if you want to follow-up, call this number, make an appointment and they'll try to help." I took the details, thanked both women and made my way out of the archive room.

The main entrance hall was teeming with people. I hurriedly walked towards the exit. I was caught up with my thoughts and what I was going to do next when I heard my name being called. I turned around.

"Well hello. What are you doing here?" I immediately recognised the soft-lilted voice of Detective Rainer.

"Oh, hello, Detective. I'm just doing some research for a future book. You know us journalists. Always snooping around." I laughed. How was I going to get out of this one?

"Do you have time for a cup of coffee? There's a coffee shop on the first floor." I wanted to get out of there so I could make the call to Concord, but on reflection, this was too good an opportunity to miss. I could find out if Rainer had any more clues on Bridge's murderer.

We sat drinking our cappuccinos on a mezzanine floor overlooking the comings and goings of the entrance hall.

"Can't resist these things," he said, taking a bite out of his blueberry muffin. Neither could I, but my expanding waistline convinced me to lay off them for a while. At least until I could get out and do more exercise.

"So, Miss Green. What book did you say you were writing?" His question caught me off guard.

"Oh, it's just an idea for a thriller set in the twenties or thirties. Nothing concrete yet, but always good to have the ideas." I had to change the subject before he pressed me on the real reason I was here.

"Hope something comes out of it," he said. I watched him as he sipped his coffee and finished the muffin.

"What brings you here, Detective?" As I asked the question, I realised how stupid it was. Police officers and lawyers were a common sight at the Coroner's office.

"Just a couple of things I had to check out concerning the Bridge case."

"How's it going? Any new developments?"

"We're still going through the evidence from the scene. No one heard or saw anything. You know, it's quite a remote place and the killer would have had to drive over there. We know that Mr. and Mrs. Farlow were sleeping like babies, so we'll have to see if there are any tyre tracks. The trouble is, people are coming and going all the time with it being a farm. Anyway, we'll keep trying. We had to send some evidence we found inside the house to the Forensic Laboratory in Boston for more intensive analysis. We should get that back any day now."

I was intrigued at the progress and looked forward to quizzing the Detective again, but I was now anxious to get my hands on any information that might be available on Emily's death.

"Well, I must be off. I have to stop at the stationery store. I need some envelopes," I lied, but I wanted to get out and make that call. I left Rainer nursing his coffee cup and picking up the crumbs from his muffin.

I walked down the steps of the building and then stopped. There it was. The black car that I'd seen the other day near Police Headquarters. It was parked across the street. I stopped at the bottom of the steps. There were lots of people milling around. I made my way over to it. There was no sign of the driver and I couldn't see in the back because of the blacked-out windows. The car had New Hampshire plates. I took the number down. The *Live Free or Die* motto seemed ironic. I knew someone back in New York who could tap into the registration database. I needed to find out who was following me.

I went back to my car and turned the key in the ignition. I was tempted to wait to see who came back to the car, but I could be there all day. I drove a few yards and parked in a side street. I switched on my cell phone and dialled the State Coroner's Office in Concord.

"Hello, Coroner's Records, Jane Forrest."

"Yes, Hello Ms. Forrest. I'm Victoria Green. Your colleague at the Laconia Coroner's Office asked me to call you about some records dating back to 1926."

"Oh yes. What can I do for you?' she said cheerily as I explained what I was looking for.

We agreed to meet that afternoon at three. I'd have to go back to the Manor and explain to Aunt Elizabeth that unexpectedly my publisher was visiting Concord and that we needed to meet to discuss the schedule for my book, and that I may not be back until the following day. That would give me enough time to sift through the records.

I had a feeling of trepidation as I drove back to Thornhill Manor. My desire to find out what really happened to Emily was stronger than ever.

CHAPTER ELEVEN

Concord, New Hampshire was founded in 1725. I remember a couple of years ago reading all about its early history. However, that was the furthest thing from my mind at the moment, as I travelled south on Interstate 93. I arrived there just before three o'clock. I found Faulkner Street and parked my car outside of New Hampshire's State Coroner's Office. Unfortunately, it didn't have the charm of the Coroner's Office in Laconia. This was a modern building, a mass of sand-coloured concrete interspersed with small windows. It reminded me of the FBI building in Washington. I walked through the automatic doors, announced myself to the receptionist and was given a visitor's badge. I was asked to go to the sixth floor, where I found Jane Forrest sitting at her computer terminal.

"Hello, I'm Jane." She was in her mid-forties, with short-cropped blond hair and large doe-like brown eyes.

"Hi Jane, I'm Victoria." Once the pleasantries were out of the way, she took me to the archive room.

"You're probably familiar with how these things work," she said, showing me the microfilm machine.

"You could say that." We both laughed. I was beginning to think that libraries and archive rooms had become my second home.

"We've also moved a lot of stuff to the database, but our microfilm system is usually an exact copy or scanned version of that document."

"If I find something, do you have the originals?" I asked hopefully.

"Yes, but we don't really like to show them. They get exposed to dust so where possible we prefer to use the microfilm." She left me to look at the files. It was just after three o'clock and the office closed at five.

I started my search of the database first. I entered Emily's name, the date of the Inquest and after a couple of minutes I saw a message on the screen *one record match*. On the screen I saw the details of the death certificate:

Name of deceased:	Emily Patricia Thornhill
Date of Birth:	February 22nd 1900
Place of Birth:	Chatham, Massachusetts
Place of Death:	Thornhill Manor, Moultonborough, NH
Date of Death:	November 25th 1925
Cause of Death:	Head Wound

If she fell from the horse, it was almost certain she would hit her head. No big surprise here. However, my eyes grew wide in amazement at what was written in the comments box about the cause of death. She'd sustained a gunshot wound. Was it an accident? Now I seriously doubted it. I thought back to the entry in the journal when Emily mentioned a pot had fallen off the roof. Now I'm reading she'd been shot. I wondered whether there had been some kind of cover-up. Strings would have been pulled and only someone like Todd Thornhill with his connections and money could have done that.

I quickly selected the information on screen and sent this to print. I walked over to the microfilm machine and found the information from the Inquest. It was a perfect copy of the report. I printed it and then went back to see Jane.

"Did you find what you were looking for?" she asked me as I sat down in front of her desk.

"Oh yes. I sure did." I was delighted with my find. I just couldn't understand why all the cloak and dagger stuff. Why did my relatives want everyone to think that Emily's death was an accident? Did they know who killed her and then it was all hushed up? Loads of questions, but I needed answers. Back in the 1920s, information was not so freely available. I knew that Bridge was onto something, but he couldn't prove it. What was the police department's version of events of that night? Maybe I had to take Detective Rainer into my confidence and see if he could unearth something.

"Jane, are there any more files concerning Emily Thornhill? Perhaps copies of a medical record, autopsy." I wanted to say anything surrounding the case, but waited for her reaction.

"Let me look," she said, and typed something into the keyboard.

"Ah, well. There are some old files down in the cellar. I can put a request in to have them sent up, but it won't be today. We're closing shortly."

"That's fine. Can I come back tomorrow morning?"

"Sure. We're open to the public from nine o'clock."

"Thanks." I said, as Jane escorted me to the door.

"You know, I read one of your books. I love history and looking at all those photos of Kings and Queens from a bygone age. It must be absolutely fascinating to be able to gather all that information and then churn it out in the book.

"Well, it is rather a challenge, but one I rise to every time. I'm in the middle of writing a book about Queen Katherine of Aragon, Henry VIII's first wife."

"I would love to read it when it is published." Jane said, holding the door for me.

"I'll remember to send you a signed copy. Thanks again and see you tomorrow, Jane."

"See you tomorrow, Victoria." I started to walk down the corridor, and then paused. "Jane, can you recommend an inn or motel nearby?"

"Well, there's a motel a few blocks away, but to be honest, it's not so good. I would recommend The Inn on Shipley Street, just around the corner from here. It's very good, but I'm not sure if they have any vacancies."

"Maybe I'll stop by there and see."

"Victoria, I have an idea. I have a spare room. You're very welcome to use it."

"That's very kind of you. My overnight bag is in the car."

"Great. It will be nice to have some company. My husband is out of town at a convention."

"Okay then and thanks so much. My car is parked across the street."

"Fine let's meet up around ten past five outside the main door and you can follow me. I only live about a twenty-minute drive from here."

———•———

Jane lived in a Georgian-style house with a long lawn, just on the outskirts of Concord. She told me she worked part-time at the Coroner's Office, while studying for her Master's degree in psychology. She'd qualified as a nurse when she was in her twenties, but left to have her two children, who were now away at universities in Europe. She hoped to return to the medical profession as a psychologist, especially helping young people with eating disorders. Her father was a doctor in Boston, her grandfather had also been one and she'd married one.

"I'll be in safe hands if I get sick," she joked as we sat in her lounge sipping our Pinot Noir.

"The house is too big for just me and Bob to roam around in, but we love it here and we don't really want to sell. It's nice when the children visit from Europe, especially the holidays. At Thanksgiving and Christmas the house is absolutely full of people. The kids invite all their friends over and Bob and I love having an *open house*."

When she mentioned she had a spare room, I conjured up pictures of a tiny box room with a single bed. However, the room she gave me had a four-poster bed with a floral print duvet and matching pillowcases, cream carpets and lacy curtains. It looked out over perfectly manicured lawns.

During dinner that night she listened sympathetically as I told her about my aunt and Thornhill Manor. I also mentioned my desire to find out the truth about Emily.

"Well, every family has a secret of one kind or another. My grandfather worked on some cases way back in the twenties. He was always in the news." I put down my fork and looked at her.

"I thought you said he was a doctor."

"He was. He still likes to regale us with some of his most famous cases. You see, he was the Assistant to the State Coroner for New Hampshire between 1926 and 1945."

"So he was here when they sent the information through for Emily? Would he have had to review the case?"

"Yes. All county cases then get reviewed by the State Coroner and, as his assistant, he would have seen something." I quickly rummaged in my bag and found the copy of the Inquest report. It was signed by the County Coroner and then the State Coroner with a counter signature. I couldn't make out the signatures, but Jane told me who had counter-signed it.

"Samuel J. Pembury. My maiden name is Pembury. It doesn't sound American at all, does it? Our descendants came over on the Mayflower. They were from Kent in England. I still have some distant cousins living there. Never get a chance to see them very often. The children are catching up with our long-lost relatives while they're in Europe."

"Yes, interesting." I wasn't paying attention to what she was saying about her ancestors. The words just floated over the top of my head. All I wanted to know was whether I'd be able to speak to her grandfather at some point.

We finished our dinner and took our coffee into the lounge. I was excited at the prospect of going back to the archives the following day to look at the files, but I was even more excited at the possibility of talking to Dr. Pembury. Would he remember a case that far back?

"Jane, do you think I could speak to your grandfather, before I head back to Moultonborough tomorrow?"

"I don't see why not. He lives about a ten-minute drive from here. I'll call him first thing in the morning. He likes to receive visitors every now and then. He gets a bit lonely, now that my grandma is dead."

I went to bed that night with a head full of questions and not a lot of answers.

The following morning when I came downstairs, I found Jane in the kitchen making pancakes.

"Hi, Victoria. Would you like some breakfast?"

"I'd love some. Those pancakes smell great." I sat at the breakfast bar in the centre of the kitchen and poured myself some coffee. I was thinking about the meeting with Jane's grandfather. Jane saw the serious look on my face.

"I'll call my granddad in about half an hour. His nurse usually comes in to help him dress and make sure he has his breakfast." She put the plates full of steaming pancakes onto the table. The pancakes were delicious and I added some blueberries, which Jane had picked from her garden. We chatted over coffee about our respective lives and my work as a writer.

"Well, I'll make that call." She dialled his number and quickly filled him in on the reason for my visit.

"Sure, that will be fine. We'll drop in around half past twelve and join you for lunch." She put the phone down and walked back to the table.

"He's in fine fettle. He's remarkable for his age. Well, we'll see him at lunchtime." It was approaching twenty to nine when we both left Jane's house. We arrived at her office and while she headed for her desk I decided to wait at the coffee bar for the files I had requested the previous day. I sat at one of the small tables nursing a latte, checking my cell phone for any messages. Detective Rainer had called and said he had some news and Mrs. Winton left a brief message to ask if my journey down to Concord was okay and would I just call the Manor to reassure my aunt that I had arrived safely. My aunt was a real worrywart.

"Hi, Victoria." I looked up from the phone and Jane was standing there.

"We've got those files you asked for. They're on my desk; when you're ready, just drop by." I quickly finished my coffee and followed her back to her office.

"Now, let me see," she said, as she shuffled through the buff-coloured folders sending clouds of dust particles into the air, making her sneeze.

"Well, what would we expect after all these years," she laughed. Although I'd only met Jane the previous day, I'd grown to like her. She handed me a file marked *Confidential, Emily Thornhill*. I couldn't believe my luck, as I took the file and sat down at a small table in Jane's office.

The file contained the official autopsy report on Emily. She had died from a wound to the head, but not the type of wound associated with a fall. Jane heard my sharp intake of breath.

"What is it?" Jane got up from her computer terminal and stood behind me.

"I can't believe it. Emily didn't die from the fall from the horse. She was shot. The wound to her head was made by a gun." I looked at Jane in bewilderment.

"She obviously fell from the horse, but she did not die from the injuries sustained in the fall. The gunshot killed her," I told Jane. Things were getting more and more sinister the more information I uncovered.

"I need to make some copies of stuff in this file, so I can discuss them with your grandfather, Jane."

"Sure. I'll show you where the photocopier is."

———•———

Just after midday, Jane and I made our way to her car to embark on the journey to see the man who I thought could answer a lot of the niggling questions that I had. By this time, the situation had become more and more complex. Was the death of Emily connected to Jason Bridge's death? Who was the driver of the mysterious black car that I had seen parked in various places? My enquiries through my friend at the vehicle licensing centre had drawn a blank. The plates were false. They had previously belonged to a 1985 red Pontiac that had been sent to the scrap yard.

Jane's grandfather lived in a small bungalow, certainly not as ostentatious as the grand house of his granddaughter. We were greeted at the main door by a plump woman with salt-and-pepper hair.

"Hello Mrs. Farnsworth. How is Granddad today?"

"He's just fine, Mrs. Forrest. He's got me rushed off my feet though." I could see that this lady and Jane were old friends from the cheerful banter they exchanged, as we made our way into the house.

The bungalow was tastefully decorated with lots of family pictures adorning the walls.

We were shown into the garden, where Dr. Pembury was seated at a table surrounded by wicker chairs. He tried to get up as we approached.

"No, stay there, Granddad. This is Victoria Green. I told you about her on the phone this morning." I shook hands with him and we sat down.

"My, it doesn't seem that long ago since I was working in the Coroner's Office, on the case of your relative." He looked thoughtful as he recalled the events.

"It was my great aunt Emily. I was hoping, Dr. Pembury, that I could ask you some questions regarding her death." I took the copies of the reports out of my handbag and handed them to him. He took a few minutes to look through them and then he stared at me.

"Miss Green. It wasn't an easy case. There were some very influential people around then, who, for whatever reason, didn't want the truth to become public knowledge. As Assistant to the State Coroner, I could only observe what was going on. My boss was ultimately responsible for the final decision." He looked sad and reflective as we sat at the table.

"Why all the secrecy?"

"Well, I can only suspect foul play. The evidence proved that the head wound your great aunt sustained was from a hunting rifle. Some people heard shots that evening, but it is a place that is full of wildlife and hearing gunshots is not uncommon. Those sorts of things don't really arouse much suspicion."

"She was involved with a man called James Flynn, the son of the estate manager. He sounded like a bit of cad." I wasn't sure if Dr. Pembury was aware of this.

"Yes, I recall someone telling me that. You know, he was one of the suspects at the time, but my guess is that the family protected him because of his connection to Emily and they didn't want any scandal. He was paid off, apparently, so that action speaks for itself."

The more I listened to what Dr. Pembury had to say, the more I realised that I had indeed opened a hornet's nest.

"What happened to James Flynn, by the way?" Jane asked. She had been following the story with interest.

"He died in New York in 1946. He'd returned to New York where he worked as a journalist. He was coming out of his office one day and was hit by a car, but the driver and car were never found." Even as I relayed this information to Jane and her grandfather, I couldn't help thinking that the whole story sounded like something out of a Mary Higgins Clark novel. I had a hunch that if I could get some information on Flynn's death in New York, it might shed some light on how Emily had died.

"It sounds like there's a lot more to this than meets the eye," Dr Pembury remarked. We ate our lunch and I said goodbye to Dr. Pembury.

"Thank you for your time, Sir." I shook his hand and I was caught by surprise as he gripped it tightly.

"A word of caution, Miss Green. I think this business is a lot messier than we realise. I know that Todd Thornhill made a lot of enemies in those days with his various business interests. There were all kinds of rumours of how he arranged for people to be killed. Of course these are rumours, but like the saying goes—there is no smoke without fire. Who knows, maybe someone seeking revenge took a pot shot at Emily to get back at Thornhill." He let go of my hand and smiled at me.

"Be very careful," he said. Those parting words sent a shiver up my spine.

———•———

Later that day, I collected my things from Jane's house and loaded them into the car ready for my trip back to Moultonborough. I thanked her for all her help and we promised to keep in touch. She said she would visit me the next time she came to New York.

Before I knew it, I was on Interstate 93 North heading back to Moultonborough and Thornhill Manor. I took the long winding road that I was getting used to by now.

When I try to recall the next series of events, everything seems to be a blur. I hadn't noticed the car behind me until it got really close and we were bumper to bumper. As I tried to keep on the road, I couldn't tell what make of car it was or the colour because of the darkness. I accelerated in the faint hope that it was just one of these nuisance tailgaters who would quickly get bored with the cat and mouse game. Then, when I was bumped several times, I realised that the driver meant business. All I could see was a mass of headlights through my rear view and side mirrors.

Apparently, I was found two hours later by a passing motorist who had been visiting one of the houses near the estate and who had seen smoke coming from the car. All I could remember was my car swerving and hitting a tree. The car had ended up in a ditch. I had a severe concussion and woke up several hours later in Laconia General with the biggest headache I have ever had. As I opened my eyes, I saw a welcoming face.

"Aunt Elizabeth, what happened? I was coming home and then my car was hit." I started to cry and she put her arms around me.

"There, there. You probably skidded on some leaves or something. It was dark. Perhaps you were tired, my dear."

Was this a bad dream? Did I imagine a car was following me or did I really skid off the road and into a tree? My aunt left me then and I called Jane in Concord and told her that I had been in an auto accident. She couldn't believe it when I told her I'd been bumped off the road. I could still hear those cautionary words of her grandfather—be very careful. I was just finishing the call when there was a knock on my room door.

"I've got to go now Jane. I'll call you soon. Bye for now."

I pulled myself up onto the pillows. "Come in." I said, feeling every little ache and pain.

Detective Rainer popped his head around the door clutching a bunch of tulips.

"Hello. Thanks for the flowers, they're lovely," I said, as he handed me the tulips and sat in a chair opposite me.

"Miss Green. I'm sorry to see you here in hospital. Can you tell me exactly what happened?" He placed a small tape recorder on the table beside my bed.

I told Rainer that I was being followed and that some crazy person had tried to run me off the road as I drove back to the estate.

"I was unable to get a make on the car," I said.

"Why would someone want to run you off the road?"

"Detective, I strongly suspect that the driver of the car was probably the same person who has been following me. I knew I had to come clean to Rainer. He sat there for the next hour while I told him about Emily's death, her romance with Flynn, my visit to the newspaper office, the Coroner's Office in Laconia and Concord and my recent visit to Dr. Pembury. He heard the whole story of how I suspected that someone didn't want me to uncover the truth about Emily's death and that I suspected it was all connected to the Bridge murder.

"Well, that's quite a story," he said, when I paused. I also told him about my visit to Annie Farlow and the tape I'd found and its subsequent disappearance, all of which I was convinced were connected to this. Rainer sat in the chair with a pensive look on his face.

"Who would want to hurt you, Miss Green?"

"Good question, Detective. Simon Flynn has been acting strangely; always popping up when I least expect him to. There's also my aunt's housekeeper. I've always thought of her as a bit of a busybody and that has never bothered me until now." I sighed. "I need to uncover the truth about Emily's death and then I might find some answers to the events of the past few days. When I spoke to Dr. Pembury, he told me about Todd Thornhill and implied he might have had some enemies from his business interests, but why would someone want to kill Emily? If they were going to kill someone, why not Todd?" I was grasping at straws, trying to think through the whole mess, but not really coming up with any answers.

"Well, I'll have your statement typed up and ready for your signature tomorrow. In the meantime, I'll have a guard positioned outside this door," the Detective replied. "I spoke to your doctor and he said you'll probably be released tomorrow afternoon. After that, I suggest you stay at the Manor and don't leave." He left me and I tried to get some sleep.

CHAPTER TWELVE

I was running down a long corridor, a white corridor with swirling mist. The faces started to come out of the pictures lining the walls, leering eyes following me as I ran and ran and ran. Where was I running? It was like a tunnel with no end in sight. I then heard a telephone ringing, but I couldn't see one. The ringing got louder and louder.

I woke up with a start. The phone was still ringing, but on the side of my hospital bed. Where am I? What time is it? I briefly looked up towards the window. It was almost light and I remembered I was in hospital. I picked up the receiver.

"Victoria, why did you talk to the police?" The caller's voice was distorted, high-pitched. It had clearly been disguised, I was sure.

"Who is this?" I could hardly breathe as I sat clutching the phone.

"Never mind who it is. You're too nosey, Victoria. Why didn't you let the past rest? Sleep well, Victoria, it might be the last time you ever do." The line went dead.

I sat there holding the phone for what seemed like an age when in fact it was only a couple of minutes. This certainly wasn't a dream. I had to call Rainer. When I finally had the energy to look at the clock I realised it was only twenty past six. I pulled the phone out of the socket and then got out of bed. I peeked outside the door and the young police officer smiled at me.

"Everything okay, Ma'am?"

"Why yes, officer, I just wanted to get a cup of coffee; I'm an early riser." He asked me to press the buzzer at the side of the bed to call for a nurse. I went back to bed and rested my head against the pillows. I didn't even hear the door opening. I jumped as I saw Detective Rainer standing there.

"Oh, you made me jump."

He sat down in the chair. "We tried to trace the call, but it wasn't long enough, but we heard everything."

I let out a sigh of relief. Now they would believe me. There was a nut case out there trying to kill me.

"I can't believe what's happening. Someone is following me, has stolen something from my room at the Manor, has tried to run me off the road and is now making crank phone calls. What more could a girl ask for?" My feigned sarcasm did not fool him, and he saw the despair in my face as tears slid down my cheeks.

What had started out as a simple case of finding out what happened to my relative was now looking like something out of a Nancy Drew thriller on prime time TV.

"We'll get to the bottom of this, don't worry." I wasn't reassured by his words and I don't know why. I wanted to put all this behind me and go back to New York. I felt disheartened and was now realising exactly how much danger I was in with some crackpot on the loose. I realised that it was probably the same crackpot who had killed Jason Bridge.

"Try and get some rest." He made for the door and then turned to me.

"By the way, Miss Green, it looks like we've found the car that ran you off the road."

I looked up at him. "Where?"

"It was abandoned in a side road a couple of miles from Laconia. It was a black sedan, covered in mud, but someone had given the inside a thorough clean. Our Forensics Team are taking a closer look."

"I hope they find something, Detective." Even though I said this, I strongly suspected Simon.

"One good thing though. The front bumper is badly dented, which is consistent with it hitting the back of another car. We found tiny traces of blue paint which match the paint from your car." I was relieved when he told me this.

"The license plate was false, but we managed to get a serial number from the chassis and it's a car registered to Thornhill Enterprises."

"This must be the same car that I saw outside the County Coroner's Office in Laconia, Detective."

"Well, this car is just one of many from a pool of cars that people on the estate can use. It was reported stolen about six months ago. The keys to all the cars are kept on a rack near the kitchen door at Thornhill Manor. Someone just walked in took the keys and drove off in the car. No one saw or heard anything."

Rainer left my room and I tried to gather my thoughts. The call scared the living daylights out of me. Who would want me to drop this investigation? My head was buzzing with questions as I stared up at the ceiling. Sleep did not come easily for me that night.

———————

The following morning, I was given the all clear by the doctor. I could leave that afternoon. He told me to rest and eat three meals a day, the usual thing. Rainer picked me up just after half past three and we drove to Thornhill Manor. I looked out of the car window, lost in my thoughts as I went through the events of the past few days.

"You're quiet; the cat got your tongue?" he said, trying to humour me, but I was in no mood for it.

"I don't know what to think anymore. I'm coming back here and perhaps I'm putting myself in more danger."

"We won't let anything happen to you. We've got a few of our officers up here, keeping an eye on things. Don't worry," he said reassuringly. "By the way, one of the Forensics Team found a small helium canister wedged underneath the driver's seat of the black sedan. So we now know that the person who drove you off the road and the one who made that threatening call are the same."

I let out a long sigh. "I wished you hadn't told me that Detective. I'll be frightened to close my eyes tonight."

Detective Rainer suddenly pulled the car over to the side of the road and switched off the ignition.

"Listen, Miss Green. No one is going to hurt you. We'll catch whoever did this." He said touching my arm.

"Oh, I forgot to mention, a Mrs. Forrest called your aunt and she's coming to stay with you for a few days. She should be here when we arrive." My mood improved. It would be nice to see a friendly face and one I could trust. I wasn't sure who to trust anymore.

"Thanks Detective, for the good news. Perhaps it's about time you called me Victoria." I smiled at him.

"Okay. Please call me Bill," he said, starting the car. When we finally arrived at Thornhill Manor around five, I was still filled with apprehension. As the car approached, I saw my aunt, Mrs. Winton and Simon Flynn waiting at the door. It was quite a welcoming party. Who could I trust? Simon, whose grandfather was the catalyst in all this. My aunt, whom I adored, or Mrs. Winton, the kindly seeming housekeeper who looked as if she wouldn't hurt a fly? As I got out of the car, I noticed Jane standing behind the group. It was nice to see her.

"Hello, everyone, I'm back. Did you miss me?" I tried to make light of the situation, but I wasn't fooling anyone. Detective Rainer helped me with my bag and we all went inside the house. There was the usual exchange of hugs and kisses and expressions of concern.

"Hi Jane. Thanks so much for coming. Hope I'm not breaking up your happy home and your husband doesn't mind?"

"No, not at all. Bob had to stay out of town for a few more days, so I just closed up the house and came up here. I've never been to this part of New Hampshire before."

"Well, you'll get plenty of fresh air here," I replied.

After dinner, Jane and I sat in my room and chatted about the events of the last few days. I told her everything. I had no one else to confide in, other than Bill Rainer, but he was a police officer and I'm sure he had to remain impartial.

"I'm sure things will sort themselves out," Jane said, as we said goodnight and she made her way to one of the guestrooms on the first floor. As I climbed into bed, I was both emotionally and physically exhausted. I really wondered who had tried to kill me and whether they would try again. I went to sleep, hoping I wouldn't have another bad dream.

I was awakened by the pounding rain on the windows. There was so much cloud cover over the mountains that I couldn't see a thing. I turned over and pulled the duvet closer to me, but I couldn't go back to sleep. All the events of the past week were swirling around in my head like the mist outside my window. As I lay there I heard voices in the corridor and then a tap on the door.

"Come in," I managed to shout. The door opened and Mrs. Winton came into the room carrying a tray. She set it on the table near the window. I sat up and looked at the tray laden with a pot of tea, milk and sugar, a couple of slices of toast as well as a small bowl of raspberries.

"Morning Miss Victoria. How are you today?"

"Fine, thank you, Mrs. Winton. You've brought my favourite breakfast. That's very kind of you."

"You're very welcome and I hope you're feeling better."

"Well, I thought I'd have a lie in, but it's difficult to go back to sleep."

"Some people have no problem going back to sleep. They could sleep on a clothes line,' she laughed as I got up and walked over to the table and sat down.

"Thanks again for bringing me breakfast."

"Your aunt thought you'd like to have breakfast in your room. She likes to make a fuss. She worries about you. We all do." She had the gentlest look of concern on her face. It almost brought tears to my eyes. I thought about what Bill Rainer had said about the black sedan. Could this gentle old lady drive a car like that and run me down? The thought sounded so bizarre that I almost laughed out loud. However, my face didn't betray any emotion as she headed towards the door.

"I'll collect the tray later. You should get some rest." She disappeared out of the door as I spread some honey on my toast.

My cell phone started to ring just as I'd poured myself a nice cup of Earl Grey Tea. Who could that be? I looked at the incoming call information. Hell's bells, it was the agency calling about the book. I'd completely forgotten in the hurly burly of everything. I was supposed to send them the next chunk of text. So much had happened since the last time I'd spoken to them. I very much doubt if they would believe me if I told them the truth: *Oh, by the way, I was too busy to work on my book; someone tried to run me off the road and I've been getting mysterious phone calls.*

"Hello, Victoria Green speaking. Hi there. Everything is fine. Of course, I'm just finishing a really interesting piece. What, I thought he was giving me two weeks. I still have four more days before that deadline expires. Why the big rush?" I cursed agents for being such pains in the ass at moments like this.

"He's received a couple of other manuscripts and his work is backing up a bit," Connie said sympathetically.

"That's not my problem," I replied, trying not to sound irritated. It wasn't her fault, but I was really browned off. I didn't need this.

"Well, Victoria, that's the official excuse. He's actually off to Maine at the weekend for his annual fishing trip with some old college buddies. He's not the most organised person in the world, as you know, but even he can see a swamp coming towards him at a fast rate of knots. The publisher is on his back, so he's on yours."

"Tell him I'll send what I have by the end of the day. Probably only 5,000 words and I can send him another chunk early next week by fax."

"I'm sorry. He gets my goat too. I'll be glad when he goes to Maine. We'll all get some peace." I got the contact number in Maine and promised to call again in a few days.

I finished breakfast, showered and dressed in blue jeans, pink shirt and a pair of moccasins. It was still raining outside and the mist hadn't lifted. I went to the library and found my aunt reading a magazine.

"Morning, Dear. Did you sleep well?"

I planted a kiss on her cheek and sat down in the chair opposite her. "Morning, Aunt. Yes, I had a good rest. Lovely breakfast too. It was nice of you to suggest I take my breakfast in my room. Pity about the weather, though. I can usually see those wonderful mountains from my window, but not this morning."

"Never mind, they'll still be there tomorrow. You should have a lazy day, Victoria."

"I wish I could." I thought about my conversation with the agency. "I have to do some writing. My agent is practically having a hissy fit back in New York. He wants some material by the end of the day."

"Why don't you work in Uncle Todd's old study? You'll have plenty of room, a big desk. It might be better than using your room."

"That sounds like a great idea." I wanted to speak to Aunt Elizabeth about what I'd learned from Sam Pembury in Concord, but thought I'd touch base with Jane first.

I found Jane in the breakfast room sipping some coffee and reading the *Laconia Herald*.

"Hi, Jane."

"Oh, Victoria, you did scare me. I was so caught up with this story, that I didn't hear a sound."

"Sorry Jane. Did you sleep well? I hope the guest room that Mrs. Winton put you in is alright for you?"

"I slept like a baby and the room is perfect. I have a magnificent view of the mountains. You know I won't be able to go back home." She put the paper down and smiled.

"I know it's such a peaceful place and the mountain air really helps you sleep." We both laughed.

"What are you going to do today, Victoria?" Jane asked, as she helped herself to some more coffee.

"I've got to work on my book. I need to get some pages to my Agent. He's on my back, so I'll have to chain myself to the desk in the study."

"It must be hard keeping to all those deadlines. Do you ever get writer's block?"

"Sometimes, but when the ideas start flowing I find I haven't got enough fingers to type them into the computer. Fortunately, I did a typing course a couple of years ago in between college courses and I'm glad of it now. I'd get a bit frustrated trying to type with two fingers."

"Yes, that sounds like what I do." she said laughing.

"What I also like about writing is the research, especially now that I'm delving into history. Anyway, I must get moving. What are your plans Jane?"

"I thought I'd go for a walk."

"That sounds like a good idea. There are some nice trails around the estate."

"I could do with the fresh air."

"You know I wish I could bottle that fresh air. I'd make a fortune."

She laughed. "I'm looking forward to exploring. Do you think I could borrow a jacket from you? I only brought a thin one with me."

"Sure. I've got one with a hood. It can get a bit fresh up here, so best to wear one. I'll leave it on the table by the front door. Let's catch up later for lunch, shall we? Say one o'clock in the summer room. You'll like it in there. We'll have a fabulous view over the mountains and it looks as if the clouds are lifting."

Jane laughed. "That sounds good. See you later, Victoria. Don't work too hard."

"I'll try not to. Enjoy your walk and wrap up well."

I left Jane to finish her breakfast and headed to the study.

According to Aunt Elizabeth, Todd's study hadn't changed too much over the years, despite the fact that Aunt Elizabeth used it occasionally. I sat back in the brown leather chair that was cracked with age. A picture of Todd, Emily and Eleanor sat on the edge of the desk. I wondered if he had had anything to do with his niece's death. Why the mystery and if she died from a gunshot, who fired the gun?

I wondered about this secret closet that Emily had referred to in her journal. I decided to go into the library to see if I could find it.

I walked down the corridor in anticipation. I suddenly heard a voice and stepped into the shadows.

"You can't say that. How do I know if I give you the money you won't come back and ask for more?" It was Mrs. Winton talking on the telephone. What on earth did she mean? Was she being blackmailed? Could there be a simple explanation? Perhaps one of her children was after a loan? I didn't want to make a mountain out of a mole hill, but something was going on.

"You won't get another penny from me, so don't call here again." She slammed the phone down.

If it was one of her children, it was a very harsh way to deal with them. The blackmail idea was a more likely answer, but by whom? I put aside all thoughts of blackmail as I quietly opened the library door and walked over to main bookcase. Now, which set of books would the lever be hidden behind?, I wondered. I found a book of short stories by Leo Burns and removed it from the shelf. No, nothing behind that. An Art deco book. No nothing. I could be here all day. Then I found the book that Mrs. Banbury had written about the estate. I took it off the shelf. Bingo, I could see a lever behind. I pulled it to the left and a door, which had always looked like a bookcase to me, slowly slid open. I hadn't realised that the library even had a false door. I peered inside. It was dark and I saw a light switch. I flicked it and the bulb slowly came to life. It was very faint and looked as if it was on its last legs. I heard voices in the distance and quickly flicked the switch and closed over the door. I managed to get back to Todd's study without anyone seeing me. Very interesting, I thought switching on my laptop.

My head was full of secret hiding places as I plunged back into my book. Once I started writing, it was easy to get lost once again in the comings and goings of Tudor England. I'd lost track of time and before I knew it, it was ten past one. I picked up the phone and buzzed the summer room. Jane was probably waiting for me. After several rings, Mrs. Winton answered.

"Mrs. Winton, it's Victoria. Sorry I'm a bit late for lunch. I promised Mrs. Forrest that I'd meet her for lunch at one. Can you tell her I'll be there shortly."

"She's not here. I haven't seen her since this morning. Saw her going out the front door just after ten thirty."

"That's strange; I can't imagine she would prolong her walk," I said, concern creeping into my voice. "Mrs. Winton, I'll just finish up here and I'll be in for lunch in about five minutes. If you see Mrs. Forrest tell her I'll join her shortly." I said, replacing the receiver.

I saved my work and e-mailed a copy to Connie at the agency with a nice note about meeting my first of two deadlines and wishing Hal, a good holiday. The next instalment would be sent to them later.

I arrived in the summer room around twenty past one. It was deserted. The table was set, but no sign of Jane. I was pacing up and down the room when Mrs. Winton walked in.

"Have you found Mrs. Forrest yet?" she asked.

"No, I haven't. I think I'll go out and look around the grounds."

"Shall I call Mr. Flynn; maybe he's seen her?" Mrs. Winton said, looking concerned.

"That's a good idea. I'll head towards the stable block. I can borrow one of the horses to look around if necessary."

When I arrived at the stable block, my aunt was there talking to Simon.

"Hi Victoria. I didn't see you at lunch. Did you finish your writing?" She stood next to Flynn who was brushing down a horse. He looked at me and then turned away quickly.

"Yes, I've done what I had to. Sorry about lunch, I had arranged to meet Jane at one o'clock, but she hasn't come back from her walk yet. Have you seen her by any chance?"

"No, I haven't seen her since this morning. I spoke to her briefly in the breakfast room, but that was hours ago. She was knee deep in the newspaper, so I didn't want to disturb her."

I looked at Simon. He'd continued to brush his horse.

"Simon, Have you seen Jane?"

"No, I've been in the stables practically all morning. She didn't come by here," he said coldly.

"I think I should go and look for her. I'm getting really worried. Can I borrow one of the horses?"

"Okay. I'll come with you," he said. I wasn't particularly interested in Simon's company, but what the heck. We could split up if necessary. Two sets of eyes and ears were better than one.

"Victoria. Be careful. It's been raining and the ground might be slippery." My aunt waved us off and we headed out into the forest. The rain had dampened everything and had left a wonderful smell of leaves and pine.

We decided to split up and I took one of the paths. I set the horse into a gentle trot and then we walked for a little while. I thought I heard something moving in the bushes, a branch breaking. My eyes darted around. Probably an animal. I trotted again and came out onto a wider gravel road. I saw Jane in the distance, not walking like I expected, but lying face down by the side of the road, my distinctive orange jacket covered in mud, now acting like a beacon. I got off the horse and quickly tied it to a tree. I turned her over. She was covered in mud and had blood pouring out of a head wound. I felt her pulse. It was slight. I tried mouth-to-mouth and prayed that she would breathe. I heard a horse approaching.

"Simon!" I screamed.

"My god, what happened?"

"I don't know. I found her lying here like this. She's hit her head, but I can feel a faint pulse."

"Don't move her. She might have broken something. We'd better wait for the ambulance." Simon quickly flipped open his cell phone and dialled 911. He told me that the ambulance was on it's way and they'd be about fifteen minutes."

By the time the ambulance arrived I felt numb from shock. It was like watching a scene from a movie. Was this really happening to me? The ambulance crew hoisted Jane onto a stretcher and bundled her inside. I'd given them some basic details and then they tore off into the distance. I wondered whether to go with her, but it felt as if my feet were glued to the floor and I was operating in slow motion. I knew it would take them at least thirty minutes to get to Moultonborough Memorial Hospital. One of the drawbacks of living up in the mountains away from town.

"Everything will be okay, Victoria. She's in safe hands," Simon tried to reassure me.

"I feel so responsible. She was staying here with me and now look." A sob caught in my throat as I got back on my horse and rode back to the Manor.

———·———

I'd made a brief visit to the hospital, but was sent home as there was little I could do. I called the hospital just before midnight and they told me there was no change in Jane's condition, but the next twenty-four hours would be crucial. Jane's husband had been contacted and was expected within the hour.

Sleep did not come easy to me that night. I couldn't stop thinking about Jane, lying there in the intensive care unit.

When I awoke the next morning just after nine o'clock and made my way down to breakfast, Simon was sitting in the breakfast room with Aunt Elizabeth.

"Victoria, Dear. Please sit down." I could see from the look on her face and her eye contact with Simon that something wasn't right.

"She's gone, Victoria," my aunt said.

Tears welled up in my eyes. "I feel so responsible. If it wasn't for me, she wouldn't have been visiting Thornhill Manor." I sat at the table with my head in my hands.

"Now Victoria, you mustn't blame yourself. Accidents happen and what with all the rain, it would be so easy to take a tumble," Aunt Elizabeth said, putting her arm around me. I noticed then that Simon had left the room.

I was absolutely gutted at Jane's death. I told the police exactly what happened that day, even down to the tiny detail of how she borrowed my jacket. I couldn't help it. I know I was being overly cautious. It could have been an accident, but what if it wasn't.

It was hard to concentrate on my writing, and I then had to face Jane's funeral the following week in Concord. I decided I had to go out of respect for a really kind woman, who I'd grown fond of. I was pleased when I heard that Bill Rainer would also be there and Aunt Elizabeth also wanted to attend.

———•———

The following week we gathered in the small cemetery just outside Concord. Jane's husband was very sweet and understanding as he clasped my hand by the graveside. Jane's two children just about got through the service. They had abandoned their studies in Europe to return home to attend their mother's funeral.

"Victoria, thanks for coming," Bob Forrest said to me.

"Bob, I'm so sorry for your loss. How are you all holding up?" I enquired.

"Not too bad. It's a comfort that the children are here."

"Well, if there's anything you need, do let me know."

"Thanks," he managed to say, through his tears. He put his arms around his children as they walked to the car. Jane's grandfather had glared at me during the service. After the burial, I walked over to him.

"Dr. Pembury. I'm very sorry for your loss. If there's anything I can do." He looked up at me from his wheelchair.

"Haven't you done enough. We were a happy family before you came along. Will my daughter's death also be covered up, Miss

Green? You people seem to have a knack for doing that," he said, and looked away.

"Whatever do you mean?" I was completely confused by his outburst.

"Seems strange that my granddaughter goes to stay with you, goes for a walk, and then gets killed. Or should I say murdered." I couldn't answer him. I saw Bill Rainer in the distance coming towards us. Another grieving relative pushed Pembury away and I could hear his sobs as he was helped into the car.

"Bill, I don't know what to say. Jane's grandfather has just made an amazing accusation. He seems to think that her death wasn't an accident, that she was murdered."

"He's right. The Medical Examiner's report says that she died from a blow to the head. We already know that she was pushed down the embankment. We believe whoever did this thought it was you. After all, she was wearing your jacket."

"My god, then whoever did it is still out there."

I felt Bill's arm around my waist as I slid to the ground.

When I regained consciousness, I was sitting in the back of Bill's car. Aunt Elizabeth was holding a wet handkerchief to my forehead. Had I been dreaming or did Bill tell me that Jane had been murdered? A case of mistaken identity, he said. No, it wasn't a dream.

"Here, Dear, take a drop of this." Aunt Elizabeth said holding a small hip flash to my mouth. I caught a faint whiff of brandy as I took a tiny sip. The liquid warmed me as my head fell back on the seat.

"We'll have you home in no time,' Bill said, starting the car.

Thankfully, there wasn't much traffic as we headed back to the Manor. I managed to get out of the car without too much trouble, despite the fact that my legs felt like lead. I felt as if I'd been kicked by a mule.

"Oh, Miss Victoria, you're as white as a sheet," Mrs. Winton said, as I walked through the front door.

"Mrs. Winton can you please bring us some tea in the library. We could all do with a cup."

I sat in one of the leather chairs near the fireplace, grateful for the warmth from the fire.

"Here, drink this, Dear." Aunt Elizabeth handed me a cup of sweetened tea; I drank it, grateful for the refreshment.

After I finished my tea, I went to my room, where I slept for several hours. When I woke up, I had no idea what time it was until I switched on the bedside light. It was twenty to three. I got out of bed and walked to the bathroom. I drank some water from the tap. It was nice and cool, from a well on the estate. I was just about to go back to bed when I heard a noise outside in the garden. I ran over to the bed and switched off the light. I suddenly saw a dark shape outside the window. I could hear a pin drop in the room. My heart pounded in my chest. I felt as if I'd just run the New York Marathon. I opened the bedroom door and walked slowly along the corridor trying to avoid some of the creaking floorboards.

That's when I heard it. A scream that seemed to penetrate the walls. I ran down the corridor as fast as my legs would take me and reached the library hardly able to breathe. As I opened the door, the moonlight guided me to the hiding place. A place also familiar to Emily. She'd mentioned it in her journal.

Feeling my way along the bookcase, I found the lever. Please make it work, I thought. Turning it to the left, the heavy door creaked open. The air was thick and heavy with the smell of old books and wood. Something touched my hair and I flinched, moving my hand to wipe away the remnants of a spider's web. As I closed the door, I heard footsteps on the parquet floor, getting louder and louder. Closer and closer to my hiding place. My heart pounded and I felt as if it would leap out of my chest. I wanted to scream, but I had to stay calm. The heat inside the room was stifling. The thick dust clung to my nostrils. It was difficult to breathe. A shaft of light under the door penetrated the inky blackness. The wooden floor creaked. Suddenly the door swung open.

"Ah, there you are. Why are you hiding here? Did you think I wouldn't find you?" I was pulled up by the scruff of the neck. I felt the coldness of a gun pressed against my forehead as he looked straight at me. His face was pressed close to mine; his blue eyes cold and empty like a cobra's. I tried to move, but it was impossible. He had quite a grip. He threw me down in one of the chairs. I sat there stunned trying to catch my breath as he hovered over me.

"Simon, please why are you doing this?" I managed to say when my breathing had returned to normal.

"Too much snooping around is not good for you. You had to be stopped."

"You've been spying on me, haven't you?"

"You're quite the little detective, aren't you?" He looked at the gun and then back at me.

"Did you kill Jane?"

"Sorry about that. I thought it was you." he said sarcastically.

"That explains your surprise when I reached the stable block looking for Jane."

"Yes, it was a bit of a surprise. When I saw that orange jacket and its owner tumbling over the embankment, I thought all my problems were over," he remarked coldly. "Then you appeared a few hours later large as life."

It was difficult for me to think. What would he do next? Would I also be added to his growing list of victims. Murder number three? My vivid imagination which I so exploited as a writer was now working overtime, but this wasn't fiction, this was for real.

Simon continued, "I couldn't let you destroy the family name, Victoria." *Where would his loyalty get him now?*, I wondered. A couple of years in the slammer for killing my friend and not to mention Jason Bridge's murder; the only way this nutcase would be leaving prison was in a body bag.

"Why should you want to protect the Thornhill name? Do you have something to protect?"

"My father loved this estate. My grandfather's downfall was his dalliance with sweet Emily," he said cynically. "She didn't really care about him. Look what happened. He got run over in New York. My guess is old man Thornhill paid someone to do that."

"Did he kill Emily?" After all my research, would I now finally hear the truth?

"No, he didn't. Someone else did." I assumed then he was talking about Todd, but that didn't make sense. He absolutely adored Emily, according to Aunt Elizabeth. He would never want to kill her and I couldn't imagine Eleanor Thornhill taking a shot at her. This was weird and the scenario had more holes in it than a Swiss cheese. I was still none the wiser.

"Why did you kill Jason Bridge?" I was like a dog with a bone and didn't want to let go until I had some answers.

"What makes you think that I killed him, Victoria?"

He was goading me. *Who else could have done it*, I thought. I felt dizzy and wanted to go back to bed.

"Because it would have taken someone with a lot of strength to get Jason into his chair and then push him down the stairs."

The floor creaked and I was suddenly aware that someone else was standing in the room. I looked up and gasped. Mrs. Winton stepped out of the shadows, brandishing a gun.

"Jason Bridge knew more than he let on. We couldn't let him reveal the truth."

"And the tape?" I looked at this sweet old lady who now stood perfectly still as she pointed the gun directly at me. I didn't doubt for one minute that she wouldn't use that gun.

"I stole it, Victoria," Simon said. "We realised that it had all the answers you were looking for. It would have been best if you'd have let things rest. Now we'll have to get rid of you. I've already taken care of your aunt." Simon laughed. I'd completely forgotten about Aunt Elizabeth. Where was she? Oh my god, was she okay?

"Don't hurt my aunt. She's not responsible for what I've done," I said shakily.

"You're all the same, you people. You think because you have money you can buy whatever you want. Well, let me tell you something. You can't." Mrs. Winton looked as if she was going to explode with anger. Was she insane?

"Mother, please." Simon went over to her and put a comforting arm around her shoulders.

"Don't look so startled, Victoria; yes, he's my son. I'd just arrived at the Estate when I started an affair with Simon's father. We kept it a secret and I continued to work here, but then I discovered I was pregnant. I was sent off to a convent about a hundred and fifty miles from here. I couldn't look after my baby, so he was eventually adopted by Mr. Flynn when his wife died and I returned to New York to live with my sister. I got married and had my family and then we moved up here. I was able to see Simon. He didn't find out until his father died, but he had to know the truth." She looked lovingly at Simon.

"Jason Bridge did some snooping into my mother's past after she'd had the affair with my father. Through his contacts in Great Britain, he'd discovered she'd been involved in a scandal at the Royal Castle of Balmoral in Scotland. I'll give him his due, that guy was like a bloodhound when he got hold of the scent of something."

"Did he have to die? What harm could he do to you now?" I was sickened by it all.

"He would have destroyed everything!" Simon shouted. "My mother has suffered enough. Why couldn't he just leave well alone?"

The sound from the clock ticking away on the mantelpiece penetrated the silence. The next thing, a bolt of lightning lit up the sky. It was raining heavily and the strong wind made the branches knock against the window.

"What are you going to do now, Simon?" I said finding my voice.

"Why don't you just shut up? Can't you do that for once?" I was shocked at his anger. An anger that had probably been festering for a long time.

Before I had a chance to dwell on what was going to happen to me, I heard a commotion outside the window. I could see flashlights and then I heard a voice over a loudspeaker.

"This is the Police. The building is surrounded. Come out with your hands up." At that moment the relief at hearing Bill's voice seemed to float over me like a soft blanket. Another bolt of lightning lit up the sky as the driving rain lashed against the windows.

"Not bloody likely," Mrs. Winton mumbled.

"We'll never get out of here alive, Mother," Simon said nervously.

"If you have a better idea, then let's hear it," she said, walking towards the door.

"Maybe we should let her go. She's no use to us now."

"No." Mrs. Winton snapped. "She's our passage to freedom." She pointed her gun at me. "Stand up and don't try any funny business Nancy Drew."

I walked slowly towards the library door. Simon had walked ahead of me. I couldn't imagine what they were going to do to me. Were they going to make a run for it and take me hostage?" As Mrs. Winton turned to close the door, I grabbed her wrist. We struggled and I was amazed at her strength. Finally I managed to knock the gun out of her hand. It dropped on the floor and I quickly grabbed it. Apart from some clay pigeon shooting a couple of years beforehand, I'd never fired a gun in my life, but I prayed I wouldn't have to use this one. Simon looked on, startled, as I strengthened my grip on his mother's arm. He raised his gun, but even he wasn't going to risk shooting his mother if he missed hitting me first.

"You'll never make it to the front gate. The place is surrounded," I said. He suddenly raced towards the front door. I wasn't going to chase after him, even if I did have a gun. I'd had enough exercise for one night. Suddenly, I heard a hammering on the front door and the sound of hinges splintering, as Rainer and his officers crashed through the door. Simon fired, but thankfully the shot hit the wall. Rainer was luckier with his shot. Simon slumped to the floor clutching his left arm. A uniformed officer quickly handcuffed him.

"Read him his rights and get him out of here," Rainer barked. "And don't forget her," he said, pointing to Mrs. Winton.

I looked on, bewildered, and released my grip on the ashen-faced housekeeper, who collapsed in a chair near the entry hall. I was certainly glad to see Bill and his team.

"Victoria. Are you alright?" He put his hand on my arm.

"Yes. I'm okay. I can't . . . can't believe it." At that moment, I felt as if a huge weight had been lifted from my shoulders, but my relief was short-lived.

"Bill, my aunt. I've got to find her." I suddenly remembered what Simon had said about Aunt Elizabeth. We both raced upstairs to my aunt's bedroom. She was lying on the bed. Her eyes were closed and she'd been bound and gagged. We quickly released her and I was relieved to see her slowly open her eyes.

"Oh my. What's happening? Where's Mrs. Winton?" She sat up and started coughing.

"Aunt Elizabeth, it's okay. Everything's going to be fine. Here drink this." I grabbed the glass of water from the bedside table and put it to her lips.

"Simon tied me up," she said, in a state of bewilderment.

"Aunt Elizabeth, you must rest now. You've had a terrible shock." *She wasn't the only one,* I thought. "I'll call Dr. Melrose to check you over."

She lay back on the pillows. I didn't tell her that her housekeeper and her housekeeper's long-lost son had just been hauled away in handcuffs. She would hear about the evening's escapades soon enough.

I closed the door to her room and, after calling the doctor, Bill and I made our way downstairs to the library.

"Simon confessed to killing Jane and Jason Bridge."

"Well, we suspected him. Thank god for forensics. We found a hair on Jason's pyjama top and when we extracted DNA and ran it through our crime database, we matched it to Flynn. He had a prior arrest for drunken driving a few years ago.

"How did you link him to Jane's murder?" I enquired.

"We found a set of footprints near the area where Jane had been pushed down the hill. They matched the tread from a pair of Flynn's riding boots that we found when we searched the stables. After he killed her, he must have walked back through the trees and got back on his horse. On the back of the jacket that Mrs. Forrest was wearing, we found traces of an oil Flynn had used to clean his saddle. He must have cleaned his saddle that morning and didn't wash his hands. That guy's been on our radar for a while now. We had a feeling he'd make a move tonight. You were getting too close, Victoria."

I was too shocked to speak. I'd had enough shocks to last me a lifetime. Flynn had confessed to the murders, but would he come clean to the police. He'd told me probably in the knowledge that I'd be added to his list of victims. As Bill had said, thank god for forensics. They wouldn't have a problem nailing him.

"Victoria, I thought you'd like to know that during our search of Flynn's stuff, we also found a helium gas canister. We traced the canister to a supplier in Concord. Three canisters of the stuff had been purchased a few weeks ago. The shop assistant recalls that the man drove a black car. She remembers because it had a bump on the front and the license plate was almost hanging off. She wasn't able to describe what the man looked like or even remember the plate number, but we're convinced it was Flynn. He had the motive and the access to the car. He won't be making any more nuisance calls to you.

"Bill I'm relieved it's all over." He stood up and clasped my hand.

"Now you make sure you get a good night's sleep."

"That sounds like a good idea." I said smiling and longing for a hot bath. I wanted to soak away all the aches and pains, after being manhandled by Simon.

I walked Bill to his car. The driveway was choked with police cars and forensic vans. Bill told me that the Crime Scene Investigators would continue with their work, *but that was the least of my worries,* I thought, as I watched his car disappear down the driveway.

CHAPTER THIRTEEN

New York City, 2000

woke to the sounds of the alarm clock and as usual the incessant traffic. Was it only a quarter past six? I didn't feel as if I'd been asleep. I reached for the water glass beside my bed. It was another hot summer and we were in the midst of a heat wave. The forecast said that temperatures were expected to climb to the high nineties by mid-afternoon.

It was cool in the room now and I wondered whether to go for a run in Central Park. If I leave in the next half an hour, then I might beat the crowds and the heat.

My cat Nahla snuggled next to me as I took a sip of water. I thought about the letter that I'd received a few days ago. Aunt Elizabeth wanted to see me. Resting my head back on the pillow, I closed my eyes and caught a faint whiff of lavender oil that I religiously sprinkled on my bed linen each night.

As I lay there under the duvet, I thought again about the letter that Aunt Elizabeth's personal maid had written to me. According to the doctors, she didn't have long to live and she wanted to tell me something. I decided to drive up to New Hampshire the following day. I hadn't been to the estate for over a year and, to be honest, I couldn't bear the thought of going back to Thornhill Manor after what happened with Flynn and Mrs. Winton, but I had no choice. If Aunt Elizabeth didn't have long to live then I had to see her, to say my goodbyes.

I got out of bed and walked towards the bathroom. Nahla, a black bundle of silky soft fur, was sound asleep. If I didn't know any better, I'd think that cat had been at the sleeping pills. As I dressed in jogging pants and t-shirt for my morning usual, the same niggling thought was going through my head. What exactly did Aunt Elizabeth want to speak to me about?

In the past, I had so enjoyed the drive up to Thornhill Manor and under other circumstances, I would be happy to go back. I was getting strong feelings of *déjà vu* as soon as I turned off the highway. It had been a difficult twelve months. I kept having flashbacks to the July day last year when I was practically murdered for investigating the real cause of Great Aunt Emily's death and the other events surrounding it, not to mention the court cases for Simon and Mrs. Winton.

I found one of the ways to put the past behind me was to plunge back into work. I'd finished my book about Queen Katherine of Aragon and it was due to be published in the coming weeks. The usual book tours would follow and I was busy doing research and gathering ideas for my next project.

I parked the car close to the fountain, grabbed my bag and walked towards the front door. After ringing the bell, the door was opened by a tall thin woman with shoulder-length auburn hair, who I guessed was in her mid-forties. This was my aunt's companion and nurse.

"Miss Green. I'm Jessica Wentworth," she said, as she shook my hand and smiled.

"Mrs. Wentworth. I'm so pleased to meet you. Please call me Victoria." A warm smile spread across her face and seemed to emanate from her laughing green eyes.

"And you must call me Jessica."

"How is my aunt today?"

"She's stable, but the doctor only gives her a few weeks maximum. She wants to speak to you as soon as possible."

"Do you know what it's about?" I quizzed.

"She would only say it's a family matter."

"Okay. Let me know when it's a good time. I'd like to take a shower and change. Which room shall I use?"

"The ground floor guest room. The one with the French windows that looks out over the rose garden. Your aunt said it was your favourite."

"Oh, yes. That's fine." I wasn't absolutely sure I wanted to stay in that room after all that had happened, but I tried to hide my doubt. I took my bag and made my way to Aunt Emily's old room. It felt strange to see it again. The same wallpaper, bathroom with the antiquated plumbing, the bedspread and bookcase. The same bookcase where I'd found the journal that started a chain of events that almost cost me my life.

I showered and changed and was towelling my hair dry when the telephone rang.

"Hello." I sat down on the bed and noticed it was a call from inside the house.

"Victoria. Your aunt would like you to join her for dinner in her suite around seven o'clock."

"That's fine." I replaced the receiver and finished drying my hair. I still wondered what family business my aunt wanted to discuss with me.

I knocked at the bedroom suite promptly at seven. Jessica opened the door and I walked over to the bed where my aunt lay. Her eyes were closed and her face looked pale. I thought she was asleep, so I sat on the chair near the window.

"Victoria, is that you?" I went back over to her bedside. She smiled at me. She looked thin and frail, lying in the bed. The events of the past year had taken their toll.

"Yes, It's me, Aunt Elizabeth. It's so nice to see you." I clutched her hand and leaned forward to kiss her forehead. Jessica brought me a chair.

"Move closer, Dear. I have something to tell you. Mrs. Wentworth, you can leave us now. I'll ring when we're ready to eat dinner." I listened intently as she started her story.

"I couldn't let James Flynn get away with what he did to her," she said. "One day, I waited for him to come out of his office at his newspaper in New York. He was standing there on the street corner smoking a cigarette. I drove my car straight at him. I was in such a rage, I couldn't think straight.

"Uncle Todd managed to quash any real investigation into Flynn's death and I just carried on as normal. It's been hard to keep this secret, but now that my days are numbered, Victoria, I feel I need to tell someone." She closed her eyes for a few seconds and gripped my hand.

"You reminded me of myself. So determined and persistent, wanting to know what happened to Emily," she said, and managed to smile.

"What did Flynn do to her, Aunt Elizabeth?" I wanted some more information. This whole episode still had some unanswered questions.

"He had an affair with Mary Riley, one of the maids. She became pregnant. She was shipped off to a private home for young ladies in that condition and we discovered she'd had a baby boy. You see, Mary went to live with her relatives in New York after that. She couldn't possibly return to the Manor. The scandal and everything. Emily, understandably, was heartbroken. She loved Flynn and I know she'd grown fond of young Mary." We sat in silence for what seemed like an age.

"Well, let's have some dinner, shall we?" She reached over and rang the bell for Mrs. Wentworth.

"It still doesn't explain how Emily died," I said. My aunt looked shocked that I should still be raising the subject.

"She fell from her horse, Victoria."

"Why won't you tell me the truth," I pleaded.

"Because it's too painful to talk about it. The truth . . . ." She sank back against the pillows and closed her eyes.

———•———

"Emily, I thought you went riding this morning?" Elizabeth was almost knocked to one side as her elder sister came storming out of her room in full riding habit.

"I did but I have to meet James before he goes back to New York. Please don't tell Uncle Todd or Aunt Eleanor," she pleaded as she grabbed her riding crop and hat from the hall table, where she had left them that morning.

"Please be careful. Flynn is in such a rage. He met with Uncle this morning and I could hear raised voices coming from the study."

"I'll be fine, Lizzie. See you later."

As Elizabeth returned to her room, Uncle Todd was coming down the stairs.

"Hello, Elizabeth. Have you seen Emily? I thought she was with your aunt."

"No, Uncle, I haven't seen her for a while." Elizabeth's face glowed. She wasn't a good liar.

"Where's your sister?" He grabbed her by the arms and shook her. "Has she gone off to meet that scoundrel Flynn?" he shouted. "I ought to wring his neck and one of these days I'll wring hers too."

Elizabeth shook with fear. Her uncle's face was within inches of her own.

"Come on, out with it, girl. Tell me, where is she?" he raged.

"She's gone riding."

"I don't believe you. She went out this morning. I want the truth, otherwise I'll take a riding crop to you my girl and you won't sit down for a week."

"The clearing near Flynn's cottage." She'd seen them together many times and sometimes he was there with his other girlfriend.

"Todd. What's gotten into you? Really, leave the poor girl alone, can't you see she's petrified. Lower your voice. The whole household will hear you." Eleanor Thornhill said as she calmly walked down the stairs.

"There, there, Elizabeth, don't you cry now." She put her arm around the child's shoulders as her husband stormed into his study and slammed the door.

Todd Thornhill opened the top right-hand drawer of his desk, took the small key and unlocked the gun cabinet. He removed one of his hunting rifles, grabbed a handful of bullets and closed the cabinet. He returned the key to the desk.

When he went back into the hall, Eleanor and Elizabeth had gone. He made his way to the stables, saddled up a horse and took one of the paths around the side of the house. As he approached the clearing, he could see Flynn and Emily embracing. He fired a shot into the air and they looked startled. Emily broke free of Flynn's embrace and tried to calm her horse as her uncle approached.

"I told you never to see this villain again."

"Uncle Todd, please, I only wanted to say goodbye."

"Well, say goodbye, get back on your horse and go home." Emily climbed back on her horse.

"You'll never be able to keep us apart, Thornhill,' James spoke up. "If you think $10,000 will keep me away from Emily, then you're mistaken."

"You're dirt, Flynn. I don't want you coming anywhere near my niece."

"Me dirt, you've got a nerve. You're no saint Thornhill. We know all about you and the little servant girl Mary. Looks like I wasn't the only one she was having an affair with."

"Uncle, is it true? All the rumours floating around. Tell me are they true?" Emily shrieked. "You had an affair with Mary, Aunt Eleanor's maid?"

"Don't listen to him, Emily. He's trying to save his own neck. You're not the only one he's been courting."

Elizabeth stood silently looking through the bushes. After her encounter with her uncle, she'd rushed out of the house. She wanted to warn Emily that Uncle Todd was looking for her. She realized now that it was too late.

Todd lunged at Flynn and they struggled with the gun.

"Stop it, please stop," Emily shrieked atop her horse. The two men wrestled to the ground as Flynn tried to take the gun away from Todd. Flynn managed to grab the gun and held it aloft.

"So I have this and I'll use it if I have to."

"You haven't got the guts, Flynn. You use that and you'll book yourself a place in the gas chamber."

"Put the gun down James, please," Emily said, as she tried to control her mount. Flynn threw the gun in the bushes and grabbed the reins.

"Uncle, please listen. We want to be together, can't you understand that?" Emily said trying to dismount.

"Flynn." Elizabeth rushed forward and was now holding the gun. "Let go of the horse."

"Elizabeth, dear god. Put the gun down." Todd said.

"No I won't. I want Flynn to move away from my sister. Haven't you hurt her enough? Why don't you just go back to New York and leave her alone!" Elizabeth said, as tears sprang up in her eyes.

Todd tried to grab the reins from Flynn and they fell against the tree. Suddenly the sound of gunfire echoed across the forest. Emily's horse reared up and she was thrown to the ground. She lay on the ground, blood pouring from the side of her head.

"Elizabeth, dear god, what have you done?" their uncle screamed.

Elizabeth dropped the gun and rushed over to her sister.

"Emily. No, I didn't mean to . . . Oh my what have I done?" She dropped the gun and ran through the trees. Her hair caught in the branches and she could feel a sharp pain from a cut on her left cheek.

She arrived back at the house hardly able to catch her breath as the tears streamed down her face. Her beloved sister had been mortally wounded, maybe she was even dead. As she raced into the hallway, she almost collided with Mrs. Banbury.

"Hey there, Miss Elizabeth, careful how you go. You look like you've been shot out of a cannon. What happened to your face."

"Mrs. B . . . Banbury, Em, Emily," she sobbed. She ran up the stairs, before the housekeeper could ask any more questions.

"What's up with her?" Mrs. Banbury wondered. Suddenly the front door burst open.

"Eleanor, where are you? Eleanor." Todd's voice boomed down the hallway as he carried Emily through to the library followed by an anxious Flynn. They laid her on the sofa. Flynn's jacket had been wrapped around her head and was now saturated in blood.

"Mrs. Banbury quick bring some towels and hot water. Get someone to telephone the doctor. Miss Emily's been injured."

Eleanor entered the room. She stood staring at the scene of chaos before her. She couldn't take in what was happening. No, it couldn't be. Not her dear niece lying helplessly on the sofa, blood gushing out of the wound.

"Todd, tell me what happened. Is she dead?" Please tell me," she shrieked.

Todd Thornhill looked at his wife."No, she's not dead."

"What happened?" Eleanor cried. He turned away from his wife unable to look her in the face.

"She fell from her horse. Where in heaven's name are the towels and water?"

The doctor eventually arrived and Emily Thornhill was taken to her room.

"Eleanor, you need to trust me. It was a terrible accident. Elizabeth is completely distraught and she needs our help now. We must stay strong and hope that Emily will pull through," Todd said, as they stood next to Emily's bed.

"How did she fall Todd. She's such an excellent rider?"

"Her horse stumbled and she was thrown. Please Eleanor, try not to upset yourself. We must be strong. Strong for Emily. Now try to get some rest." He kissed his wife's forehead and she left the room.

Todd stood next to the bed staring at Emily. How could this have happened? I know that Elizabeth would never hurt her sister. It's all Flynn's fault. If he hadn't come back to Thornhill Manor to see Emily, this would never have happened. A single tear slid down his cheek. "I will get even with you Flynn if it's the last thing I do," Todd muttered as he left the room.

Emily died from her injuries five days later. She would never see her beloved rose garden again.

———

As my aunt lay there with her eyes closed, she seemed more at peace now that she had unburdened herself of the terrible secret. I honestly thought she was dead, but she gripped my hand and then opened her eyes.

"Victoria, please forgive me for not telling you this sooner, but I had to protect the family. At the time of my sister's death we were all in a terrible state. Aunt Eleanor was beside herself and, well, you can imagine Uncle Todd. The whole house was in turmoil. I'd tried to aim the gun at Flynn. I was sick and tired of his treatment of Emily and his two-timing. Before I knew what was happening, the gun went off and instead of hitting Flynn, I hit Emily. Please believe me when I tell you it was an accident. I only wanted him to leave my sister alone. To frighten him."

"It must have been a terrible thing to witness, Aunt. I know how much you cared for her." I felt genuine sympathy for her. She'd had to carry that terrible burden around with her all these years. I knew she wasn't capable of murdering Emily; she had adored her sister.

"Victoria, I didn't get in that car with the intention of killing Flynn. It just happened. I was in a state of such anxiety. When I saw him standing there on the street corner smoking a cigarette, I was overcome with emotion. It was on reflection a moment of madness. You know, he was trying to blackmail Uncle Todd. He said he would spill the beans on what had happened to Emily if he didn't pay him $20,000." She started to cry as I held her hand. I had mixed feelings as to who was the criminal—Flynn for blackmail and for his part in the tragedy or Aunt Elizabeth for mowing the man down.

"Victoria, can you bring me that box on my dressing table?" I found a Japanese-style box on the dressing table and gave it to my aunt. It was almost identical to the one that I'd found in Emily's bedroom the previous year along with her journal.

Aunt Elizabeth opened the box and removed a cassette. She handed it to me. It was the tape that Bridge had made surrounding Emily's death.

I stared at her in disbelief. "How did you get this?"

"Simon took it from your room. He was listening at the window. He then gave it to May and then she passed it to me. I'm sorry to have put you through any anguish, Victoria, but I knew that Jason Bridge pretty much had all the answers. His career as a journalist would have been finished if he'd have printed anything about us. Uncle Todd had friends in high places."

At that moment, Jessica came into the room with our meal. She put the serving dishes on a table under the window. I put some food onto a plate and gave it to my Aunt. I sat down by the side of her bed and pushed a piece of chicken around my plate. After ten minutes, not one single morsel of food had found its way to my mouth. I had little appetite. One last question kept creeping into my thoughts. I wondered what had happened to Mary Riley's child.

The servants' quarters buzzed with the news that Miss Emily had taken a tumble from the horse and was gravely ill. A huge cloud seemed to hover over the house as every little snippet of news was passed on and the rumour mill swung into action.

Mary Riley lay on her bed crying softly. This was the most miserable day of her life. Miss Emily, who had become a friend, had had a terrible accident and was on death's door. Mary was pregnant and now feared for her unborn child. Emily knew about her affair with James, but had refused to believe it. Mary had tried to keep her pregnancy secret. She drifted in and out of sleep. Her eyes were stinging. She didn't think it was possible to shed so many tears.

She heard banging on her door. What time was it? *Oh god I must have overslept. Old Banbury will beat the living daylights out of me.*

Mary jumped up and then fell back onto the bed; the nausea gripped her like an iron fist around her throat. She'd had it for a few days now. The first time she had it, she'd known instantly what it meant. Her older sister had had so many kids, Mary knew she was in the family way. *What is he going to say when he finds out?*

She managed to raise her head off the pillow and walk to the bathroom. She splashed cold water on her faced and dressed hurriedly before old battle-axe Banbury came looking for her.

As she came out of her room, Banbury was walking down the corridor.

"So here you are. Where have you been, girl? What's wrong with you?"

"Nothing, Mrs. Banbury. I overslept. I'm a bit sad about Miss Emily."

"Well, yes, we're all sad. I cried my eyes out last night, I did. She is such a sweet child. Well, shake a leg then. Mrs. Thornhill wants her tea and she wants to speak to you about something."

Mary smoothed down her dress and tied her apron around her waist. It was becoming more and more difficult to conceal the child. She knocked quietly on Eleanor's door.

"Come in." Eleanor was looking out of the window.

"Such beauty when we are surrounded by such grief. Dear sweet Emily, I still can't believe what is happening. She turned to face Mary.

"Sorry I'm late, Ma'am. I've brought ya tea."

"Never mind the tea, Mary. Please sit down." Eleanor Thornhill's voice had a sharp edge to it.

"I know that my husband has been having an affair with you. I also know that you are pregnant. You'd be surprised what news reaches my ears." Eleanor didn't mince her words. "As you can imagine, I can't allow you to stay here any longer. Simply out of the question. The scandal would ruin us. We've arranged for you to stay at a convent and then I'll find a place in service for you, perhaps near your family in New York. A car will take you to the convent shortly and we'll see that you have enough money and we'll pay all the doctor's bills. We can arrange to have the child adopted once it's born and we'll find . . . ."

"No. I won't let you take my child. You've taken everything else, but not my child," Mary screamed.

"Mary, please calm yourself. I can see you're upset, but don't you think it will be for the best? What kind of life will the child have with the label of being illegitimate?"

"I'll raise this child myself, if it's the last thing I do." She said turning on her heels and slamming the door behind her.

—————

Mary Riley got off the tram that had brought her from her sister's house. She walked quickly to the house where she now worked as a parlour maid. The tall imposing house built in 1920 stood on Hornby Street and housed the Morgan family. Despite her ranting, Mary had been glad of the job after her baby was born. Money didn't grow on trees and the money given to her by the Thornhill's only covered the basics. Her baby was happy and settling down nicely at her sister's house. Her placement with the Morgan Family had been arranged by Mrs. Thornhill, who knew Mrs. Morgan from her charity work in New York. Of course, the Morgan's had no idea who had fathered her child. They didn't concern themselves with such things. This sort of thing happened all the time. They were kind to Mary letting her go to visit her sister and her baby twice a week.

"Excuse me, Miss." She swung around. A man wearing a flat cap and a dark brown overcoat stood before her. He had what looked like three-day-old stubble. She caught a glimpse of his rotten teeth as he attempted a lopsided smile. The smell of beer floated off his breath and Mary took a step backwards.

"I'm looking for the Morgan residence." He doffed his cap.

"What's your business there?"

"Need to deliver a letter to the gentleman o' the house." Another waft of alcohol assaulted Mary's nostrils.

"Well, I'm in service there." Mary said, eying him suspiciously. "I can give the letter to Mr. Morgan myself," Mary insisted. He looked a bit shifty. She would never turn her back on him, that's for sure.

"No, I have me instructions. Deliver it to the man o' the house personally." Mary felt uncomfortable walking along the road with him.

They reached Burlington Street and then turned left into Hornby. They stopped at the service entrance.

"Wait here and I'll fetch the butler." The man removed his cap and stood outside the door as Mary walked inside looking for Sims, the Morgan's butler.

"He said he had a letter to give the master, Sir." Mary informed Sims. When he opened the door, the man had gone.

"So, a man stops you in the street and says he has a letter for the master. Then where is he? Has he vanished into thin air? I can't waste my time on this nonsense." Sims stormed off, leaving Mary Riley perplexed and worried. She wondered who the man was.

A few days later, Mary was walking from the fishmonger's a few blocks from the Morgan house. As she glanced across the road, she saw the same man standing in a doorway smoking a cigarette.

It's him, she thought. The man who said he wanted to see the master. She tried to cross the road, but a tram sped past. When she looked across the road, he was gone. She hurried back to the house.

———•———

Mary Riley's body was found in an alleyway two days later. She'd met her end only two blocks from her sister's house. She'd been savagely beaten around the head and then strangled. According to police, the motive was robbery. The contents of her purse had been taken, and the purse itself had been discarded not far from her body.

As the man stood, cap in hand, his benefactor handed him three crisp $100 bills.

"A good job done. Now she won't be talking to anyone."

"Yes, Sir. Not a problem anymore." He smiled to reveal his rotten teeth, put his cap on and headed out the door.

The man sat back in his chair quietly enjoying his cigar. *I had to take care of her; she could have ruined me.*

CHAPTER FOURTEEN

New Hampshire

I pulled my coat around my ears. The wind had an icy chill to it as I stood next to my aunt's grave. I was still coming to terms with what she had told me on her death bed a week earlier. What was I supposed to do with this information, tell Detective Rainer? I noticed that Houghton from the *Laconia Herald* was there. He'd written my aunt's obituary, and he'd had a field day with the story of Simon and Mrs. Winton.

At least one part of the mystery was solved—The pearl-drop earrings. With a bit of investigating, I'd discovered that in 1950, May Winton had worked as a young maid for the British Royal Family at Balmoral Castle, Scotland. She had been linked to the theft of some jewellery and there was also the unsolved murder of a Royal housekeeper, who had been pushed down some stairs. Naturally, the Police were very keen to get to the bottom of that mystery.

From photographs taken of Queen Elizabeth around that time and with the help of an expert jeweller, the police confirmed that the pearl-drop earrings that I'd found in Emily's Japanese box were the same as one's that had gone missing back in the 1950s. Mrs. Winton had found Emily's box when she arrived at Thornhill Manor and thought this was a good hiding place.

According to the Scottish police, at the time of the theft, a young groom was accused and was sentenced to five years in jail. They'd said he'd probably sold the earrings in the local pub. Needless to say, the New Hampshire police through Interpol had arranged the return of the royal trinkets to their rightful owners—The House of Windsor.

Detective Rainer also told me when they searched May's quarters at the Manor they found all kinds of things. Apparently, she'd been suffering from kleptomania from a young age. I recalled Aunt Elizabeth telling me a few years ago that she couldn't find a ring her Papa had left her in his will.

I knew that May had read Emily's journal. How else would she have known about the secret closet? Obviously, she told her partner in crime, her son Simon. Whether Aunt Elizabeth had read the journal or not, I would never know.

I shuddered to think what would happen if Houghton knew the whole story. I can just imagine the headlines *Little old lady bumps off sister's sweetheart to protect family name.*

"Penny for your thoughts." I recognised the voice immediately.

"Hi Bill. How are you?"

"I'm fine, but more importantly how are you doing?" I looked away trying to fight back the tears.

"Okay, I suppose. It's still a tremendous shock. She's all the family I had."

"How about I buy you a cup of coffee and we can talk." The thought of a nice hot cup of coffee was inviting, but I wasn't willing to talk to him about Aunt Elizabeth and the family secrets. I wondered if he'd even believe half of it. I had a hard time keeping up with it myself. I had never believed that Uncle Todd would ever harm Emily. It was just a tragic accident. The struggle between James and Todd had set off a terrible chain of events resulting in Emily's death. With the limited medical treatment way back in 1925, no wonder she didn't live. I knew one thing, I had to protect the family name, now that I was the sole heiress. Thornhill Manor was mine, and I would have to keep the Thornhill Secret.

"Shall we go?" Bill and I got into his car and headed towards the Cottage Tea Shop in Moultonborough. A cup of coffee and a slice of homemade cheesecake was just what I needed.

A few years ago, I'd been to a typical Irish Wake in New York. The husband of one of my friends had died from cancer. It had been a fitting celebration of a life of a well-loved man who had never forgotten his roots. Earlier that day, we had all attended a rather moving service at St. Patrick's cathedral. In the evening we started talking about his life and then jigging around to traditional Irish music in between glasses of some of the finest Irish whiskey. I remember dancing so much I could hardly walk the next day and that had nothing to do with the whiskey, I can assure you.

When Aunt Elizabeth died, I knew that I wanted to celebrate her life. I obviously couldn't do anything on the scale of an Irish Wake; the conservative members of the community would have thought it a terrible scandal. So, with the help of Jessica, I organised a memorial service with classical music and a children's choir from Moultonborough School. I read one of my aunt's favourite poems and the current Chair of the Conservation Committee gave a lengthy speech about my aunt's work on the Environment and her contribution to the community through the Thornhill Trust.

"Thank you for coming." I sounded like a broken record as I greeted people outside Moultonborough Church.

"A wonderful service, Miss Green." I recognised the voice as I spun around.

"Mr. Houghton." I hadn't invited him to the service. Although he knew my aunt from her work in the community, I now didn't want him asking too many questions. Once a journalist, always a journalist. The *Laconia Herald* had sent another reporter to cover the service.

"I thought I'd pay my respects," he said, staring at me.

"Well, that's kind of you. Everyone has been very thoughtful." I smiled uneasily, I really didn't want to invite him back to the Manor. How could I get rid of him?

"Victoria, do you want a lift back to the Manor?" Bill Rainer said holding my elbow. I'd been pleased to see him and his wife sitting amongst the congregation.

"Bill, good to see you. Thanks for being here. I'll be fine going back to the Manor. I have my car. I'm pleased you and Sheila can join me for lunch."

"Our pleasure. See you there." I was relieved to see that Houghton was nowhere in sight.

I was amongst a mini-convoy of cars heading back to the Manor. The long-winding roads now so familiar to me, acted like a magic carpet as it swept us up to Thornhill Manor in next to no time.

"We'll get you a nice cup of tea," Sheila Rainer offered as we headed toward the main door. Jessica had left the service earlier to get everything ready at the Manor and to organise the caterer. She was an absolute godsend. She was now greeting the other guests and showing them into the library. I'd invited about fifty people to a buffet lunch. I was frankly not in the mood at this moment for chit chat. I knew I could leave the arrangements in her safe hands. The service was very moving and I wanted to compose myself before I faced the crowd again.

"Here you are, hon." Sheila Rainer handed me a cup of tea. I took a gulp and noticed she'd added some brandy. I was glad of it.

"Thanks." I said smiling at her, feeling the warm liquid as it slid down my throat. I sat there gripping the tea cup as if someone was going to snatch it from me.

Bill and Sheila Rainer had found their way onto my Christmas card list and were such a nice couple. It's funny how we meet people in strange circumstances. If I hadn't followed up on the events surrounding Emily Thornhill's death in 1925 and Jason Bridge's murder, then I never would have met Bill. I wouldn't have met Jane either and I fought back tears when I thought of how kind and helpful she had been. It was more than a year since her death and I silently cursed Simon Flynn for her murder.

The door to Uncle Todd's study opened. "Victoria, there's a telephone call for you. Shall I put it through here or do you want to take it in the hallway?" Jessica enquired.

"I'll take it here, thanks and I'll be joining the guests in a little while." After a few minutes the phone in the study rang.

"Hello, Victoria Green here."

"Ms Green. Jim Houghton here. Just thought I'd let you know that I was clearing out my storage room and came across another file about the Thornhill death. Would you like to see it?"

It was difficult to absorb the information that he had just given me.

"Hello, Ms Green, are you still there? . . ."

I was torn between putting everything to rest and my inquisitive nature. What else could I find out about the events of 1925? I was also hesitant for another reason. Houghton might start asking questions.

"Yes, sorry. Mr. Houghton, that will be fine. I'll drop by in the morning and, er, Mr. Houghton, thanks again for attending my aunt's memorial service."

"Don't mention it Ma'am. See you tomorrow." I replaced the receiver and let out a sigh.

"Everything okay, Victoria?" Bill asked, seeing the expression on my face.

"Houghton's found another file for 1925. I told him I'll come over tomorrow to take a look."

"Are you sure?"

"At this moment, No, Bill. Anyway, don't want to think about it right now. Let's go and get some food down us before we all fall over." I laughed as we all made our way to the sumptuous buffet that awaited us in the library.

Despite downing a couple of glasses of chardonnay at the buffet lunch, I slept fitfully that night. I had persuaded Bill and Sheila to stay over in one of the guest rooms. We'd ended up talking about all kinds of things until well past midnight; his plans for retirement and move to Maine to the latest shenanigans of Washington politicians.

The Rainer's had left for home long before I headed down to breakfast just after nine o'clock. They'd left me a note to thank me for inviting them to the service and for my hospitality.

As I sipped my coffee, I thought about the file that Houghton had found. Now in the clearer light of day, I wondered if I was doing the right thing. By the time I'd finished my second coffee, I'd convinced myself; what harm could it do? I just had to be wary of letting the cat out of the bag concerning Aunt Elizabeth's involvement in Emily's death, even if it was an accident.

The road was quiet down to Laconia. As I made my way to Houghton's office at the *Laconia Herald,* the lingering doubts resurfaced. What could the file possibly tell me that I didn't already know. Again, curiosity got the better of me and I pulled up in front of the newspaper office lucky enough to have found a parking space. I wasn't in the mood to walk. I still had a slight headache from the wine the previous night. The *Herald's* office hadn't changed since the last time I'd been here. A young couple dressed in leather gear came out of the door as I locked my car. I looked up at the slate grey sky. We would have some rain before the day was out. I thought I'd perhaps stop at Frankie's Diner after my visit with Houghton and say hello to Cindy. I wonder if she still works there, I thought, as I opened the door. A gust of wind swirled around the door and the dusty Venetian blinds clattered against the glass as it closed suddenly. Houghton looked up from his phone call, startled, as I mouthed *sorry.*

"Sure, that's what they all say," he said showing his yellowing teeth. I was surprised he still had a tooth in his head. I would have thought they'd have fallen out by now.

"Well, keep on it. It might lead to something and don't take no for an answer." He replaced the receiver in its cradle.

"Ms Green, can I get you a coffee?" He stood up and made his way over to the machine.

"No thanks, just a glass of water. I need to take some aspirin. Too much wine last night," I said, smiling.

"Here you go." He placed the glass in front of me. I popped the pills into my mouth and took a long gulp of water. Houghton was staring at me and I felt uneasy. Was he going to hit me with some questions that I didn't want to answer? I could even see his face through the bottom of the glass as I emptied it.

"So, you found another file from 1925?"

"Yes, I was doing some sorting out. Long overdue if you ask me and what do ya know. There it was. It must have got buried underneath all our other stuff." He leaned back in his chair, his eyes never leaving my face.

"Well, I'll take a look and see if there's anything new." I tried to hide my nervousness. The one thing I didn't want to find in the file was any possible reference to Aunt Elizabeth.

"Right then, come with me." He turned over the door sign to closed. We went down the same rickety wooden stairs to the archive room where only a year before I'd rummaged until I could rummage no more. Light was provided by a single light bulb and there were cobwebs everywhere. It was still a sorry sight with files and papers heaped on desks. How someone could make any sense of all this stuff was beyond my comprehension. So much for Houghton's attempt at organising things.

"It's just in there," he gestured towards a smaller room. "Take a seat. I'll be with you in a minute." He went inside the small room and closed the door. I looked around on the table next to me. On the top of a mountain of paper there was an article concerning the assassination of Dr. Martin Luther King. It had been written by the *Laconia Herald's* chief journalist Jason Bridge. There was also an article which had been published in the *San Francisco News* in March 1963 about the closure of *Alcatraz* prison. I noted that certain parts of that article had been highlighted. I leaned forward to take a closer look.

"Victoria, you are still as curious as ever." I caught my breath. *No, it can't be—the voice.* The sound that could only be achieved by inhaling helium gas. I slowly turned around.

"Houghton." I screamed. He was pointing a gun straight at me.

"What in the name of god are you doing? Have you completely lost your mind?"

"No, I haven't, Victoria. Now, you don't mind if I call you Victoria, do you? Ms Green, sounds so formal. I feel like I know you so well," he said, laughing." *If I ever get out of this situation alive, it will be a miracle,* I thought. *When will this nightmare ever end?*

"Houghton, please put the gun down. I only wanted to find out what happened to Emily Thornhill. You can't blame a fellow journalist for that, now, can you?"

"Shut up," he barked, pushing over a stack of files. The dust that rose up from the pile as it cascaded onto the floor looked like a mini volcano.

"Why are you so concerned about the Thornhill family?" It then crossed my mind that he had found out about James Flynn and the hit-and-run back in 1946 and Aunt Elizabeth's involvement, or perhaps he'd heard the true story about Emily and how she died. All kinds of thoughts were floating around in my mind.

"What makes you think I have any interest in your family? I'm more interested in mine," he said sarcastically, his voice no longer distorted by the helium gas. He pulled out a chair and sat down. His grip never weakened around the gun. There was no way I could make a run for it without receiving a bullet in my back.

"Your family. What, I don't understand . . . ."

"I had some unfinished business to take care of, Victoria, and then you arrived to upset the apple cart," he interrupted. "You like a good story don't you? Well, let me tell you one." He leaned back in his chair.

"My father, Arthur Winton, was released from prison in 1963. He'd been incarcerated in *Alcatraz* for robbery and blackmail and . . . ."

"Just a minute, did you say Winton? Are you related to May Winton at Thornhill Manor?"

"Yes, she's my aunt by marriage. Her husband Eddie was my father's older brother."

I let out a long sigh. I couldn't believe what he had just told me.

"I knew all about May's past and her involvement with a theft at Balmoral Castle in Scotland. You know what they say: once a thief, always a thief. It didn't stop even when she married Eddie Winton. My father knew all about her. May and my father hated each other's guts, but he never spilled the beans on her, a sort of family loyalty so to speak. I also found out that May had had an illegitimate son before she married Eddie."

"Yes, Simon Flynn, her son and partner in crime," I added sarcastically.

"Well, at the time, a lot of people didn't know about her child, especially those nice folk up at the Manor."

"May Winton is safely locked up in prison. Why would she now want to tell the police about you? She'll only implicate herself in her other crimes."

"It's not May I'm worried about. It's her idiot son, Simon. Well, I fixed him." Houghton sneered.

"But the police found the empty helium gas canister amongst his things at the stables. Let me guess, you made it look as if he was making the calls to me."

"Someone give this girl a prize," he added sarcastically. "Yes I wanted him to take all the heat. I put that canister there, when I went to meet May Winton one day. She was becoming a little difficult about paying me my money."

So I was right. Mrs. Winton was indeed being blackmailed. That would explain the call I'd overhead the day when I was searching in the library for the secret closet.

"What about the black car that was following me?"

"I borrowed it from the car pool and then changed the plates. It was easy to return it and put the keys back in place. Then, after I'd done what I had to do, I dumped it. The police would never trace the plates."

"Look Houghton, please put the gun down. If you let me go, I won't mention that we had this conversation to the police."

"Not possible. How do I know you didn't find anything in Bridge's stuff to link me to May Winton? I couldn't take the chance of you ever finding out."

In the hour that had passed since I'd arrived at the *Herald*, I'd grown to utterly despise this man. Not only had he tried to kill me the year before by running me off the road, he'd scared the living daylights out of me with an anonymous call, not to mention this nasty experience in the archive room. I didn't think I had an ounce more of hate left in me since the business with Simon and his mother May.

Houghton continued, "I wasn't the only one who had found out about May's past. Simon's wife Sarah knew about her. Her and May didn't always see eye to eye. The next thing, Sarah was killed in a hit and run accident. To this day, they never found out who killed her."

"It wasn't you then, Houghton?" I said confidently.

"You have got a vivid imagination, Victoria. You should save it for one of your books," he snapped.

I heard a creak above my head. Houghton stood up.

"I put the closed sign on the door. Who the hell is that?" he said, taking off his necktie. "Right, turn around and put your arms behind your back." After tying my hands together, he pushed me towards the small room, where he'd inhaled the helium gas.

"Don't attempt to make a sound or whoever is up there will be pushing up daisies before you know it." I wasn't in the mood for his attempt at humour. Houghton closed the door. It was as black as night in the room. I stumbled into a box in the corner and sat on it keeping perfectly still.

Houghton had tied the necktie so tightly around my wrists it had started to dig into my skin.

Suddenly, I heard voices overhead, an argument and then a scuffle. It sounded like furniture was being overturned. I jumped when I heard the gunshot. I sat there, a million and one things going through my mind. Has Houghton now added murder to his list of crimes? I didn't doubt that he would come down those stairs any minute and finish me off. I sat there, tears slowly trickling down my dusty cheeks. I tried to loosen the necktie, but it was no use. There was no way I could get out of this situation.

"Victoria, Victoria." I listened.

"In here." I croaked through my tears. The door swung open and a flashlight was shone in my face.

"I'll have to stop rescuing you like this; it's becoming quite a habit."

"Bill. Oh thank god it's you."

"Here, let me untie you." He undid the necktie from around my wrists and pulled me to my feet.

I managed to laugh through my tears as we went upstairs. Houghton lay on the floor, blood pouring from his chest.

"Is he dead, Bill?"

"Yes he is."

I closed my eyes, stunned at the latest events.

"What made you come to see Houghton?" I asked, rubbing my wrists, as Bill ushered me to one side.

"I followed you. I thought it a bit strange that he would suddenly find another file. It was now obviously a ruse just to get you here. Also, the girl in the shop where the helium gas was bought remembered that the man who'd bought the stuff had rotten yellowing teeth. We all know that Flynn has a perfect set of pearly whites."

"Houghton was related to May Winton. Her nephew by marriage. That reminds me, can I show you something Bill?"

"Sure, what is it?"

"Come with me." We went downstairs, navigating the wooden staircase, which I prayed would not collapse under our weight.

"Look, something interesting concerning Houghton's past." We both read the article, published in March 1963:

Alcatraz finally closes its doors

Alcatraz, once home to some of the country's most dangerous prisoners including Al Capone, and Machine Gun Kelly, said goodbye today to the last of its prisoners before it closes its doors for good.

One of these lucky prisoners will not be transferred to another state penitentiary when he reaches San Francisco. Arthur Winton has served his entire sentence for armed robbery and will now join his wife and son for a new life of freedom.

In the accompanying photograph, a group of six men could be seen boarding a small boat to take them off the Rock to San Francisco. Arthur Winton was the third person in the group. He bore a striking resemblance to Houghton.

"Well, well. Like father like son," Bill said, putting the article on the table.

"Houghton was blackmailing Mrs. Winton about the incident in Scotland and her illegitimate child."

"We did a little bit of investigating into his background. He left home a couple of years after his father returned from prison. Neighbours describe constant arguments between Houghton and his father. He managed to put himself through College and then settled near Laconia. His past caught up with him and there's a possibility that Bridge may have stumbled on something. Houghton didn't want people to know about his connection to May Winton, but Bridge found out. The old guy dying the way he did at the hands of Simon Flynn was clearly a godsend for Houghton." I reflected on what Bill said as we climbed the stairs to the main office, which was now swarming with police.

"I suppose you could say that Houghton was the last person to blackmail anyone," I said, as we went outside into the sunshine. It had been raining and I welcomed the cool air after my adventure in the dark and dingy archive room.

"Yes. Now young lady you have a safe trip back to the Manor. I think you've had enough excitement for one day."

"You said it. As my English father would have said, *I'm going to pour myself a large one when I get home*." We both laughed as I climbed into my car.

EPILOGUE

After I had recovered from my latest ordeal—as if one ever does, I had the unenviable task of going through my aunt's things. No one is prepared for this, even though we expect our elderly relatives to die at some stage. It was still a painful thing to do. My aunt's companion helped me sort out her clothes. Elizabeth had kept all her clothes over the years and her closets were full of all the wonderful gowns made of silk and duchess satin, as well as furs, scarves and an endless number of shoes that would have made Imelda Marcos look shoe-poor. I had to decide what to do with them. Some would go to charity, but some could be remodelled. After all, some styles never go out of fashion. My friend's older sister works in the Costume Department of Universal Studios in Hollywood. I'm sure they could be used. Who knows, one day I could be watching a movie and think, hey there's Aunt Elizabeth's wine-coloured gown with the low back.

"Would you like some tea, Victoria?" I was shaken out of my reverie, sitting in one of my aunt's closets daydreaming, running my hands over these wonderful fabrics. I hadn't heard anyone come into the room.

"Oh yes, I'd love some, Jessica."

The floor was covered with letters, postcards from far-flung places such as St. Moritz, Paris and Biarritz and various Christmas cards that Elizabeth had kept over the years.

One item that suddenly caught my eye was a cream-coloured sealed envelope with my name on it with the words, *To Be Opened After the Death of Elizabeth Thornhill* written underneath. How spooky, I shivered as the reality of my aunt's death sank in. I was looking at the envelope when I heard the bedroom door creak.

"Here you are." Jessica placed the tea tray on on a small table near the window.

"Jessica, did you know about this?" I held the envelope up as I walked towards her.

"Yes, I did. Your aunt said I was to ensure that you received it after her funeral." Jessica turned and walked quietly out of the room.

I sat down on the edge of the bed and opened the envelope:

> Elizabeth Thornhill
> Thornhill Manor
> Moultonborough, NH

Miss Victoria Thornhill
Apartment 1b
East 54th Street
New York, NY

July 9th, 2000

My Dearest Victoria,

By the time you read this letter, I will have departed this life. Finally reunited with Mama and Papa, Emily and your dear Grandmother Mary. I've had a good life with my family all around me and our last few years together have been most enjoyable. I cherish the day that I came to Thornhill Manor. It hasn't always been easy being a Thornhill. The Manor is yours now Dear. To do as you wish. I ask of one thing, which is to honour our legacy. To protect the family name.

You know what happened back in November 1925, but there is something that I want to ask you to do now, for me, as the sole heiress to this estate. I've lived with this final secret for some years and as I'm about to breathe my last I must do something.

Mary Riley did indeed have a son. She called him John after her father. He eventually married and settled in New York with his wife. Their daughter was born in 1958; her name is Jessica Wentworth. Please look after your cousin; I do feel that she is a nice young woman and cannot be blamed for her grandmother's mistakes. I know you will do the right thing. That's what I always admired about you. You remind me so much of your grandmother.

With much affection and all my love.
Great-Aunt Elizabeth

I put the letter down. It was all about the Thornhill name and it's no wonder everything was kept quiet about Emily's death. Maintaining the Thornhill Secret was the most important thing and I dreaded to think how many people were in on it.

"Can I get you anything else, Victoria?" Jessica said, shaking me from my reverie. I didn't hear her come in.

"Jessica. I didn't realise. I had no idea . . ."

"My father had told me about Todd Thornhill and his affair with my grandmother Mary. You know, she was murdered in New York soon after my father was born. They never found out who did it."

When she told me this, I shuddered to think. I'd unearthed some very interesting stories about Uncle Todd. He had an angry streak and some say he had a habit of getting rid of people who stood in his way. Was Mary one of those people who had to be silenced?

I looked at Jessica and realised we were both caught up in events that were still having repercussions now.

"What made you come here, Jessica?" I asked.

"Well, I applied for the job as personal companion to your aunt. I thought it was a good way to meet her and I realised it would give me a chance to explore my roots. I told her straightaway who I really was. I wanted to be up front from the start. Of course, I didn't know how she'd react. I thought she would show me the door, but she didn't. She said she was relieved. I also had a DNA test and I am related to your aunt and of course to you," she smiled hesitantly.

As I sat listening to Jessica, I recalled how I'd stood at my aunt's graveside next to Rainer, telling him that I had no other family. Suddenly I had a cousin, albeit a distant one.

"Your aunt wrote the letter to you the day she found out she didn't have long to live. She swore me to secrecy." She gave a weak smile. "She said when you found out you would know what to do."

Jessica had no legal claim to the Thornhill estate, but there and then I decided that she could stay on at the house to manage it. She readily agreed and I suggested she could use the Flynn cottage. After we removed all signs of Simon and had it redecorated, it was quite a cosy place. It had two good-sized bedrooms and a small garden. I'm sure it would be just right for her. I felt it was the least I could do and I knew I'd only use part of the main house in summer. In the short space of time that I had known Jessica, I had grown to like her.

I was thinking that I'd use part of the house as an educational centre through Aunt Elizabeth's Conservation Committee. Yes, that would be a good idea. I could just imagine budding horticulturists wandering around the grounds, not to mention the children wanting to learn all about the different species of wildlife. Yes, a very fitting gesture in memory of the Thornhill girls, Emily, Elizabeth and my grandmother Mary. Another thing I've decided to do is to use the name Thornhill. I've contacted my lawyer and I will now be known as Victoria Green-Thornhill. It sounds a bit corny, I know, and I laughed at the thought that it would strike a note for all those environmentalists. Aunt Elizabeth would have been proud.

Changing my name, or rather adding to it, was rather a big step. I didn't want to forget my dear Papa, but it would now be nice to honour my mother's side of the family. It would also mean that the name would not die. I thought I would start a tradition that if I had children, each child would bear the name Thornhill as well as part of their other names.

The house seemed to sense that Elizabeth was gone. The walls seemed to sigh as if to say, that is it, why go on? Who's going to live here now? I was the keeper of the Thornhill secret. I had to protect the family name at whatever the cost.

I walked down the hallway, the parquet floor creaking under my weight. Jessica had put some fresh flowers in a vase on the hall table. I immediately recognised the scent from the hyacinths, one of my favourites.

Looking through the house now, I thought it could do with a fresh look. I would refurbish the guest rooms. I had enough friends and colleagues that could fill them. I really wanted to see the house full of people. I know I couldn't recreate the 1920s, when the house had been a hive of activity, but it would be sad if it was left to go to rack and ruin. I knew my undertaking would cost money, but I could dip into the trust fund that Aunt Elizabeth had left me. It had been a pleasant surprise when I'd had a call from her lawyer a couple of weeks ago advising me that over $2 million had been left to me, as well as the Estate.

As I walked into the library, I caught that familiar whiff of old books and polished wood. I could now come into this room without feeling a sense of panic and thinking of the time that I'd feared for my life and had a gun pointed at me. I would get rid of the secret closet and use the extra space to extend the library. The extra space would be useful for the mass of books I already had.

I stood at the bay window looking out over Lake Winnipesaukee and the surrounding mountains. The sun made a feeble attempt to break through the clouds, but within minutes it had started to rain. I looked across the garden and noticed that some of the roses needed pruning. The dead heads bobbed up and down under the weight of each raindrop. As part of the house renovation, I would also restore the garden to its former glory. Aunt Emily wouldn't have wanted it any other way.

———•———

ABOUT THE AUTHOR

Caroline Curran grew up in England and studied Sociology, English and Creative Writing at University. She now teaches English as a foreign language in Switzerland. Before she turned to writing, she worked as a Conference Organiser in Geneva. She is an avid reader, particularly historical novels and crime fiction. Her other interests include cooking, gardening and interior design. She now lives in France. The Thornhill Secret is her first novel.

Lightning Source UK Ltd.
Milton Keynes UK
UKOW050303010212

186416UK00001B/93/P